Ace of PALMS

k. jaspersen

To request permissions, contact the author at
katrionajaspersen@gmail.com

The story, all names, characters, and incidents portrayed in this production are fictitious. No identification with actual persons (living or deceased), places, buildings, and products is intended or should be inferred.

ISBN: 979-8-3304-1997-5 (Paperback)

Self-published by the author in May 2024

Edited by K. Jaspersen
Cover Art created by author, November 2024 (Photos by Omid Armin and Derek Thomson on Unsplash, Rionaldo Angelo font by Creative Fabrica)

katrionajaspersen.com

To all the girls that rooted for Team Damon. He always did what was necessary to protect her and even after everything, he still got the girl.

Chapter One

A piece of me has been missing for most of my life. Not just a piece, but a person. And not just anyone. *Him.*

He was taken too soon. Too short lived. The only things I have now are the vague memories of him. Of us.

I'm not the only one. I know others have had the same experience, but it's difficult sometimes to think of the past. To think of the things that could have been. And it only makes things worse that my least favorite time of the year is coming. *Fall.*

What's worse is when I pass someone on the street that vaguely looks like him. If someone from my past was standing in front of me, would I even realize it? Someone whom I was so close with? Someone who I spent so much time with in my youth? Or would they just be a ghost - a face I no longer recognized? A distant memory?

As my moment of reflection passes and my eyes adjust, the realization sets in. He isn't coming back. He never will. *He's gone.*

"Hey Paige!"

The loud familiar voice snaps me out of my thoughts. I look up to see Lily, about a hundred feet in front of me, standing there staring at me along with her group of friends.

Lily is my best friend. Practically my only friend that I've ever had. If anyone saw us on the street together, they would think we were sisters by how much we looked like one another. Well, I would say we look pretty similar, but maybe it's just because of our long brown hair and the way we just "get" each other.

I see Lily's eyebrows lift just as a concerned look crosses over her face.

"Are you coming or not?" Lily shouts loudly as she crosses her arms in front of her.

I quickly look around me and realize I am the only one standing there. If I hadn't gotten lost in my thoughts again, maybe I would have noticed that I stopped walking next to our group and now, I was the only one standing there alone in the middle of the sidewalk half a block behind them.

I look back up at Lily, who starts to look a bit more concerned. I must look like a deer in the headlights by the way her friends are judgmentally staring at me like I may be losing it.

Without realizing it, my feet start walking me toward Lily and the others because within a few seconds I am almost caught up with the group.

"Sorry about that." I quickly shake my head. "Where are we going?"

"I thought it would be fun to see a psychic while we're here!" Lily says excitedly, pointing her finger up, as a large smile crosses her face.

"Psychic?" I whisper to myself, as I finally close the distance between Lily and I.

I look up to see what she had been pointing to and the sign above Lily's head is black with almost illegible purple writing that reads, "Avalon's Moon Readings." The building itself is pretty generic. Large windows similar to the rest of the buildings on the street and signs written on the windows advertising what the business offers.

"Let's go!" Lily demands as she locks arms with me, practically dragging me through the door.

As Lily's friends follow behind us, we enter a pleasant and surprisingly welcoming waiting area. I had seen psychic's shops in the movies before this and they were always shown as dark, spooky places. The psychics would be wearing dark cloaks, have curly, untamable hair and would be sitting at a table with a crystal ball waiting for you to walk in so they could ask you a bunch of questions, then repeat the answers to you as if they knew all along.

This place is different though. The waiting room is bright white and open. There are several seats available, similar to the ones you would see when you walk into a nail salon, and there's a desk off to the side. I imagine if this was a physician's waiting room, there would be someone about to call my name over to come into the back, but nobody is standing at the desk, only a tall floor to ceiling brown curtain is draped behind it.

Once all of us are standing in the waiting room and the door closes behind us, the curtain behind the desk ruffles and someone emerges.

The psychic isn't at all what I was expecting. She has straight blond hair that hits her just past her shoulders and she is wearing a plain white T-shirt with a dark red skirt that goes down to the floor. Definitely not like in the movies.

"Hello! Are you all here for a reading?" She kindly asks with a small smile.

"Hi! Yes!" Lily chimes in. "We all want to get a tarot card reading because I am getting married soon and we are here for my bachelorette par-," Lily stops, taking both hands and covering her mouth.

"Oops!" Lily laughs. "Didn't mean to give away so much! I imagine you probably prefer us not to tell you anything and let the cards do the talking."

The woman chuckles. "Oh don't worry! The tarot cards will have plenty more to tell you!"

The woman glances around at the group of us standing there, then back to Lily.

"Well then, would you like to go first?" She asks.

"Yes, why not!" Lily smiles.

"Come with me then." The woman turns around and holds the curtain open enough for Lily to walk through, then follows Lily and closes the curtain behind them.

We all wait and make small talk and after about twenty minutes, Lily comes out from behind the curtain, walks over and sits on the chair beside me.

"Your turn." The woman points to Lily's friend, Heather. Heather walks over and goes out of sight behind the curtain.

"I really don't want to do this." I say as I turn to Lily.

I didn't want to hear about ghosts of my past or hear about when I'd meet my future soulmate. Honestly, I didn't even believe in this at all. I had seen movies with psychics before and from what I could tell, they all read the same generic lines. *Shuffle the cards - the cards will tell the truth. Your spirit guide will lead you.* I didn't believe any of it.

"Come on!" Lily insists. "It was fun! It almost felt like an intense therapy session to be honest, but I found out a lot about my future!"

Therapy? *Great.* I had been to my fair share of therapy sessions when I was younger after my dad passed away, but I hadn't been to a session in a long time. The last one was around the same time I had met Lily, who seemed to be the only person that helped me break out of my shell, helped me to feel like I could be myself again and became the constant in my life that I needed. I certainly didn't need another therapy session at this point in my life.

"Okay, it's not really like that." Lily chimes in, emphasizing the word "really" as she says it.

"Not like what?" I ask slowly, a little confused by her statement.

"It's not actually a therapy session." She reassures me. "It just feels invasive a bit, but in a good way! Like, she knows things you don't even realize are happening in your life."

"What did she tell you?" I ask, raising my eyebrow.

"Well," she starts. "Just about how I'll be getting married soon, we will be fortunate, and she also showed me the Empress card, which means motherhood, and said it will be in my future, she just didn't say when."

"Lily." I scoff, putting my hands up to my temples. "You literally told her you were getting married. Those all seem like things that anyone could guess."

Lily looks up, as if to think. "Well, maybe! But I'm going to believe it!"

I let out a small laugh and Lily joins.

At that moment, the woman appears from behind the curtain again and Heather walks out, looking quite puzzled. The woman looks around the room until our eyes meet. Then, she points in my direction.

"Would you like to be next?" She asks.

"Okay. Sure." I say as I stand up.

I start walking toward the woman and turn to give Lily a quick glance, but I can tell she already sees the hesitation in my eyes. She gives me a smile and it's the little encouragement that I need.

Once I reach the woman, she gestures for me to go through the curtain she is holding open. Once through, she follows and closes it behind us.

"I'm Ava by the way." She says, holding out her hand.

"Nice to meet you. I'm Paige." I say as I shake her hand.

"Lovely to meet you as well Paige." She says, walking over to a table in the middle of the room. "Please, come sit down."

The room is similar to the waiting room, with bright natural light coming in through the window, but a bit more moody. The walls are a dark purple and the room itself smells of incense, which makes the room a bit hazy where the light from the windows is coming through. On each side of the room are black bookshelves, filled with books and crystals, and in the middle of the room there is a round black table where Ava sits down. The table is covered in a purple tablecloth and the only thing in front of her is a stack of tarot cards as well as her water bottle.

I walk over to the table and sit across from her in the chair.

"So, are you going to tell me I'll find clarity in my life or I'll go down a path that will lead me somewhere?" I ask sarcastically.

"Well, I am only an interpreter for the cards." She says with a kind smile, while looking down at the cards in her hands. "The cards tell the whole story."

I'm not sure what she means, so I feel a bit confused.

"I won't be able to give you any information today if you aren't at least open to seeing what they say."

She looks up at me, placing the deck back on the table and holds out her hands toward me with both palms facing up.

"You can be skeptical, but I promise it will be worth it to see what they say." She says, nodding her head with encouragement.

I hadn't realized I was furrowing my brows, but I quickly relax my face and look her in the eyes.

It can't be that bad seeing what she has to say, right? I mean, Lily seemed to be satisfied with what she had heard, whether it was true or not. The least I could do was play along to make Lily happy, considering this is her bachelorette weekend after all.

"Okay." I say, reaching my hands out to grab Ava's. She squeezes my hands quickly, then lets them go.

"Perfect." She says with a grin. "Let's get started."

She picks up the deck of tarot cards in front of her, shuffles them and places the deck in the middle of the table.

"Go ahead and cut the deck for me." She asks.

I grab the deck and split it into two separate piles in front of me.

"Thank you." She says. "Let's see what your story says."

She takes the two decks from the table and puts them back together. Pulling the first card off the top of the deck, she places it face up on the table. She does the same with the next three cards, arranging them on the table in a diamond pattern.

She quickly glances at me, then flips the first card over. It's a picture of two people surrounded by cups in a medieval setting.

"Ah, the Six of Cups." She says as she lightly touches the card in front of her. "The first card is the love card. I see here that you are currently in a period of healing and may be seeking comfort or a way to let go."

"Sure you could say that." I say, tilting my head back and forth. "I mean, I've been thinking a lot about my dad lately."

"A loss?" She asks.

"Yes." I say, my eyes wide.

"Remember the great times you spent together and keep his memory alive in any way that you can." She continues. "But, do not live in the past. It will only haunt you more." She pauses. "I will say though, there will be a revival from the past that comes with this card. See how it faces you?"

I nod.

"You will experience a sense of familiarity. I can't tell you when or where you will feel this sensation, but it will happen."

I raise my eyebrow. I'm still not sure I believe any of this, but she told me to be willing to open up so I'm trying. I take a deep breath, trying to convince myself to trust what she says to me.

"Okay, what else?" I ask, taking a deep breath.

"When you experience this familiarity, the past will also project lessons to you. Use these to help you decide what you want in your life."

She turns and flips the next card, turning it face up.

"The Ace of Pentacles is facing you." She states.

"And what does that do?" I ask, realizing I am leaning into the table to look more closely at the cards in front of me.

"In regards to finances, you will be presented with financial opportunities. This may come from a new career choice or within your present career, or it could be given in the form of a gift. You will be happy with the financial opportunities coming your way."

"Well that's good to hear." I say.

"Yes it could be." She says with a smile. "Let's move onto the health and happiness card."

She flips the card closest to her.

"A Major Arcana card. It's the Magician." She looks closer at the card then up to me. "Do you see how it is facing me instead of facing you?"

I look closer and nod my head.

"The reversed magician is all about illusion and deception." She says. "You will be lured by it, but it may be all for its own selfish gain."

"What does that mean? I'll meet a magician?" I ask.

She continues looking down, giving me a half smile, seemingly holding back a laugh.

"Not a magician." She says. "But someone will come into your life that will be deceiving you. It can even be perceived that your own emotions can be the deceiver, but I don't see that interpretation here. This card will be most impactful in your life, so focus on those around you to watch out for the deceiver."

I look up and stare at the ceiling. I watch as the fan circles above us. At this point, I'm really unsure of what these cards even mean. If someone is going to deceive me, is it someone I already know? Someone I'm already close with? I shake off those thoughts.

"Lastly, we have the Ace of Swords for your career card."

I hadn't realized she had already flipped the card in front of me. She points down at the card showing a snake wrapped around a sword. *This can't be good.* Even the picture looks like it'll be a frightening outcome.

"Remember the word 'Ace.' It will be meaningful to you down the line." She says, looking up at me with a big grin. "The aces on the sword allow you to cut through deception. I can see this also relates to the Magician card. You will discover the truth of what has been deceiving you. There will be a start and restart that comes for you and communication is key. When it relates to your career, this card can represent a new job or opportunities, much like the Ace of Pentacles card. Remember to keep a clear vision of where you want to go with your future endeavors."

"Hm, interesting." I look up from the cards and look her in the eyes, raising my eyebrows. "Is that it?"

"Yes, that's it." She places her hands down over the four cards on the table. "How do you feel?"

I press my lips together. "It was," I pause. "Different." I shrug my shoulders. "I'm not really sure what to think of all of it."

"Well," She says, grabbing the cards and shuffling them back into the pile. "Take what resonates and leave the rest."

She stands up and gestures toward the curtain. I stand up, follow her and soon, I'm back out into the waiting room, but the group is no longer there. I glance out the window and see Lily waiting outside with her friends, who are all looking down at their phones. As I walk out to join them, Lily jumps and gives me a hug.

"I'm glad you're done! I hope you enjoyed it like I did." Lily says as she pulls back, holding each of my shoulders. With a smile she says, "Now that you're finished, we were thinking of heading back to Broadway. Are you ready?"

I shrug. When Lily's smile changes into concern, I lock arms with her, straighten myself up with a smile and pull her into a walk down the sidewalk.

"Of course I am. Let's go!" I say, smiling at her.

As we start walking, I think back to what the psychic said. A new career opportunity is always good, right? I've been hoping my drawings would take off and someone would finally see my potential using them in children's books. *Maybe this is the time?* I smile thinking about it. Maybe even some additional wealth will come with it too? *I wouldn't be too mad about that. Who would?* Then, the words the psychic said ring in my head, "*You will experience a sense of familiarity…someone will come into your life that will be deceiving you…You will discover the truth of what has been deceiving you.*" What do those words even mean?

As we inch closer to the bustling streets of Broadway, my vision blurs for a slight moment.

The group stops and Lily unlocks her arm from mine, turning to talk to her other friends behind her.

I stare down, looking at my dark brown cowgirl boots I had discovered buried in the back of my closet last week, just in time for Lily's bachelorette weekend. I think back to another strange thing the psychic said regarding the word "Ace." *Is this a place? A thing? Or possibly a who.*

Chapter Two

Paige

It was a little past nine o'clock and we had already been to several bars on Broadway by that point. We had started off the night when it was still a little warm out, but as the night carried on, it had gotten a little bit chillier.

As we walk to the next bar, I watch Lily and her friends in front of me looking at least somewhat warmer than I am in their jean jackets.

As we were leaving the rental house, everyone had grabbed a jacket, but I had insisted I didn't need it. I grew up in a colder area in my early childhood so I lied to myself when I was thinking I could handle the night without a jacket. *I cannot.* So underneath my short dress and boots, I can feel my legs shaking from the cold. At this point, I am desperate to go back into another bar as soon as possible.

While I rarely drink, I wanted to let loose just a little for Lily tonight. She has always been the outgoing one - the one who convinced me to get out, go to parties and have fun. I, on the other hand, would have preferred to stay at home during our college years if it wasn't for her. So, I wanted to try to be more outgoing this weekend for her and the only way I could do that would be to have a few drinks in me. Unfortunately, even the few drinks - four in the last two hours - didn't help to trick my mind into thinking it was warmer outside than it was.

Lily, on the other hand, was a little drunker than I had hoped she would be tonight. I want her to enjoy her bachelorette weekend with friends rather than not be able to remember it in the morning. She insisted that every bar we went to *had* to have live music, so here we were - another live music bar. I completely understand why though, I mean, it is Nashville, the magnet for live music.

"Let's go up front!" Lily shouts as we make our way through the loud crowd.

She grabs my hand and pulls me through the gathering of people watching the show and into the front of the stage where a hopeful country singer is playing. Her friends follow and stand around us as we move a few feet away from the singer on stage. I watch as he plays several songs, many of which are covers and all I can think about is his slim possibility of becoming a famous country singer someday, but what do I know?

"Aren't they amazing?" Lily shouts loudly, assuming I won't be able to hear her as she stands right next to me. It isn't *that* loud in here.

I give her a sarcastic grin and a quick nod in agreement, but she doesn't notice as she starts to sway with the music.

"Do you want another drink?" She shouts again. "I was going to go get us each another one!"

I hold my hand around her ear and lean down to speak to her.

"Don't worry! I'll go get us one!" I offer, finding an excuse to get out of the dancing crowd.

As several guitars continue to strum and the singer sings with a twang in his voice, the noise fades a bit as I walk over towards the bar.

As I approach the bar, it's almost just as crowded as the dance floor, however, I quickly find the back of a line and stand in it. If my phone wasn't in Lily's purse, I would be looking down and staring at it as I waited, but with my hands empty and nothing better to do, I take the time to people-watch.

As I scan the crowd, I see two people making out against a wall, practically sucking each other's faces off. I inch forward in line. Near the front of the bar, are several other bachelorette groups, one group with pink bedazzled cowboy hats and another with all black outfits on, except one woman who I assume is the bride and has a white hat on, is the only one dressed in all white. *Thank goodness Lily didn't make us wear matching outfits.*

I take another step up in line. Turning to a table near the bar, I see two guys sitting slumped over passed out with their faces down, most likely from too much drinking.

As I turn to stare forward in line, a figure leaning against the wall near the stairwell catches my eye. I can't really see his face hidden under his cowboy hat, but he appears to be looking down at the drink he is holding in his hand. He is tall, about six foot four, each of his arms is covered in tattoos from his wrist up to the bottom of his short sleeves, which I imagine continue to expand up and over his broad shoulders. He is wearing an all black outfit - a tight black shirt carving out the lines on his muscular chest, tight jeans and cowboy boots, which are also black. I can't help but stare as I watch him take sips from his drink while never showing his face as the glass disappears below his hat.

As I watch him take another sip from his drink, his face slowly comes into view from below his hat and I feel myself take in a quick breath. I watch as his neck, clean from tattoos, displays his Adam's apple rise and fall. His sharp, chiseled jaw surrounding his thin lips, which appear to be slightly open, looks like something I would want to recall in a dream every single night. A fantasy of this man appearing in front of me, our lips almost touching. Then, I have no doubt with my luck, I would wake up before anything happened. *A shame.*

"Hello?" I hear faintly to my side. I ignore it.

I move my eyes up to the top of his face, looking at his dark eyebrows, until my eyes slowly move just a little bit further. I stop. Piercing green eyes stare in my direction and I feel my body freeze. *It's just a dream. He can't be looking at me.*

I quickly close my eyes. *1. 2. 3.* When I open them, our eyes meet once again. My body is filled with a yearning sensation and my eyes are locked onto his eyes staring back at me and I cannot escape. It couldn't have been more than a few seconds, but I feel myself being pulled in just from the sight of this man. As our eyes stay fixed on one another's, I slightly notice one of his eyebrows raise and I can't help but glance down his face once more and onto his lips, where a slight smirk has appeared. My legs buckle at the sight and my mind starts to quickly imagine the things he would do to me, the whispers in my ear, his hands caressing my-.

"Hello!" I hear an irritated shout from my side. An unfortunate break to the invisible string between the tall man and myself.

I turn to look at the voice, only to be greeted by an annoyed bartender, giving me what appears to be his death stare.

"Are you going to order or can I get the next person?" He snaps at me.

My eyes widen as I look at him, frozen by his words. I hope he wasn't calling for me too long. He turns to look behind me, "Okay, Can I get the next-"

"Sorry!" I say interrupting him. "Two vodka crans please." I anxiously smile, hoping he doesn't get upset with me, or worse - spit in my drink. *I can only imagine.*

As the bartender looks down at the counter in front of him and starts making my drinks, my head turns back toward the mystery man near the stairwell, but he is no longer there. My eyes quickly search the crowd, hoping to catch another glimpse of the man that took my breath away, but he is nowhere in sight.

"Here." The bartender says with an irritated tone as he sets the two drinks on the counter, both spilling slightly from the force of him setting them down.

I lean down and pull out the twenty dollar bill that was tucked in my boot.

"Keep the change." I say, handing him the folded bill, hoping this will end his mini-feud he has with me. He still can't be annoyed at me for getting distracted, can he? *I hope not. I'll probably have to come back for more alcohol at some point.*

The bartender glares at me again and snatches the money from my hand before walking over to the next person down the bar. *I guess I have my answer.*

I grab the two plastic cups on the counter, trying not to linger near the bar longer than needed. I imagine the bartender would find any chance to throw another glare in my direction.

As I'm about to turn around to go, the hairs on the back of my neck raise and a chill goes down my spine. I ignore the feeling and continue to turn, but I quickly collide with a tall, dark figure that I realize must have been standing behind me. *Why was someone standing so close to me?*

The impact stops me in my tracks and out of self preservation, I reach my arms out in front of me, crushing the two plastic cups into the dark, muscular shirt before me. As I watch the cups fall out of my hands and onto the ground, I flush with embarrassment and keep my eyes locked to the ground. *I can't look up. I can't.* I watch as the puddle of cranberry juice and vodka slowly widens underneath my boots on the floor and my eyes glance at the figure's legs. Black jeans and black boots. *Could it be-*

"Are you okay, beautiful?" A deep, but calming voice asks from above my head.

With my eyes still glued to our boots on the ground, his hand reaches below my chin and slowly pulls it up, sending another tingling sensation between my legs. He continues to lift my chin up until our eyes meet. My eyes widen and my heartbeat quickens as I watch his green eyes move around, studying my face. A sense of familiarity hits me as I stare into the hint of gold on the corners of his irises. *Do I know him?* I shake off the thought. The corner of his mouth rises and I catch myself smiling as he smirks in front of me.

"I'll take that as a yes." He says, letting go of my chin. *Don't let go.*

For what feels like minutes, but can't be more than a second or two as we look at each other, I finally shake my head and snap out of the trance he has put me in.

"Sorry! I'm okay! Definitely!" I quickly say.

I break our eye contact and look down at his shirt, that is now soaking wet from the drinks I just spilled all over him. *Shit.* His abs are even more toned and visible through the fabric. Without asking permission, I take both hands and pinch the shirt, checking to see how much damage I've done, and I immediately feel the stickiness from the juice on the tips of my fingers.

"Are you okay?" I say, emphasizing the "you" as I look back up into his eyes and raise my eyebrows.

He just looks down at me and says nothing. *He's upset.* Instantly my cheeks flush and my face starts to turn red with embarrassment. Not only have I spilled my drinks on him, but I may have ruined his shirt. *Great.* His thin lips start to form into a smile as he continues to look back at me. He grabs my hands from his shirt and holds them in place between us and I freeze.

"Nothing a new shirt won't fix." He says with a laugh. *Phew. He isn't mad.*

Looking around me, he lets go of one of my hands and holds up two fingers. "Two!" He motions to the bartender.

Just when I feel my face starting to lose the red tint from my momentary embarrassment, I realize I'm now holding hands with this stranger in front of me. A handsome, charming stranger nonetheless, but a stranger whose name I don't even know! Well, I should probably introduce myself. No, I should *definitely* introduce myself, and quickly, before this gets awkward.

I pull my hand out of his and raise it between us. "I'm Paige, by the way." I say, looking into his charming eyes.

"Ryker. Ryker Blackwell." He says with a magnetic tone that draws me closer as he reaches out to shake my hand.

"Here you are, sir! Terribly sorry for the wait!" I hear from behind me. I turn to see the bartender, anxiously holding two drinks in his hands with a large grin on his face. *Seriously? He didn't smile once for me.*

Ryker lets go of my hand and pulls a black metal card out of his pocket. He reaches around me and sets it on the counter in front of the bartender. The bartender carefully sets the two drinks on the counter and swipes the card.

"All set, sir! Enjoy!" The bartender says as he hands the card back to Ryker, who puts it into his pocket, while never breaking our eye contact.

Ryker steps forward then, instinctively making me step backward until my back hits the bar counter. Breaking eye contact and closing the distance between us, he steps closer again until his chest rests a few inches from my face. As he wraps his arms around my sides to reach for the drinks behind me, I feel him lean down slightly just as his lips brush my ear. His breath against my ear makes my leg shake and I resist the urge to grab Ryker, a man I barely know, and kiss him. *Who am I?*

I can't help but savor the smell of his cologne from his wet shirt, barely masked by the vodka and cranberry juice soaking into his chest. His aromatic scent, woodsy with a hint of spice, provides a calming sensation throughout my body, reminding me of the trees near my childhood home that I have always loved. The scent lingers in my nose even after he pulls back away from me and takes a step back, his hands each holding a drink.

"Are these both for you?" He asks, raising an eyebrow curiously.

I smile. "Well, one is! The other is for my friend Lily." I gesture over to the crowd and realize I cannot see her. *Shit.* Lily must be worried. I have no clue how long I've been gone.

Ryker reaches his arm up and gestures toward the stage. I look at the cups in his hands and back to him, almost as if to ask if I need to hold them or not.

"I got 'em. Don't want you spilling the drinks again!" A small chuckle slips from his throat and I smile and nod.

I start heading toward the band, slowly moving into the growing crowd. I take a quick glance back to Ryker to make sure he is still following closely behind me, and he throws a smirk in my direction. *Dammit, I want to kiss him so badly.*

I stop just before we enter the crowd as it quickly disperses and I watch as the singer proceeds to exit the stage. As people walk by me, I search each person's face, looking for Lily to come out of the stream, but I'm unable to find her. Suddenly, I hear a familiar voice in the opposite direction of the stage shouting "Next bar ladies!"

As I turn my head towards the sound, I see Lily and her friends laughing as they walk toward the far exit. *Shit, they are leaving already?*

I quickly turn to Ryker with an anxious look on my face and start spitting out my words as fast as I can say them.

"I'm so sorry! Thank you for the drinks, but I don't want to lose track of my friend! She doesn't really do well drunk." I let out a timid laugh and before Ryker can say anything, I run toward the exit after Lily.

As I reach the door, I turn one last time to see Ryker setting the drinks on a table near him. As if he can feel me watching him, he turns and leans against the table and we immediately lock eyes once more. His green eyes gaze into mine and I let out a sigh, wishing I could stay at the bar to get to know him better.

As I hear "Party! Party!" from Lily outside the door, Ryker gives me a quick wink with a half smirk on his face before I feel pulled outside. *An image I know I won't be able to get out of my mind.*

When I get outside and join Lily and her friends, Lily stumbles into my arms and hugs me. "Glad you're back! We are heading to another bar!"

"Maybe we should take a break Lily?" I ask, desperately wanting to go back into the bar to spend more time with Ryker, but also partially wanting Lily to slow it down on her drinking. Lily pulls back from our hug.

"The night is just getting started!" She yells, turning back to the rest of her friends, who all shout "yes" at the same time. Before I can say anything, she links arms with me and drags me further down the street.

I turn and glance back at the bar that we just left, thinking of Ryker, this mysterious man that I couldn't help but feel drawn to. His calming, deep voice etched in my head. A vivid picture of his smirk that will continue to melt me from the inside out. His touch on my skin, which rattled every part of me. *Shit.* And I didn't even get his number.

Chapter Three

Paige

The rest of the weekend was similar to what anyone could expect for a bachelorette weekend. Party games at the rental house, riding around on a pink pedal bus and Lily once again getting drunker than I was hoping. All of it very typical for a bachelorette party weekend.

Despite going to several other bars that night as well as the following day, unfortunately I didn't run into *him* again. I was more disappointed than I expected after leaving Nashville. This unrealistic, fantasy dream that played in my head was nothing more than that. I knew his name, but that would be all I ever got from him. I wasn't going back to Nashville anytime soon and I never got his number, so I would only be able to replay that moment that we shared together at the bar in my head. *Just a dream.*

I walk past a building on the corner and stop as I look up to see a tree hanging over the sidewalk in front of me. The large tree, nearly forty feet tall, has started changing colors, from green to shades of red, yellow and orange. *Similar to the ones I had outside my childhood home.* The thought immediately makes my stomach turn and I blink, turning my gaze down at my shoes resting on the sidewalk.

"Hey!" I hear a call out from behind me. I turn around to see Lily standing in the doorway of the dress shop. "Are you okay?" She raises an eyebrow at me.

I look around, realizing I nearly walked past the dress shop. If it hadn't been for Lily, I would have missed it.

I shake my head and smile. "Yes, I'm good!" I say, hoping she won't ask more.

"Well, come on in!" She smiles as she gestures for me to come over. I walk over to her and hug her as we go inside.

The shop is just as I remember it from before when I went with Lily to pick out her wedding dress earlier this year. The pale walls are laced with white dresses hanging around the room from floor to ceiling and in the back are a set of couches centered around a cylinder pedestal. In front of the pedestal is a mirror that is draped at the top with an arch filled with faux greenery and florals.

Lily walks over to the mirror, gesturing for me to come over, as the woman from the front desk walks into the back room. *Was her name Barb?* When I reach Lily, who is standing on the pedestal now, she pulls me up there with her, embracing me in her arms.

"Can you believe I'll be married one month from today?" She says, looking at the two of us hugging in the reflection of the mirror.

I met Lily when I first moved into the city after losing my dad. My mom had quickly found a job to support us and I was placed in school for the first time in my life. I always felt like an outsider in my old neighborhood, so I was expecting school to be exactly the same. It didn't help that I enrolled in the middle of the school year either and most kids had already become close friends, so I assumed I would once again be isolated.

It was lunch time the first day when Lily came over to the table I was sitting at. As she made her way over to the table, I did a double take because I could have sworn she was my long lost sister, apart from having different colored eyes than mine. As soon as she sat down next to me, she informed me that we would be sitting together the rest of the year. I remember laughing at her, but I didn't question it. I did what she asked. I mean, I was always the one nobody wanted to be friends with, yet here I was at kindergarten on my first day of school, already making a friend. From that moment, we were inseparable and we sat together every single day, like Lily had predicted.

Lily has always been the more confident one between the two of us and she is the kind of person that has always known what she wanted. I expected her to be like all the other kids I knew growing up, but she wasn't. She was friendly and sincere, which made it easier to open up to her about everything that happened with my dad.

"I can't wait." I say, smiling at our reflection in the mirror.

"Alright ladies!" I hear, as the small woman from the front desk emerges from the back room carrying a large white bag that covers her entire body. "Here's the dress!"

She hangs up the long bag to the side of the mirror and unzips it to reveal Lily's wedding dress. *Wow.* It is beautiful. Even more stunning than I remember it.

Lily had assured me that the previous fittings she had attended without me were only subpar compared to the final fitting, so I hadn't gone to any of those with her, but this was it, the last fitting before Lily's big day. Something about a big reveal, I think?

It had been almost a year since I first saw this dress when I originally went with Lily and her mom to the very same dress shop. Lily said she only valued honest opinions when it came to her dress choice and so she didn't invite her other friends the first time. When I asked her why, she said she was worried that all they would do was agree with anything she said. *Like the saying goes, the bride is always right.* So, she opted for just her mom and I, trusting that we would provide blunt and honest feedback, which I know she appreciated.

I remember her trying on several dresses, one by one, and never feeling confident in them, which was rare considering who Lily was. She oozes confidence, so I could tell when she felt out of place in the dresses she disliked. When she came out in 'the one' for the first time, you could just tell by her expression that it was the winner. Lily had the biggest smile on her face and not only was she gleaming, but the dress hugged her in all the right places, as if it were meant to be.

I look at the dress again with awe as the woman removes it from the bag in front of us. The strapless pale cream dress has a princess-seamed bodice and plunges to a deep v in the middle, that I imagine is held together with hidden wire to keep the shape. The details were even more incredible than I remembered. Carefully-placed pearls from the shoulders down to the train were what made the dress not only unique, but expensive. *It was beautiful.*

I turn to Lily, whose face is lit up just like the day she first tried on the dress. I chuckle as she abruptly grabs the dress, almost ripping it out of the woman's hands as she pulls it into the dressing room.

I sit down on the couch in front of the mirror just as the dressing room door behind Lily closes. I stare at the mirror, watching the reflection of people walk past the dress shop outside. *Would I ever meet him again? Would he ever be here?*

I pull my phone out of my purse and open a new browser window. As I start typing his name, R-Y-K-E-R B-L-A-C, a silky material brushes against my feet, pulling my attention away from my phone. I look down at what tickles my foot and recognize the material. My eyes quickly shoot up from my phone as Lily, now fully dressed, stands in front of me.

"Who are you looking up?" She asks, peering over as she pulls my phone down towards her to take a look.

"No one." I quickly say, pulling my phone back and against my chest, hoping she didn't see what I was typing. I look back up at her.

"Erm, 'no one' seems to be making you very secretive." She says, putting air quotes over the words "no one."

"Let me see!" She demands. I roll my eyes and reluctantly hand her my phone. *I know I won't win when it comes to Lily.*

Lily stares down at my screen at the half-typed name I've written out, then looks back up at me. A wide grin grows on her face and she raises an eyebrow.

"Hmm, is this someone you know?" She says.

"Yes, well, not exactly." I confess, as I nervously scratch at the polish on my fingernails. "I met him in Nashville."

"What?" Lily screams. "Why didn't you tell me you met someone there?" Lily crouches down to hug me, but I stop her, making sure not a single pearl is touched on her dress.

"Oh, right!" She straightens up and steps back, sliding her hand carefully down over her dress to straighten it out.

"Well, it happened so quick-" I reply, before Lily interrupts me.

"Have you been talking to him since Nashville?" She asks. "When are you seeing him again?" She asks again quickly, trying to get out every question she can about the topic.

"Well, I don't know. I never got his number." I shrug.

Lily's facial expression slightly calms, before a grin grows back on her face. "This is perfect." She whispers under her breath.

"What'd you say? Why are you smiling like that?" I look at her, tilting my head to the side.

She quickly blinks. "What do you mean? This is just how I smile." She makes an obnoxious smile, showing all her teeth. *Okay, sure.*

"If you say so." I roll my eyes at her.

"Oh, don't worry! Maybe you two will meet again one day!" She says smirking as she hands back my phone, but I quickly delete the open browser. *I doubt it.*

Lily turns around and steps onto the pedestal, doing a quick spin in a circle as she holds up a piece of her dress. I smile as she turns back to me.

"I was thinking," she says, holding her dress as she twirls back and forth. "You need a date for my wedding!"

"Woah, no I don't!" I stand, holding my hands up in front of me.

"Of course you do!" She insists.

"I'm not even dating anyone!" I say, raising both my eyebrows with my eyes wide.

"Yet!" Lily smirks again as she turns back around to look at her dress in the mirror. "And I have the perfect person for you!" She looks back at me through the mirror's reflection.

I put my face into my hands and sit back down on the couch.

"Oh great, that's what you said the last time and look how that turned out!" I say, my voice muffled between my hands.

I lean back on the couch and open my hands slightly to stare up at the ornamental ceiling, thinking back to the last blind date Lily set me up on.

While I've casually dated one or two guys in high school and in college, I have still always been closed off when it came to dating and Lily can attest to that. After I broke up with a guy that I had dated only a couple months, Lily set me up on a blind date with one of her friend's brothers. I was reluctant at first, but in true Lily fashion, she pushed me to go.

Lily had helped me get ready that night, picking out my outfit and giving me pointers on what to say and how to act, yet I'm not sure if there was anything I could have said or done to make this guy like me. He was the typical type that I was attracted to, tall with dark features, but he made me feel second best the entire night.

Within the first hour of our date, he had not only flirted with the hostess seating us, but had gotten the waitresses' number while I had gone to the restroom. I only knew that because I saw it happen right in front of me. I had just walked out of the bathroom when she slipped a piece of paper into his hand and leaned down to whisper something into his ear. She hadn't even tried to hide it either as she threw me a contemptuous look when we locked eyes from across the room. When I sat back down, I pretended I hadn't seen anything. I didn't want to make a scene. Although, it didn't help that the waitress barely acknowledged me for the remaining two hours of the date and I could tell that the guy was far from interested in what I had to say.

After I came home to Lily, I had told her no more blind dates and honestly, I was happy about that. I loved Lily, but I didn't have high expectations when it came to the guys she picked for me. I found it was just easier for me to meet someone out on my own, but once again, here she was trying to set me up. *Great.*

Lily walks over to sit next to me on the couch, fluffing out her dress as she leans back staring up at the ceiling with me. Simultaneously, we turn our heads toward one another and Lily gives me a reassuring look.

"I promise this time will be different." She says as I roll my eyes. She nudges me with her shoulder. "You will not be disappointed." She smirks, as she emphasizes the word "not."

"Fine." I say, pressing my lips together.

"Good! I'll send you the details later. In the meantime-" She pulls me up with her from the couch and onto the pedestal with her. "-how amazing is this dress?

"It looks perfect on you." I smile, looking at our reflection.

"Right? It truly does! Thank you so much Barb!" Lily says, turning to the dress shop owner who helped us. *I knew her name was Barb!* "Can you have it delivered to Mason's?"

"Of course," Barb says smiling as she stands off to the side of the mirror. "Once my assistant gives it one last steam, I can have it delivered by Wednesday."

"Thank you!" Lily unlocks arms with me and steps down, heading back into the dressing room. Within a few minutes, Lily walks out and we head to the front of the store.

"Oh! Mason's here!" She says, looking around me.

I turn around and see a black town car parked outside the shop. Lily turns her attention back towards me.

"We're getting lunch together, but I'll see you soon, okay?"

I nod and she embraces me in a hug before swiftly running out the door. I watch as she hugs Mason, who is now standing outside of the car and they slide into the back seat together.

I turn to Barb and wave goodbye, before exiting to walk back to my apartment complex, only eight blocks away.

When Lily met her fiancé, Mason, two years ago, I didn't doubt for a second that their meeting had been similar to ours. Lily and I live down the street from a small hole-in-the-wall coffee shop, which happens to be right next to my office building, that we frequent often. We had been sitting at our signature corner table together one day, when I got a call from work that required me to go in a little earlier that day. Lily didn't seem to mind me leaving early though.

From what I heard, after I walked out the door, Mason was sitting alone at one of the tables when Lily noticed him looking at her from across the room. Without pause, Lily walked over to his table and sat down across from him, without even asking first. I can imagine Mason was fairly shocked that a stranger sat down with him that morning, but in true Lily fashion, she was able to secure a date with him less than a minute later. Don't ask me how she did it, but I have no doubt she used the same friendly demands that she used on me back in elementary school.

It wasn't long until they were engaged. Maybe ten months? I remember Lily had shown me all of the rings on her phone that she had sent Mason weeks prior, pointing to all the ones she hoped would be "the" winner. Which, in her mind, meant any one of them met her standards.

It was a Saturday night and I remember sitting on the couch in my pajamas when Lily facetimed me to share the news. Her face lit up as she went through every detail of how it happened and how she didn't expect the surprise, which I knew wasn't true. She had been anticipating it and had called me earlier that day saying she was sure it would happen that night, and sure enough, it did.

She then showed me the ring, which took over the entire small screen on my phone. It must have been two carats from what I could tell and wow, did it sparkle. It was identical to one of the photos she showed me earlier in the month and I could tell Lily was happy to get one of the rings she truly wanted.

As she started planning her wedding, she slowly started to move her things from our small, shared apartment over to his place across town. And with that, the apartment we had shared started feeling bigger and bigger as Lily started staying over at his place more and more, but she still kept a few things of hers at our place. I didn't expect it, but seeing her stuff slowly disappear was discouraging, considering it was the first time in my life that I was living on my own.

When I had left for college, Lily was right there with me, ready to move into our dorm. She made it a lot easier when I was away from my mom because she already felt like the sister I never had. She always knew the right thing to say to cheer me up when I was down and she was so optimistic, so I think it rubbed off on me at times.

When we graduated, we found this apartment complex that had been recently purchased by some real estate mogul, but had incredible rental prices, so we jumped at the opportunity. The apartment was right across the street from a small park, offering a breathtaking view of the city and it was close to my office. *The perfect place.*

I always found it strange that the price was so affordable, considering the apartments nearby were almost triple the price. I wasn't complaining though. Even though Lily wasn't paying half of the rent any longer, it was still a great deal even for one person.

Walking home from the dress shop, I stopped as I passed the park across from my apartment complex. Several kids were playing on the swingset, their parents pushing them higher and higher as they laughed. All around the park, there were large trees flaked with pops of red, yellow and orange - something that would have made me ecstatic when I was younger, but not any more.

Growing up, I always loved the trees planted down the sidewalks of my neighborhood. They were large enough to drape over the street, creating a tunnel that you could drive through when coming home. As the trees changed colors and the air got cooler, signaling the end of summer and the beginning of fall, my excitement grew each day as I looked forward to the fall activities. Jumping into freshly raked leaf piles and carving pumpkins that we handpicked from the farm outside of my hometown, it was a time of year I always looked forward to when I was younger. Unfortunately, now it also was a time that carried with it some of my worst memories.

I turn and walk into my apartment complex. Once I get inside my apartment, it is dark inside, but the light from the window illuminates the furniture in the room. I look over at Lily's remaining boxes in the corner and let out a sigh as I set my keys down on the counter.

Lily's wedding is only two weeks away, but I know I have to put on a happy face when I am around her. I don't want to worry her, especially since she won't be at our apartment any longer, but living alone will be harder than I imagine. I should be happy to have this big apartment to myself. More storage, more room for me to paint in, yet seeing how empty it really is, it's hard not to get lost in my thoughts.

I walk over and grab a photo of Lily and I that is sitting on a corner shelf and study it for a moment.

I can't wait for Lily to get married though. I'm sincerely happy for her, but whenever I think about her wedding day, it's hard not to think about my own future. I think about how Lily will walk down the aisle in her beautiful dress, happy that everyone she loves is there to celebrate with her. I think about how she found the perfect person for her that will be waiting for her at the altar. I think about her holding onto her dad's arm as he walks her down the aisle. It's going to be an amazing day for my best friend and I can't wait for it, but I can't help but think about the what if's.

The only family I have is my mom and Lily. I won't get that perfect wedding. That perfect dream. And I definitely won't have the one person I wish could be there. *My dad.*

Chapter Four

I never thought we were poor and I wasn't sure how we were able to afford living in such a nice neighborhood, but I never felt like I fit in with those around me. Despite having other kids my age living down the street from me, I didn't have friends. My parents tried to get me to play with the neighborhood kids, taking me to playdates and setting up sleepovers, but it just never felt like I was supposed to be there. Many of them had the latest toys on the market and got whatever they wanted when they asked, something that I never experienced up until recently. Others called me "different," but honestly I think they were the ones that were different. Like a typical kid, I wanted to run around outside playing pretend, climbing trees and getting messy, but these neighborhood kids refused. *Their loss.*

I have pretty standard toys, but nothing like the ones the neighborhood kids have. It wasn't until earlier this year when I turned six that I started getting more toys from my parents, specifically my dad.

I remember one weekday afternoon, my dad came home and surprised me with a brand new trampoline in our backyard. Up until that point, I had only ever gotten something new for my birthday or for Christmas, which made this moment really stand out in my memories. But, that was just a turning point and I received more and more gifts as the months went on.

With the latest and greatest toys, I finally felt like I fit in with the neighborhood kids, who had always gotten whatever they wanted. Even though my dad kept surprising me with these amazing gifts, it didn't stop me from staying true to who I was. I was still the kid that wanted to spend time outdoors, pretending to be a pirate on my ship (my trampoline) and I never once strayed away from my family.

I've been curious though how my dad has been able to afford giving me such nice toys and gifts over these past few months. The newest gift being my painting set. While I've always loved to draw with my dad, I am also a pretty talented painter for my age, or at least that's what he always told me.

As I pressed my forehead against the window, my eyes widened at the sight. I pulled on my favorite leather ankle boots as I shuffled towards the door and nearly pulled the coat rack down as I grabbed the first jacket I could find hanging on a hook. As I wrapped it around myself, I ran down the front steps to the grass and nearly tripped as I caught a glimpse of the breathtaking trees surrounding our house. The trees must have just started changing colors overnight because I hadn't taken notice the day before. I turned back inside to grab my new painting set, planning to spend the entire day outdoors. *Who doesn't love painting trees?*

I couldn't have been outside painting for more than a couple hours when a moving truck pulled up to the house next door. I didn't remember the house even being up for sale nor did I see anyone move out of the house, yet there they were. *New neighbors.*

Behind the truck, a large black SUV pulled up and into the driveway of the house. I put down my paint brush on the easel, as I looked into the SUV, trying to make out the faces of those inside through the dark, tinted windows.

After a few moments, the driver's and passenger's doors opened and two people stepped out - a man and a woman. They appeared to be in their mid thirties or forties and wore nice clothes, as if they came back from an event. The man, dressed in a black suit with shiny shoes, walked over to the moving truck that had parked in front of the house. The woman, dressed in a bright floral maxi dress with long blond hair, appeared to contrast the man in every way.

She turned toward the back seat behind her and before she could grab the handle, the door flung open. Sitting in the back seat was a light brown-haired boy, who appeared to be close to my age, maybe a little older, wearing a button down shirt and jeans.

The boy climbed out of the SUV and immediately stared at me sitting in my yard with the painting easel in front of me. Giving me a quick smile, he turned and walked alongside the woman, whom I assumed was his mom, and they both disappeared inside the house.

I was hopeful to have a new neighbor, someone who maybe I could get along with this time, but feelings of doubt crept in. I could already tell their SUV was nicer than ours, they had bought one of the biggest homes on the block and judging by the way they were dressed, they already fit in with the other rich neighborhood kids that I didn't have anything in common with.

"Ah, new neighbors!" I heard from behind me, causing me to jump.

I turned around to see my dad standing behind me and he looked over at the moving truck in front of the house.

"That's exciting!" He put his hand on my shoulder. "How's the painting coming along?"

I looked back at my painting and my dad leaned in closer to get a better look.

"Wow! You definitely have a talent for this, kiddo!" He glanced down at me and smiled, before pulling away and kissing me on the top of my head. I watched as he straightened himself up and patted my back.

"Should we go meet the new neigh-" My dad said, before pausing.

I looked up to him. His body was frozen, but I could feel his hands slightly shaking against my back, as if he was cold. *The weather wasn't that bad.* Despite me wearing a coat that day, I didn't think it was cold enough to make my dad shiver.

I looked back out to see what my dad was looking at. In the new neighbors house, the man dressed in the black suit was standing in his yard, looking back in our direction. As soon as I locked eyes with him, I felt chills through my body. *Jeez, am I cold now?* I didn't know why, but this man felt dangerous to me, like how you feel when your parents tell you stories about how to stay away from stranger dangers. It felt like that. Within a few moments, he turned away from our direction and walked inside the house, following the boy and his mom.

"Come on kiddo, let's go inside." My dad said as he stepped in front of me, blocking the view of the neighbor's house.

"But I'm not done painting." I looked up at him and gestured to my painting on the easel.

"I know, but you can finish it another day." He looked down at me with worry in his eyes. *Was something wrong?* I never made my dad upset, but I felt like he wouldn't back down from this, so I nodded.

Once inside, he turned to me, with a concerned look in his eye.

"Hey kiddo, I want you to stay away from that new neighbor." I stepped back, confused by what he said. Why was he saying this? He and mom always encouraged me to try to meet new people and yet, now he wanted me to stay away from the neighbors?

"Why dad?" I asked, tilting my head.

He placed both hands on my shoulders and let out a small laugh. "Well, they are just like all the other kids on the block." He paused. "Snobby." He scrunched his face up when he said the last word and I laughed.

Judging by the way the new neighbors were dressed, I wouldn't doubt it one bit. If I didn't get along with the other neighborhood kids, why would I get along with this family too? My dad was right. No point in trying to make friends with that boy.

My dad leaned in and kissed my forehead.

"Hey, I'll always be your friend though." He said, before pulling away. As he leaned back, he started tickling me and I couldn't help but laugh.

Through my laughs, I shouted, "That's because you're required to!"

Eventually, I fell to the floor, unable to resist his tickling against my ribs. As soon as he stopped, my mom walked downstairs.

"Alright, who is ready for lunch?" She asked.

"I am!" I shouted, raising my hand up to the air.

My dad held out his hand, pulling me up from the ground and into a bear hug, as he carried us into the kitchen.

It was a Saturday and most of the green leaves had faded from the trees and were replaced with orange, red and yellow leaves by now. Some even started to fall to the ground. The air was cool and I was able to wear my favorite sweater, a blue sweater with light pink stripes. It was my favorite not only because it was warm and comfortable, but my dad always commented on how it matched my bright blue eyes, which made me love it even more. I practically wore it every day in the fall because of my dad.

As I jumped on my trampoline, I was able to see into the backyard of the mysterious neighbor's house.

Jump.

No furniture. Even after almost two weeks of living there, they still hadn't added any patio furniture into the backyard or added outdoor decorations.

Jump.

Looking over at the trash bins, I realized I hadn't seen any empty moving boxes left outside either.

Jump.

I saw the backdoor of the house open up and the boy walked out.

Jump.

The boy locked eyes with mine as my gravity pulled me back down to the trampoline.

Jump.

Then, he was gone. I continued to jump, trying to see if there was anything else peculiar in their yard, but the boy was gone.

Jump.

"Are you spying on us?" A voice to my left caught me off guard as I came down from my jump. I nearly missed the trampoline when landing and my leg got stuck between the gap of the springs. *Ouch.*

I looked over at where the voice came from and saw the boy standing in my yard with the gate open. I pulled myself out of the gap, with only a few minor scrapes and balanced myself back on the trampoline while he stared at me.

Once again he is dressed up, just like the day I first saw him. This time, he was wearing a collared shirt with a half zip sweater over the top and jeans. Did he always look like he was heading to an event? *So typical of the rich neighborhood kids.*

I jumped off the trampoline and walked over to him, just as he pushed his brown hair back and straightened himself up.

"I wasn't spying." I insisted. "Just playing on my trampoline. That's all."

He looked down at the trampoline, then back into my eyes.

"Sure doesn't look that way." He said, raising an eyebrow.

"What is it anyway with your backyard? It's so empty. It doesn't even look like you've settled in." I said, raising an eyebrow back and giving a sarcastic look.

He let out a small laugh. "So you admit it."

I rolled my eyes at him.

"We move around often so my father doesn't want us to settle in too much."

"Your father? The suited man who looks like he's always angry." I joked.

He laughed again, a little louder this time. "Yeah, I guess he does look that way." He said, nodding his head in agreement.

I think back to what my dad had told me on the day the neighbors moved in and his words echoed in my head. *I want you to stay away from that new neighbor.* I didn't want to betray him and do the opposite of what he asked, but he never was specific as to *which* new neighbor. *Aha! Loophole!* Or maybe he just meant the boy's mom or the boy's dad? I mean his dad does have that subtle always-angry look about him so maybe that was who my dad was referring to? I decided to go with that choice and I stuck my hand out in front of me.

"I'm Paige." I said.

"I'm-" The boy said. "I go by Ace."

I smiled as he shook my hand.

"Would you want to come play with me?" I asked, gesturing over to the new swingset with a rock wall my dad had bought me the week before.

"I'm not really allowed to." He shrugged and looked back at his house.

I looked at him and frowned. "Well why not?"

Hesitantly, he said, "Well my father doesn't want me to." *Odd.*

I wondered if his dad said the same thing to him that my dad had said to me. That would be strange. Either way, we can't cause too much damage just the two of us playing together, right?

I grabbed his arm and pulled him toward me.

"Well, we are neighbors now, so it's non-negotiable. We have to be friends!" I smiled back at him as I pulled him over to the swingset. He reluctantly gave in and walked over with me.

Even though I was old enough to go to kindergarten, I think my mom enjoyed our time together while my dad worked during the day, so that is why she homeschooled me. She would give me lessons throughout the week, helping me to learn what would've been taught in school, but I always found a way to be a step ahead of her. When she was making sure I could count to one hundred, I was already able to do a good amount of basic addition and subtraction. I think it was just easier having my mom teach me versus a teacher, but I wouldn't have known that at the time. Since the lessons only took up a few hours of my day though, this meant I had more time to spend with Ace.

I never asked Ace why he wasn't in school. I knew he was about two years older than me and definitely should have been in school, but I just assumed maybe he didn't make the cut since it was later in the year when he moved next door. Or maybe his mom homeschooled him like mine did? Either way, it never mattered to me. All that mattered was that I got to spend nearly every day with him and that's all I cared about.

Ace and I grew closer and closer as the weeks went by and he quickly became my best friend. I remember the day he told me I was his best friend. It came as such a shock to me, because I had never had a best friend before, even though I had tried to be friends with the neighborhood kids. Ace was different though. He was wholesome, kind and didn't treat me like I was poor or had less than he had. He also began to purposefully dress less and less dapper, a new word I learned, which made me feel like we were equals. I mean, it probably didn't help though that every time he came over to my house his nicely pressed button down shirts and polos would get wrinkled and stained as he played outside with me. Maybe his mom felt that 'regular clothes' were also easier to clean too?

The leaves had almost completely fallen off the trees on our street and despite the dew in the morning freezing the roads, the snow had yet to fall. Ace and I were still able to play outside, which made me happier knowing I'd always have someone to jump into the leaves with. While normally I was the one who thought of different activities to do, one day Ace came over with a large white blanket that he dragged across the ground behind him.

"I thought we could build a fort!" Ace shouted, tugging the blanket up next to him.

"Great idea!" I shouted back, running to hug him. Pulling away, I grabbed the other end of the blanket and helped him set it up over the top of my swingset.

We spent the afternoon decorating the blanket with different drawings using markers that my mom had brought out for us earlier in the day. I drew flowers that appeared to be swirling in the wind across the blanket and drew leaves to match the ones scattered across the ground.

While Ace claimed he wasn't the best artist, I encouraged him to try to draw something different, but he opted to go with simple drawings of windows and doors to have on the outside of our blanket fort. When we finished drawing, Ace pulled me outside of the fort so we could admire our work of art.

"I think it looks amazing!" I said, my face lighting up with excitement.

"Well you did most of the work. Look at those amazing drawings!" He smiled down at me. "Now we have a fort for our club."

"Our club?" I asked slightly confused as I tilted my head up at him.

"Yeah! All best friends have one." He put his arm around me and I smiled up at him.

I spent nearly everyday playing with him and he never questioned what we were going to do, he just went along with it. I didn't realize we were even best friends, but I never had anyone else to compare him to. He was the one person I looked forward to spending time with and he always seemed just as eager to see me. He truly was my best friend.

"And our one club rule should be that no matter how out of touch we get, we'll always be there for one another."

"Wait, you're not going somewhere, right?" I asked, slightly worried.

"No, but you never know." He said, tilting his head. "So we have to promise that to one another!"

I stepped back from his embrace and placed my hand out in front of me. "I'll take that deal!"

"Deal!" He said, shaking my hand. "What should we name our club?" He placed his hand on his chin as if to think.

I had never named a club before, but I imagined it had to be something we could both remember.

"It should be something that combines both of our names." I said as I ran over to the blanket that we built the fort out of.

Grabbing a marker off the ground, I quickly started drawing our club logo. *Every club has one, right?* Ace patiently watched as I drew out the design in under five minutes.

"It's perfect!" He said, walking over and hugging me from the side as I dropped the marker.

"I really think so too."

From behind me, I heard the screech of the sliding glass door coming from my house. Still hugging, Ace and I both turned toward the house where my mom was standing on the porch.

"Wow! You two have done a great job." She shouted, lifting up a disposable camera to her face. "Smile guys!" We both smiled as my mom took a photo of us.

"Can Ace stay for dinner?" I shouted back, pulling back from our hug. Before my mom could answer, I grabbed Ace's arm and pulled him toward my house.

"Of course he can." She said, stepping to the side as we walked under her arm through the sliding doors.

Ace came over most nights for dinner. It was becoming a routine and I didn't mind. Not one bit. But tonight, my mom wanted us to have a family dinner. Just the three of us. When I let Ace know that earlier in the day, he didn't mind. I was happy to hear that my dad would actually be home on time for us to all eat together, as he had been working late over the past couple weeks. He said it wasn't uncommon for his job, although I didn't quite know what he did for a living.

It was just past six o'clock when our home phone rang. My mom and I had already started making dinner and I was eager to see when my dad would be getting home. I jumped out of the dining chair and grabbed the phone off the counter, before the alien-like voice announced the caller ID out loud.

"Hello?" I answered, lightly out of breath.

"Hello, this is the County Sheriff's Department. Can I speak to your mother?" The deep voice sent chills down my spine. I looked over to my mom, fear striking my face. *This wasn't my dad.*

"Who is it?" My mom asked, confused by my facial expression.

"It's the police." I slowly walked over and handed my mom the phone, as she reflected the fear she saw in my eyes.

I walked over and sat on the couch as my mom spoke to the man on the phone. I couldn't make out exactly what the man was saying, but as if I could, I knew what happened when my mom started crying. I knew it was bad. And I knew it had to do with my dad. I had always seen my mom as a strong, kind person, but at that moment, I didn't recognize her. She looked broken.

I sat there on the couch, inching closer and closer to breaking down myself. I didn't want to believe it. My dad was here just this morning, sitting with us at the dining table. How could he be gone?

The night before, I had drawn him a picture of our home, as the first signs of snow had started sprinkling the ground outside. While I was a little heartbroken to see the bare trees where my favorite colored leaves once were, I was still excited to see the changes outside. I wanted to capture the small snowfall that surrounded our home and thought it would be a fun change from my typical illustrations.

I handed it to him while we were eating breakfast together the following morning and in his typical dad-fashion, he told me it was his favorite drawing I had done. *He said that every time.*

Wanting to display it in his office, he packed it into his bag, gave me a hug goodbye and drove off into his car. Only, I didn't realize that would be the last image I would have of him in my head. Him driving away to work. Something that will now be eternally pierced in my memories.

I slowly walked over and held my mom in my arms as she hung up the phone, placing it back on the table. It was at that moment that I broke down with her. I tried to hold it back, but I no longer could. The pain had taken over and I felt sick to my stomach. I felt like the world was crashing around me. I had just lost someone.

I don't remember when she told me about the accident, but I remember the details vividly. My dad had been driving home from work when he supposedly lost control of his vehicle on the road and the car rolled, according to the police. I'm not sure how it happened, but the car caught on fire and my dad was unable to get out of the car fast enough, or maybe he lost consciousness. The police said it was a "tragic accident," but I just still couldn't believe it. He was there hours before and now he was gone.

The days following the accident were difficult. I felt like my world came crashing down and I was drowning, unable to catch a breath of air. My mom and I both stayed inside the house, trying to come to terms with the now-empty presence in our life, as the snowfall picked up outside.

Staring out into the fresh, snow-covered day, I would have jumped at the opportunity to go outside and build a snowman with my dad, but now it would only ever be a wish that would never come true.

I must have lost ten pounds in those short, but horrid days, due to the lack of eating. It was a lot for someone my age, especially since I wasn't very heavy to begin with. However, once I finally felt like I could sit down and eat something, I couldn't stop. Like my body was trying to help me recover from the rollercoaster I had ridden.

It was honestly a surprise that Ace didn't come over once the news broke throughout our neighborhood. I had my mom, but since we were both going through this tragedy together, it only made me feel like I was sinking lower and lower. I needed a friend more than ever to help me through everything that had happened.

After breakfast, I had planned to go over to his house, hoping he could help me understand my pain. Even just a little bit.

Beep.

I looked around the room, trying to find the soft, muffled noise.

Beep.

I sat down my fork on the table and looked toward the front room.

Beep.

As I stood up, I walked over to the large window next to the front door and peeked outside to see where the obnoxious noise was coming from.

I stopped. My eyes widened at the sight. *This wasn't happening. It couldn't be.*

I watched as a moving truck, at the end of the driveway, continued reversing, pulling out into the street. The truck halted, then slowly started driving down the freshly snow-plowed street. I knew Ace said that his father didn't want to get settled because they moved often, but there it was - a moving truck driving away. Had Ace already left? Had he not even cared to say goodbye? *Impossible.*

I watched as suddenly the back of a black SUV started pulling back from the driveway, stopping halfway to the street. Out from the garage, his mother, dressed in a long black coat that hung down to her black boots, started walking to the vehicle. She turned, looking back at the house and mouthed something before getting into the passenger's side. *Where was he? Where was Ace?*

The car sat alone on the slick driveway for only a brief moment, until a shadow in the corner of my eye caught my attention. *Ace.*

Without a second to think, I ran to the front door, slipped on my boots and raced down the steps of the porch, nearly falling over as I made it to the snow-covered ground. Trudging through the snow in my pajamas, I stopped in the middle of my yard, just past the bushes that surrounded our porch. I froze as soon as Ace's eyes landed on mine.

I had never seen Ace look like this before. The sorrow and desperation behind his eyes made him unrecognizable. Ace always had a calm, composed demeanor, knowing exactly what to say when the time needed it, but seeing him there, I briefly forgot about what had happened to me in the previous days. All I could think about was that I needed to make sure Ace was okay. I needed to help him at that moment. Tell him all the things he needed to hear. *He needed me.*

If time had stopped, I wouldn't have even realized it. I could only see Ace standing next to the SUV and I could tell he was on the verge of breaking down. I felt a pit in the bottom of my stomach. Time was fleeting. I knew that this was perhaps the last time we would see one another.

"I'm so sorry." I saw the words mouthed in my direction as a tear fell from his eye. I didn't want to hear that. I wanted to hear that everything would be okay. That we would be okay.

"In. Now." I heard the sharp words pierce my heart, as his father demanded he get into the vehicle. Our eye contact broke and swiftly, Ace disappeared into the vehicle.

I watched as it pulled down the driveway and slowly vanished as it drove further and further down the street. This was just another stab to my heart. My knees buckled as I collapsed to the ground and my vision blurred as tears uncontrollably fell down my cheeks and disappeared into the snow.

This couldn't be happening. My heart, that had already been shattered days earlier when the news of my dad's accident had been dropped on me like a bomb, was being ripped into shreds again.

The one person that could have made me feel better during this low point in my life, or could have at least helped make it somewhat easier, was gone. I didn't get to ask why he was leaving. I didn't get to ask him where he was going and why it was so sudden. I didn't get to say goodbye - to either of them. My dad is no longer here. Ace is no longer here. Both of them. Gone.

Chapter Five

Lily and I would go to our favorite hole-in-the-wall coffee shop, Hanleys, every Monday morning to catch up before work and it had become our little tradition over the years.

As I exit my apartment building, I put my arm up to hail a taxi despite being only a few blocks away. I just want to try to avoid the color-changing trees around me that remind me of the past.

Coffee shops were always easier for me to sketch in because I could draw inspiration from those sitting inside, as well as watch the world around me through the large windows outside the shop. At most though, when I was with Lily at our coffee shop, I could barely get one drawing out before we dived deeper into another conversation. We would end up talking the entire hour and regretting it each week, but that didn't stop us from going every Monday.

Despite Lily now living with Mason full-time, I couldn't imagine going to Hanleys without her, but I truly needed to catch up on work after taking a few days off for Lily's bachelorette weekend. To me though, it didn't even feel like work and was more of an excuse to do what I love.

I work for a children's book publisher as a design assistant, helping to create book cover designs and working closely with the illustrators, but I'm not quite in my dream job yet.

I had always had a love for drawing. It was my one, true passion. My dad was the one that led me to it. While not a professional himself, he taught me about shading, creating characters and focusing on the small details. I remembered every detail when he would describe and explain it all to me, as I would sit on his lap, examining every mark he made with his pencil. Those were some of the happiest memories that I had from when I was younger and I couldn't have been more than four or five years old.

Keep his memory alive in any way that you can. The words from the psychic rang into my head.

Ever since he passed away, illustrating has become not only a coping mechanism for me, but it's also made him feel close to me, even as I get older. I'm happy that his memory will always be kept alive from our shared passions.

If I were to become a full-time artist at this company, I would finally be able to do more than assist. I'd be able to not only illustrate the images within the story, but the words within it as well. That's my dream. My next step, but I didn't know if that would ever happen. I had been a design assistant for years and it was starting to wear on me, despite it still allowing me to continue my passion for illustrating.

As I arrive at the coffee shop, it is busier than I anticipated. Most tables are occupied around me and it is filled with people talking to one another, working on their computers or the rare few that were just sitting silently enjoying their morning coffees.

After ordering a mochaccino, I am relieved to see the table in the corner is empty, as Lily and I would usually arrive right when the shop opened, getting first dibs. I still loved the table though. It not only gave me space to draw, but allowed me to people-watch with the perfect view.

I walk over and sit down at the small table, but before I can pull out my sketch book from my bag, the bell above the door to the coffee shop chimes.

Leaning over, with my hand still on the top of my open bag, I look up and catch sight of the back of a tall man, his face turned away from me. As he walks over to the counter, his broad shoulders tighten against the back of his gray suit. I watch as the barista speaks to him, smiling as she swipes his card. His hand runs through the back of his dark hair and his muscles swell against the fabric of his sleeve. *Could it be him?*

"Order for Paige!" My eyes shoot over to the left, where another barista places my order on the table top for pickup. My eyes quickly move back to where the man is standing at the counter, but now his head is turned facing in my direction. I let out a deep breath, not realizing I had been holding it in. *Damnit.*

The man has a similar physique and is wearing glasses, but looks nothing like the image I still have piercing in my memories. The eyes that made me melt where I was standing. The smirk that tingled every ounce of my body. Of all the men in the world, why would I even think Ryker would be in this coffee shop? Thousands of miles from where we met? *Get over yourself, Paige.*

I straighten myself back up into my seat as the man turns back to the barista. Shaking my head as I walk over to the counter, I grab my coffee before quickly hurrying back to my seat.

I take a sip of my coffee before placing it in front of me and pull out my sketch book from my bag on the floor. Opening it, I start doodling, hoping my mind will get me back into work-mode. *How could I even think of work when my head is filled with images of Ryker?*

My phone dings next to my sketch book on the table. I smile as I see a text from Lily, hoping she can take my mind off of my ridiculous thoughts.

Happy Monday! Are you at Hanleys?

I pick up my phone and reply.

Yes, it's different without you.

I know. I wish I was there!

Me too.

Soooo, your blind date is set up for Friday!

My eyes get wide and I remember the conversation with Lily that we had at the dress shop. I didn't think she would actually be serious about setting me up again.

I let out a sigh, hoping I'll be prepared once again for another embarrassing blind date courtesy of Lily. But, maybe it'll help take my mind off things? We both know I need it. My only worry though is that if somehow this guy she sets me up with turns out to be okay, I'll feel guilty either way. *How could I go on a date with a guy when all I could think about was someone else?*

Do I have to?

Yes, but you won't regret it! I promise it won't end like last time!

How do you know that?

Hey, just trust me, okay? It's not like I'm your best friend or something!

Fine, but I won't be dressing up.

Oh yes you will! You'll be meeting him at Forrester's at 7pm.

Geez!! Who is this guy? That's ridiculously expensive.

Just wait and see! Also - what are you doing on Wednesday?

What do you think…?

Pjs and TV?

Yup! It's like you can read my mind!

Well, change of plans! I want you to come see the new apartment!

And miss out on my favorite show? Well, since you are my best friend and all, I'll do it just for you!

Yay! I'll send you my address later! I gotta go, but order a mochaccino for me, okay?

Already ahead of you!

I send her a quick picture of my drink on the table before looking up at the time. *Shit.* I grab my sketchbook and shove it into my bag on the floor, nearly knocking my drink over. I stand up and quickly rush out the door, as I head to my office building next door.

Just as I sit down at my desk, I hear my name get called from above my cubicle. I peer out into the aisle to see Anna, my team lead, standing in the doorway between her office and the aisle. I look around, then stand up, wearily walking over to Anna's office, as she steps back inside. *Shit.* What did I do wrong? Am I getting fired? This is not going to end well.

"Sit down please." Anna says, gesturing to the chair in front of her as I walk into her office, closing the door behind me. I walk over and sit on the edge of the chair, hoping I can quickly escape once the news gets delivered.

"How are you doing today?" Anna says, smiling at me. *Please no small talk, just get to the point.*

"I'm good." I cautiously say, waiting for the words to come out of her mouth.

"It's been a tough couple months on you," Anna picks up a folder from her desk. *Here it comes.* I stare at the folder in her hands. "But I think this is the right time-" *Just get to the point.* "-for you to finally get a shot at what you've been wanting."

"Wait." I cock my head to the side and raise an eyebrow. "What are you saying?"

"You've proven to me that you can handle anything we throw at you and I think it's time for your first solo project. Finally see what you can truly do on your own." Anna hands me the folder. *Wait what?*

Opening it, I look down at a manuscript for a book, covered with small sticky notes with illustration requests. I lean back in the chair, unaware I am slumped over at the edge of the seat.

"As you can see, we've already added some notes on what we are looking for." Anna continues. I look back up at her and realize my informality, straightening myself back up into the seat. "But of course, we want to see your own visual interpretation as well."

"I don't know what to say." I stutter. I blink several times, then reality hits and a smile grows on my face. "All I can say is thank you!"

"You're very welcome!" Anna says, smiling back. "And as you may already know, we are wanting another full-time artist to be added to our team, so if this goes well, your name will definitely be in the running."

"Of course. Thank you! I promise I won't let you down!" I quickly say as I stand up, the smile not leaving my face. Anna nods her head in approval as I walk out of the room back to my desk.

I can't believe this is happening. I don't want to believe it, yet here it is. An opportunity that's been dropped in front of me, just like the psychic said would happen. *Must be a coincidence.*

I shake my head as I sit down at my desk, opening the folder. I've been a design assistant for a few years now and a ticket to my dream job has been handed to me. *Finally!*

I quickly skim through the manuscript - a book about a frog that finds a home in a pumpkin patch. I like to think that the pictures of a children's book are what really makes the story come alive. I mean, if you read a children's book, is it truly fun to read if there aren't beautifully detailed images to look at?

I know that the only way I can move up is to make sure this is the best work I've done. *It has to be.* If my dad were still with me, I know how proud he would be. His little artist whom he taught everything to, potentially becoming a full-time artist in the industry. *My dream.*

Chapter Six

While Lily had mentioned that Mason had "some money," I didn't expect them to live in one of the nicest neighborhoods in the city. The complex itself was regal, with gold gilding lining the sides of the building and beautiful gargoyles in the corners that resembled Roman sculptures, rather than frightening figures like in the movies. It was definitely not like our, or rather my, apartment complex across town.

As I walk through the entrance, I am greeted by a doorman and essentially escorted to the elevator. I couldn't tell if this was a normal occurrence from the doorman or if he just thought I looked like a deer in headlights. I mean, I wouldn't blame him. I certainly must have looked out of place in his mind. My go-to ripped jeans and a plain t-shirt looked slumpy compared to the others in the lobby, who radiated wealth in their three-piece suits and elegant dresses.

I arrive at the door to Lily's new apartment, which is on the top floor of the complex. *Of course.* If I was still a child, this would be equivalent to when I went over to try to become friends with the rich neighborhood kids, however, this time, I'm already friends with them apparently.

I knock on the door and Lily opens it almost immediately.

"Paige!" Lily pulls me in and hugs me.

"Hi Lily! Thank you for-" I pause, as I peer over her shoulder while she still holds me in an embrace.

The living room, which has expansive ceilings twice as tall as that of a normal room, is kingly. The room is filled with velvet blue couches, a piano in the corner and on one side of the room there is a bookshelf that fills the entire wall, with a ladder on wheels to help reach the top. On the other wall, are pristine windows that make it appear as if there is nothing there on the wall and the curtains, which are at least twenty feet long, drape the edges of the windows. The room itself is larger than my entire apartment, which I thought was already big for its price, but not compared to this.

Lily pulls back from our hug and places her hand behind my back. "Come on in!"

I quickly take my shoes off by the door, afraid I might track something in. I wouldn't want to ruin anything in Lily's living room. I mean, who knows how expensive everything is.

I walk over to the windows to look out and my mouth immediately drops.

"Pretty nice, huh?" Lily says, turning to me.

The view overlooks the river with the city in the background, making it feel like we are sitting up in the clouds. Not only can I see the entire city and the streets creating rows for miles, but I can even see some landmarks in the background that I know are close to my apartment.

"I don't know." I sarcastically say to Lily. "I still think our - I mean my - apartment view has the best view!" I scoff, but I know it's a lie.

When we first moved into our apartment, I was so amazed by the view that we had. It is and always will be breathtaking to me. Lily's view here was definitely up there though on my list of the best views of the city - which was now a list of two. However, nothing will beat the price I pay. That may be the cherry on top that makes my apartment view even better, knowing I'll always be able to afford living there.

It wasn't until years later when we moved into the complex, after we graduated college, that Lily and I found out that we were the only ones paying a third of the average rent compared to everyone else. It was honestly a shock to us when we found out. Several of our neighbors thought one of us had slept with the owner, whoever that was, but neither of us had even spoken to the landlord themself, at least not in person. We signed the rental agreement and had been making payments all through the online portal, so there was never a moment when we could compare rental prices. Even to this day, I still wonder how we slipped through the system. *Maybe we just got lucky?*

"I have to quit saying 'our' every time." I say to Lily, letting out a small laugh.

Lily throws her arm over my shoulder and hugs me from the side. "Hey, it'll always be 'our' apartment! I was there for almost ten years!"

"That's true!" I say, turning to Lily as she pulls back from our hug. "Wait, how can you both afford all of this?"

"Here! Come! Sit down!" Lily ignores my question and walks over to one of the velvet couches, where she sits down. I follow and sit on the couch across from her.

"No, seriously, how?" I ask again, raising my eyebrows. Lily laughs.

"Well, you know Mason kind of grew up with some money. You know, passed down from generations." Lily says.

"Just some?" I furrow my brows together.

"Oh, I guess I forgot to tell you!" Lily chuckles then smiles at me. "Wedding planning really takes a lot out on a girl! Well, when Mason took over his father's business, he inherited this thriving business, but also some additional money. Well, by some, I mean a lot."

My brows relax and my eyes widen. *Well that explains a lot.* I listen as Lily continues.

"And when we got engaged, Mason wanted us to have a place for just the two of us that was also close to the business, so we hired the best real estate executive in the city to help us - oh!" Lily shouts.

She stands up with a smug grin on her face and walks over to me. I feel myself leaning back into the couch, like an animal expecting to be pounced on as she inches closer. *What did she do?* Lily sits down next to me and purses her lips together, as if she's keeping a secret.

"What?" I slowly ask.

"You know that date on Friday?" Lily says, as a wide smile crosses her face.

"Yeah?" I skeptically ask, leaning forward. I wait a few moments for Lily to speak, but she doesn't. To close the silence, I add, "I really haven't been looking forward to it though."

Lily laughs, then quickly holds her hand up to her mouth, as if to quiet herself. After a moment, she moves her hand away and says, "I just forgot to tell you a little about him, but-" She pauses.

"But what?" I ask, trying to get her to spit it out.

"Well, actually," Lily sits up straight. "I think it's best if it's a surprise." She smiles.

I slump back onto the couch, disappointed that Lily won't tell me anything about this blind date. *She's never this secretive.*

"That's what you said the other day!" I say, a bit frustrated that Lily is being so discreet. Lily puts her hands on both of my shoulders.

"I know, but I'm just really excited for you!" She smiles, pulling me in for another hug. *Why is she hugging me so much? Maybe she misses me?* I put my arms around Lily and return the hug.

"Well, thanks Lily." I say, trying not to sound sarcastic.

I know Lily is really looking forward to me going on this blind date, but I just can't help but think about the worst possible outcomes.

"Hey babe?" I hear a familiar voice call from the other room. *Mason.*

"Yes?" Lily shouts.

"Can you help me real quick?" Mason asks, peering around from behind a wall near their very sleek and modern kitchen.

Despite only seeing his upper body, I can already tell he is getting ready to go somewhere. His sleek blonde hair is pushed back and his face is freshly shaven. He is wearing a dress shirt which is slightly unbuttoned making me think he is in the middle of getting dressed. I will say though, I have no doubt Lily picked the shirt, since the color compliments his blue eyes.

His gaze turns to me and he flashes a quick smile before turning to Lily. "You didn't tell me Paige would be here tonight."

Lily stands up, not losing eye contact with Mason.

"Babe, remember I put it on the calendar? I wanted Paige to see the new place!" Lily glances down at me quickly and gives me a quick smile.

"Oh okay, that's fine." Mason's smile turns to a grin. "We can just all have dinner together then once everyone's here!" Mason steps out from behind the wall and finishes buttoning his shirt.

"Everyone?" I ask, furrowing my brows again.

Lily anxiously looks down at me, then immediately looks back over to Mason.

"Yeah." Lily slowly says. "Everyone?" She tilts her head to the side, as if she is also unaware of who 'everyone' is.

"Yeah babe, to celebrate, remember I invited over-" Mason gets cut off.

"Shoot!" Lily shouts. "I completely forgot!" Lily shakes her head. "Damn wedding brain!"

"He said he'll be here in ten minutes." Mason says before disappearing back behind the wall, into what I assume is their bedroom. Before I'm able to say anything, Lily turns around and stares at me.

"You have to go." She demands, grabbing my arm and pulling me up from the couch forcefully.

"Ouch, Lily!" I say, rubbing my arm where she grabbed it. "I thought we were going to dinner?"

Lily grabs her phone off the coffee table and looks down at it quickly. "I know, but it's getting late."

I grab my own phone from my back pocket and check the time. *6:21.*

"It's not late at all." I snap. I look up at Lily and hold my hands up in front of me. "What's your deal?"

"I just want it to go perfectly. This is not the right time." Lily almost whispers before quickly turning and rushing over to the front door.

"Lily!" I shout before quickly walking over to her standing by the front door.

"I just don't think you should meet Mason's friend yet. That's all." Lily says, giving me a slightly deceiving smile. *Is she lying to me? That's not like her.* Lily then opens the door.

"Okay, so you're kicking me out because you don't want me meeting a friend of Mason's?" I tilt my head. In a sarcastic tone, I say, "You know I'll probably meet whoever this is at the wedding, right?"

"Well, of course, but it'll all be fine then." Lily says, placing her hand behind my back. "But not yet!" Lily starts pushing my back through the open front door and all I can see is how anxious she is getting. *What's her deal?*

"Oh my gosh, fine!" I say with frustration in my tone. "I'll leave, but you owe me!" I start taking steps toward the elevator on my own and her hand releases from my back.

"Definitely! I promise!" Lily quickly says, as she tries to give me a reassuring smile. *I hope she means it.*

"Well, I'll see you soon then, okay?" I hesitantly ask as I look back at her, waiting in the doorway. I turn back and click the button to the elevator, which opens almost immediately.

"Of course! And don't forget to dress up for your date on Friday!" Lily shouts as I step into the elevator.

I peer out quickly to reply, but she has already closed the front door before I can say anything. *Geez.* I click the button for the ground floor. I have no idea why Lily is acting like this, but she has to be up to something. I just don't know what.

Chapter Seven

Paige

As I started working on my solo project, the week had gone by faster than I anticipated. While the book took place during my least favorite time of the year, I tried to think of my dad while drawing the sketches. I used to love the fall and we would go to our local pumpkin patch every year together, a tradition I had looked forward to. When I started sketching the pages for the books, I thought back to those memories. The good ones. The ones where my dad was with me. As if a burst of creativity went through me, I was able to sketch six pages over the course of the week, which surprised even me. It didn't sound like a lot, but typically it would take me twice the amount of time.

I look down at the time on my computer that reads five thirty. *Shit, not again.* I grab my bag, race into the elevator and click the button for the floor level. My blind date is in less than two hours and knowing how excited Lily was about it, I can't be late.

Earlier this afternoon, I had decided that I wasn't going to go on this date especially after how she acted the other night. Lily only set me up on this date for me to potentially have a partner for her wedding, which I maintained I didn't need. However, as if Lily could read my mind from across town, she texted me a reminder about the date and told me I had to go, no exceptions. I could tell she was excited for me to go and had planned the date out a little too much for my liking, so I shoved my thoughts to the back of my head. The least I could do was go on one date, no matter how bad it turned out. *Can't be worse than last time.*

I tap my foot against the floor as the elevator slowly rides down, until I hear a ding. I squeeze my way past the opening doors and walk quickly toward my apartment complex, knowing I won't have time to hail a taxi.

Before I know it, I'm in my apartment with enough time to shower and do my makeup. I check the time. *6:40.* Opening my closet, I grab the nicest dress I own - a slimming black dress with a square shaped neckline, long sleeves and a length that hits just past my knees. I look at myself in the dress as I stand in front of the mirror and smile. *It's perfect.* I look down at my shoes - a pair of black strappy heels. Clicking my toes together, I can't resist the urge to roll my eyes. *I hate heels.* If it weren't for Lily's little voice in my head telling me I have to dress up, I'd have preferred to wear my boots.

I take a step back shaking my head as I realize I'm already putting more effort into this date than I had wanted to. I didn't even want to go on this date in the first place, yet here I was in my nicest dress. I know it's at Forrester's, which is one of the nicest restaurants in the city, but what if this guy is awful? He can stand me up and I'll have gotten cleaned up for an expensive date with nobody. I shake my head. *Do this for Lily.* I take a deep breath, smile at myself in the mirror and grab my purse on the counter before leaving my apartment.

It's two minutes past seven when I stop on the sidewalk in front of Forrester's. Despite being late, I need to know who this blind date is. Lily didn't tell me one thing about this mysterious man, so I have no idea how she expects me to find him in this crowded restaurant. She didn't even tell me his name, which only makes my search more difficult than it needs to be. *Does he even know my name?*

Peering around the side of the building into the large glass window, I look into the restaurant. Crowded, as I expected. I scan my eyes past the tables with groups of people and couples already sitting down, searching for any men sitting alone. I spot one man, who has blonde shaggy hair and a t-shirt on. *Seriously? In this restaurant?* I doubt that's him.

I spot another table across the room, which has a muscular man in a suit seated, however his back is turned away from me. I step forward, trying to peer into the window a little more to see his face, but suddenly I see him turning around toward me, as if he knew I was watching. I immediately duck down to avoid him seeing me. As I slowly inch back upright, I catch a glimpse of his face. The man, who appears to be in his late fifties, has dark eyes under bushy eyebrows with a mustache hiding most of his upper lip. His hair, which from the back looked normal, was extremely combed over to the side. *Yeah that's not him.*

A couple walks by me on the sidewalk and I can see their faces in the reflection of the window. I watch as the girl looks down at my shoes and her eyes move up my body, studying my outfit. Before I can turn around, she scoffs before continuing behind me down the sidewalk. *Shit.* How bad does this look right now?

Sighing, I straighten myself up and walk towards the door to the restaurant knowing I can't keep avoiding this blind date forever. Lily said I'd be pleasantly surprised, but did she mean in a good or bad way? I never got the chance to ask.

When I get to the door, I reach down to grab the handle when the door opens. A doorman greets me with a smile as I walk inside and I let out a small "thank you" as I pass him.

"Hi, I erm," I stumble. "I have a blind date. It was at seven." I peer around the hostess at the stand and attempt to look around the room more. "I'm not sure if he is here or not."

The hostess looks at me and then back down at her book as if she didn't hear a word that I said. I look down at my heels and click them together, waiting for her to speak. After a moment, she looks back up at me.

"I have a reservation for Paige. Is that you?" The hostess raises an eyebrow.

"Yes!" I quickly answer, speaking a little too loudly over the soft music playing.

"Follow me please." The hostess walks me over to a table in the corner close to the restroom. *Great, the worst table.* "Here you are. Your date has not yet arrived."

I sit down at the table with my back against the wall and quickly realize the table isn't as bad as I expected. From my view, I'm able to see almost the entire restaurant, as well as the bar and the entrance. It's almost like the table at Hanleys. *An ideal spot.*

I hang my bag on the back of the chair, but take a quick glance at my phone first. 7:12. *Great.* Not only am I late, but so is my date. *At least I hope.* I put my phone back into my bag, drop the bag so it is hanging from my chair and sit upright just as someone walks up to me.

"Hello, how are you doing this evening?" A skinny blonde dressed in a white button down top with black pants, smiles down at me. I can only assume she is the waiter dressed like that.

"I'm doing well, thank you." I smile back at her, crossing my arms, feeling slightly awkward as I sit alone at the table.

"I'm glad to hear it." She places a menu down in front of me. "Will it be just you this evening?" She starts to remove the plate and glass sitting across from me at the table.

"Oh, no!" I quickly say, placing my hands on the table to stop her. "I have a blind date. They are just late."

The waitress looks around and then starts replacing the dishes on the table. "Would you like me to come back when they are here?"

"Yes please, but can I get a water first?"

"Sure." She smiles awkwardly before placing the other menu down across from me. *Does she think my date ditched me?* I can imagine it certainly looks like that, considering it's well past the time the table was reserved for. "I'll be right back." She turns around and walks away.

As she turns and walks through a double swinging door, I catch myself looking behind her at someone sitting at the bar. A dark-haired man dressed in a navy suit sits at the end of the counter, his back turned away from me. I watch as he raises his hand that's holding a drink and his muscles swell beneath his suit. I lean closer to him over my table, hoping to catch a glimpse of this man. *Could this be my date?*

As he takes a sip of the drink, he rotates his wrist, checking the time on his silver watch. Without pause, he quickly puts the drink down on the table and slides out from the chair. I grip my chair, hoping to catch a glimpse of his face as he walks away, but to my dismay, he walks along the side of the bar and out of sight. *Damn.*

I sit back in my seat and reach for my glass, only to realize there is still no water in it. *Where is that waitress?*

As I scan the room hoping for a glimpse of the waitress so I can politely ask her for the water she hasn't brought me yet, I see a tall dark figure by the entrance. *I freeze.* If I had water in my cup, I would be spitting it out at the moment. This is definitely a dream. I'm imagining it. It can't be.

I stare at him as he stands behind the hostess stand, looking as handsome as the day we met in Nashville. He looks different, but in a good way.

From my memories, I only ever imagined him in a cowboy hat, always wondering what color hair he might have or what his searing green eyes looked like in the daylight. It was surprising to see this different look from him. He looks polished in a navy tailored suit, which hides his extensive tattoos that fill his arms. His dark brown hair, no longer covered by a cowboy hat, is cut shorter on the sides, with a few curly pieces on the top, but still neatly pushed back. I look down at his face, recognizing the dark features, ones I remember so vividly, but are so much easier to see now. My gaze turns to his green eyes illuminated by the chandelier hanging above him. *Just as striking as I remember.*

I had felt something the night we met and knowing this man had been in Nashville, so far away, made it easier for me to forget about him. Or at least I tried to forget about him. Yet, here he was in front of me. Well, across the room from me, but he was here. In the same restaurant as me.

He can still leave though. He can still walk out and I'll find a way to forget about him again. But, what if he sees me? What if our eyes meet from across the room? Every detail about the night we met would flood back into my mind and I don't know if I would be able to forget him as easily as before. And, if I saw him here once, who's to say I won't see him in the city again?

I look back down at my table, trying to avoid accidentally making eye contact. As much as I want him to see him, I'm about to go on a blind date. I can't. *For Lily, right?* But, I can't help it. I have to look. I want him to see me. I want him to look at me. I want him to come over to me.

I turn my eyes back toward the entrance and watch as he turns his head scanning the restaurant, but just as he's about to turn toward my direction, a figure blocks my view. *Shit.*

A man dressed in a tan suit stands between Ryker and myself. *Well there goes my chance.* I lean over my table slightly, hoping to overhear their conversation. Luckily, the restaurant is quiet enough for me to make out some of it.

"Hello Mr. Blackwell," the tan suited man joyfully says. "I didn't see you there! Is there anything else I can do for you this evening?"

"No Ryan, there isn't," Ryker calmly replies.

Ryan? Woah, Ryan Forrester. I remember seeing his name in the newspaper when the restaurant first opened a few years ago, wishing I could afford to dine there just once. It quickly became one of the nicest restaurants in town, according to the papers. Lily must've been excited too that the person she set me up with picked this restaurant. I mean, I definitely was.

"And please, call me Ryker."

I could feel my heart pounding through my chest. It was him. It was definitely him. I had tried to remember his voice from Nashville, but over the loud and crowded room, I had forgotten until now. *His deep, yet calming voice.*

I tighten my legs together under the table, as every thought about him from that night comes rolling back.

"Sorry, Mr. Blackwell," Ryan stutters. He shuffles the hostess off to the side before grabbing a menu from the hostess stand. "Would you also care to sit down for dinner tonight?" *How does Ryker know the owner of the restaurant?*

I turn to look back at the bar where the man that was sitting there earlier has yet to return. The man's broad shoulders pressing against his suit, the dark hair... Wait. I turn back to the entrance where Ryker is standing, his left hand resting on Ryan's shoulder, and I see the expensive silver watch around his wrist. *It was him.* Did he even realize I was sitting behind him?

"Hey Ryan, don't worry! I already have a table." Ryker says, lowering his hand from Ryan's shoulder. Ryan steps to the side and I can see Ryker's face again.

His eyes quickly scan the room once more, before he gazes in my direction and our eyes meet. Just like the night we first met. His face lights up and he sees me, then his smile quickly turns to a smirk. I shyly smile back and within a moment, Ryker is heading in my direction.

Realizing I'm still hunched over my table from trying to listen to their conversation, I quickly straighten myself up and nervously pull my hair out from behind my head and over my shoulders. I slowly lean back into my chair as he inches toward me. *Shit.* What do I even say to him? I had liquid courage to help me talk to him before, but what about now? Where is that damn waiter?

Ryker stops in front of my table and places his hands on the back of the chair in front of me, never losing eye contact with me. I can feel my heart start to race and my eyes widen as he leans closer to me over the chair. It feels like minutes go by as we look at one another, with the silence growing between us. *What am I doing? Say something!*

"I'm on a date." I quickly push the words out. Instantly, I regret it. *Why did I just say that?* I haven't even thought about this blind date since Ryker walked into the restaurant. I mean, the guy hasn't even shown up yet and I don't even know if he will at this point, since it's definitely past the "just a little late" stage of the night.

"Oh, are you now?" Ryker replies with a smirk. *Oh, great.* He probably thinks I'm lying about it. I'm the one that feels out of place in this restaurant and Ryker knows the damn owner. I lightly bite my lip.

"I mean, I will be. He's just a bit late is all." I lie, knowing fully well that the guy will probably never show up. Probably best considering the last date Lily set me up on. And honestly, I could care less about this date now that Ryker is here.

Ryker looks around the room, scanning the people sitting at the tables around us, then once again locks eyes with me.

"Well, you wouldn't mind me sitting here while we wait for this date to arrive, would you?" Ryker teases, pulling out the chair and sits down before I can reply. Within a moment, the waitress arrives at our table with a pitcher of water. *Where has she been?*

"Hello, Mr. Blackwell." The waitress says with a smile as she looks down at Ryker, ignoring me.

She starts pouring the water from the pitcher into the glasses on the table, watching to make sure she doesn't spill. "I'll be your server tonight. Is there anything I can get you to drink?" She turns back to Ryker, who looks at me.

"Is there anything you'd like?" He says.

I watch as Ryker places his hand on top of mine resting on the table between us. *This can't be happening.* I know nothing about this man, apart from his name, yet his hand on mine just feels right. When we first met, his touch sent tingles through my body and it was happening again.

I look down at his hand and look back up at Ryker, his eyes eagerly waiting for mine to meet his again. *I can't believe he is even here. Thousands of miles away from where we first met. This has to be a coincidence, right?*

"A glass of wine." I ask, almost in disbelief, but it comes off sounding like a question. Like I'm asking for permission. I rarely drink, but better to get some liquid courage now, or else I don't know how I'll make it through tonight with this spectacle of a man sitting across from me.

The waitress looks down at our hands touching on the table, then looks at me with an amused look on her face. *I can't believe it either.*

"We'll get a bottle of the 96 Margaux." Ryker confidently says, looking up at the waitress.

"Of course Mr. Blackwell." She says, nodding her head. Ryker looks back at me before she can finish. "I'll get that right out for you." Like before, she quickly turns and exits back into the kitchen through the double doors.

"I want to tell you-" He says, pausing. "I want to tell you something." He pauses again, slightly shaking his head. "No, I have to tell you-" I step in before he can say another word. *I gotta get this out now.*

"I really want to apologize for just ditching you a few weeks ago." I start. "I had no intention of running off after you bought me drinks, but my best friend Lily - it was her bachelorette party and she was really drunk that night and I wanted to make sure she wasn't going to do anything crazy." I catch my breath before continuing. "And then I just left without getting your number or anything and I wanted to get to know you more-"

I stop as a smile grows on Ryker's face before he lets out a deep chuckle, then squeezes my hand, which I had almost forgotten that he was still holding.

"You have nothing to apologize for." He says.

I furrow my brows, worried he's just saying that.

"Are you sure?" I ask, slightly embarrassed.

"Positive." He says.

"Well, at least let me make it up to you in some way." I look around the room, then down at our empty wine glasses, yet to be filled. Holding one up, I ask, "How about I buy us these drinks?"

Ryker scoffs as he looks down at the table, then back up at me.

"I have another idea." He says, raising his eyebrows. "Since I happened to be in this restaurant tonight by pure coincidence and your date decided not to show up, you can make it up to me by staying for dinner."

I purse my lips together as I feel my cheeks turning red. I wasn't planning on leaving this table even if my date showed up, especially now that Ryker was here. I would have turned the guy away in an instant, no matter what Lily had wanted.

I nod in agreement and Ryker smirks.

Every time he gives me that seductive, half smirk, I can feel my heart beating faster and faster. I can only imagine how it would feel for his hand to reach behind my back and pull me close to his chest. My breasts pressed against him as our lips get pulled closer and closer together by an invisible thread between us. My heart would be beating out of my chest and I would have no doubt he would be able to feel it against him. As our lips finally touched, I would melt into his arms as-.

I quickly blink away the thoughts, just as the waitress arrives back at our table with a bottle of wine. Ryker pulls his hand away to grab his glass and I quietly sigh, saddened his hand was only there for a moment.

"What would you two like to have tonight?" The waitress asks, pouring the wine into our glasses.

I look down at the menu and skim through the options. Several things look delicious, but my eyes widen as I see the prices. *Fuck*. Even the cheapest thing on the menu - a salad - is still $60.

My eyes glance up at Ryker and his smile fades as he sees the uncertainty plastered on my face.

"Erm," I say quietly as I keep my eyes glued to the menu. Generally on dates, I know the guy will pay, but I can't expect Ryker to pay for this. It's ridiculously expensive. Even more, this isn't a date. It's just dinner. I definitely can't expect that from him, but how am I going to afford any of these options? The only option I really have would be a piece of bread and butter, but what would he think if I ordered that?

I look up from the menu slightly and see both Ryker and the waitress' eyes on me.

"I didn't really look at the menu." I say, looking back down at the menu as I grit my teeth.

"Hey." Ryker says, lowering my menu until our eyes meet again. He raises one eyebrow. "Trust me, okay?"

I slowly lower my menu and set it down on the table as Ryker turns to the waitress.

"We'll have the usual. Thank you." Ryker says. *He has a usual?*

The waitress smiles at him and grabs both menus in front of us. "Of course, Mr. Blackwell." Once again, she turns and walks away.

This is the first time I've ever been to this restaurant and yet, Ryker is being treated like he owns the place. *Shit, does he?* I think back to the newspaper article about the restaurant opening, trying to remember what it said. The article mentioned a private partner, but no name in specific. I mean, he does know the owner. *Could he be that private partner? No, he can't be.*

My eyes turn to look at my wine glass sitting on the edge of the table. I grab the glass and take a sip. As the flavor hits my lips, my eyes widen. *Woah.* While I didn't drink often, I could taste the difference in this wine compared to the five dollar bottles I got from the convenience store with Lily during college. This was not cheap. The richness of this wine and the hint of blackberry had to be one of the best things I've tasted. I can only imagine the price. *Fuck.* And the menu prices. I look at Ryker and my mouth slightly drops open.

"Who are you?" I ask, saying each word slowly.

Ryker lets out a small laugh before giving me a smirk. "I take that you like the wine then?"

Before I can say another word, I watch as Ryker takes a sip out of his glass. I watch as his Adam's apple rises and falls as he swallows and his facial expression doesn't change like mine did when I took a sip. It's as if he isn't even surprised by the taste. It's as if he's had it many times before. Like it was water. Yet, even I can taste the subtle differences in water.

"I mean, yeah, it's delicious." I quickly say, taking another delicious sip. I shake my head, trying to find the right words. "I mean, what do you do for work?"

"I dabble in real estate now and then." Ryker suavely answers.

"Oh." I ask, slightly turning my head. "What kind?"

"A little bit of everything." He says, keeping his answers short.

"I ask because I saw you talking to the owner, Ryan Forrester." I try to get it out of him, raising my eyebrows.

"Oh, that's what you meant." He smirks again. "Well, I saw an investment in an old building a few years ago and took a chance, but this one was more for fun." *Ah ha! Knew it!*

He takes another sip of wine and I follow suit, waiting for him to give me more details.

"The one I'm most proud of is Florian Apartments. Do you know it?" He raises an eyebrow.

My eyes widen as the wine glass stays pressed against my lips. I slowly lower it and place it on the table.

"You own Florian Apartments?" I ask in disbelief as I lean back in my chair.

"Yes, it's been my most successful purchase." He looks off into the distance slightly, but keeps an eye on me as he takes another sip, waiting for my reply. *It's as if he knows, but he couldn't possibly.* I push the thought away.

"That's actually where I live." I say with a scoff. He leans forward slightly, as if he's eager to hear my next words. "My best friend Lily and I moved there after we graduated."

"Hmm." Ryker snickers and then coughs, before turning his head back towards me. "You don't say."

"Well, actually it's just me living there now. Lily - the one that was in Nashville with me - she's getting married in a few weeks and she and her fiancé just moved into a new place across town."

"Ah, okay." Ryker says, nodding at me as he leans back into his chair, taking in my words. I quickly continue, trying to avoid any silence between us.

"And the view! Wow!" I look up for a moment as a grin grows on my face. As I look back at Ryker, whose eyes lock with mine, he smiles back. As I say the words "It's breathtaking actually," his eyes move down my face and I can feel them watching my lips as the words come out of my mouth. I blush and his eyes shoot back up to meet mine.

"You are." Ryker says quietly under his breath. I feel my face brightening up and immediately turn my focus to his eyes, an easy way to distract myself from blushing more. When we first met, I was barely able to make out his eye color in the dark bar, or even his facial features. Yet now, clear as day, I was able to notice a small hint of gold that sat within the corners of his green eyes.

Ryker is the kind of man I could only ever imagine being with, yet here we were - having dinner at one of the nicest restaurants in the city. While I was supposed to have a blind date tonight, it turned out to be the best coincidence that Ryker was here. His charming personality is a breath of fresh air from the men I'm used to dating, or should I say, from those I've gone on dates with. And now, the last thing on my mind was that blind date. All I could think about now was Ryker sitting across from me.

Hours pass and the ever-lingering sense of familiarity with him made it that much easier to let me guard down as we talked. While I did most of the talking, he seemed content sitting there listening to me. It was probably the wine that made me more talkative, but the entire time he was smiling as I spoke to him about every little thing in life. He said a few things here and there, but I could tell he was genuinely interested in what I was saying and only wanted to know more about me each time I finished one topic of conversation.

As we finished eating the most delicious dinner I had ever had, I half-expected for a bill to arrive at our table, but it never did.

Ryker stands up from the table and pulls his suit jacket off the back of his chair, where he had placed it after our first glass of wine together. He looks down and smiles at me before reaching his hand out toward me.

"Ready to go, beautiful?" Ryker says. I was given compliments from men in the past, but something about the way Ryker said it made me instantly blush. I quickly stand up and look around for the waitress.

"What about the bill?" I ask, worried to leave the expensive restaurant without paying.

Ryker raises his eyebrows at me and reaches his hand out to me, as if to mentally tell me not to worry about it.

"Oh, yeah." I chuckle.

I grab Ryker's hand as he leads me toward the entrance of the restaurant. As we are about to leave, Ryan quickly rushes out from the back room and stops Ryker at the entrance.

"Mr. Blackwell, thank you again for coming. I hope everything was perfect this evening." Ryan frantically says. Despite being a partial owner, Ryan acted like Ryker had been his saving grace with the purchase. Or maybe Ryker just has a lot of friends in a lot of places? *Who knows.*

"Ryan, thank you. It was delicious as always." Ryker pats Ryan's shoulder before pulling me over to the door. Turning back slightly, Ryker chuckles and says, "Hey, and remember, call me Ryker!"

Ryan nods as we exit the restaurant and a rush of frigid air hits my chest, immediately making me tense up from the cold. When I had arrived at Forrester's earlier, I had warmed up from the walk over and the long sleeves on my dress helped to keep me warm, however, after sitting inside the restaurant for hours, the wind had picked up outside and the temperature had definitely dropped.

I look up at Ryker standing next to me watching as I begin to shiver and he takes his suit jacket off, wrapping it around my shoulders. I smile up at him as he grabs my hand once more. *I could get used to this feeling.*

"Can I walk you home?" Ryker asks, raising an eyebrow.

"I'd like that. It's-" I say before stopping.

Before I can finish, Ryker turns to the right, with his hand still holding onto mine, and we head toward my apartment complex. *Of course he knows the way, he owns the damn place.*

The ten minute walk from Forrester's to my apartment felt like a lifetime as we quietly walked next to one another. We did pass a few glances over to one another here and there during the walk back, but not much was said. I felt like I had told him just about everything about me during dinner, yet I still didn't know much about him. I had hoped he would speak up during our walk back, but he stayed quiet, which I assumed was due to nerves. I mean, I had never been this nervous in my lifetime. I had only just met this guy - this amazing man - yet he was already walking me home. I didn't know what kind of person he was, or what his intentions were, but all I wanted was to have him come up to my apartment. I would have died if I had thought these thoughts only a few years prior. *Me? Paige? Asking a man to come up to my apartment on the first date?* But when I stared into those green eyes of his, it didn't matter to me. He could do anything in the world to me and I would be happy about it.

As we reach the complex, I turn and quickly walk up the couple steps to the door and before I can key in the numbers into the door, I quickly feel Ryker right behind me. His warm breath along the back of my neck sends shivers down my spine as we stand outside in the cold. I stop what I'm doing, waiting for him to grab me right then and there and pull me inside, but he doesn't. Time feels frozen as we stand there. My heart beats out of my chest as I feel his chest lean in against my back. I slowly turn around and our faces are mere inches away from each other. I stare into his eyes, then down at his lips, before he inches closer to my face. I feel my heart beat faster as he gets closer and closer to me. All I want to do is pull him in. Have his lips touch mine. I couldn't imagine anything sweeter than that.

"I want to show you something." Ryker whispers, stopping just before our lips touch. I feel his breath against my lips as the words are spoken. *You can show me anything.*

Before I get a chance to reply, he leans around the side of me and enters the pin next to the entrance doors. As I listen to the beeping from the lock, I furrow my brows for a moment, confused about how he knew the code, but my brain quickly reminds me.

Ryker takes a step back and holds his hand out, gesturing to the door.

"After you, beautiful."

I smile as I stare up at him, before turning and heading into the complex. Ryker follows.

I walk over to the elevator and instinctively click the button to go up, forgetting that Ryker wanted to show me something.

"Sorry! Force of habit." I say turning around to look at him. Just then, I hear the elevator door open behind me.

"You're good, Beautiful. It'd be a long way up if we took the stairs." He says, sneering.

I chuckle quietly before turning around and entering the elevator. I don't know what Ryker wants to show me, but if I had any say, I'd want to bring him back to my apartment tonight.

This dream of a man in front of me takes my breath away, literally, and I can't help it when my mind wanders. Thinking of what his muscles look like without his shirt on. How it feels to touch his body. Tasting the flavor of his lips against mine as he kisses me.

As he steps inside next to me, I lean over and try to click the button for my floor on the keypad. Ryker leans over and clicks a button labeled "R" before I have a chance to click my own.

The elevator quickly rides up and dings as we reach the floor. It opens up to an unwelcoming white, cold room with no windows, except for a double door on the other side. *Oh great, am I about to get murdered?*

Ryker grabs my hand once more and leads me through the double doors, where another burst of wind sends shivers throughout my body. Before I can turn around and escape the cold, Ryker puts his arm around my shoulders and pulls me in close. In that moment, I get a whiff of his cologne again, woodsy with a hint of spice, and I instantly feel warm within his arms.

"Come on." Ryker says, pulling us away from the doors we exited through.

I turn my body away from him, still letting him hold me in his arms, and I'm surprised when I see what's around us. I don't know how I didn't realize it before, but instantly I understood what the "R" meant on the elevator. I look around as we are surrounded by lights and tall buildings, as well as the most beautiful view of the city around me. Honestly, I'm completely awestruck.

As I turn my head in one direction, I see the view of the river that I see from my living room window, the water down below lit up by the buildings in the distance. In another direction, I see a view of the city I didn't even know I could see. Looking down one street, I am able to see it continue for miles from where we are standing. If I look closely, I can even focus on each individual person walking up and down the street. As I look around in a different direction, I see the rooftops of several buildings that partially block my view of the city, yet I can still get a glimpse of the bigger skyscrapers all the way downtown.

"Wow." I say, as I gaze around us, not sure which direction to look at next. "This is definitely number one." I whisper.

"Number one?" Ryker asks. I look up to see him smiling at me, not realizing he could actually hear me.

"Of my best views of the city." I reply, smiling back at him. "It was the view from my apartment, but now that you showed me this," I pause. "It's definitely my new favorite."

I start to turn my head, but Ryker quickly adds, "It's definitely my favorite too." He looks back out at the view. "I've actually been coming here for years."

"Really?" I ask.

"Yeah. It's become one of my favorite places to just get away." He says.

"I'm shocked we never ran into one another before." I say, raising my eyebrows.

"Yeah, we must have always nearly missed one another." He scoffs.

I lean my head against Ryker's chest, hearing his heartbeat beneath my ear. I fully expected his heart to be racing like mine has been the entire night, but his is as quiet as can be. A steady beat against his chest.

"Trust me?" Ryker asks, breaking the silence. I pull back and look up at him.

"Yes?" I cautiously ask, even though I imagine I can entrust him to know every worry, fear and secret of mine. There wasn't a doubt in my mind.

Ryker lets out a small laugh, then unwraps his arm from around me, joining our hands together as his arm falls down to mine. He pulls me over to the edge of the rooftop and only a small three foot barrier separates us and the ground far below.

"Look." Ryker says, pointing to the small park below - the one I try to avoid looking at because of the sad reminder it gives me from my childhood memories.

I look down anyways, hoping Ryker doesn't see the discomfort I'm feeling. Except, the feelings of sadness I normally experience don't surround me as usual. Not even in the slightest. All I think about is this moment. I don't think about my least favorite time of the year or the bad memories of my dad. I look down at the colorful trees, lit up by the lights below them, and all I see is beauty. A profound thought that I didn't ever expect to hear myself think. Yet, how can I not? I mean, I'm standing on the rooftop seeing the most amazing views I've ever seen of the city with a man I've only just met. Well, I've met twice. But, I feel like I've known him for years and the only thing I can think about at this moment is him. *Ryker.*

I look up at Ryker, his eyes illuminated by the lights surrounding us. My eyes move down his face to his chiseled jaw, then up to his lips. He grins as he catches me looking. *Kiss me now.*

I feel his other hand slide up behind my neck, pulling me forward as the space between us closes. His other hand drops from mine and wraps around my lower back, pressing my body against his.

As he swiftly pulls me toward him, his lips are on mine and I finally taste his sweet, yet savory flavor as his lips ravage my own. He kisses me deeply, like he has been starving to kiss me. Longing to kiss me since the moment he first laid his eyes on me and I feel the exact same. I had craved his lips against mine and craved what he would taste like against my mouth. His beautiful, delectable flavor. As I get lost in the softness of his lips, the air no longer feels cold around us and my body melts into his warm embrace. Surrounded by this marvel of a man, holding me close, I give in to his movements, following his lead as he kisses me. His hands on me. His touch. His lips against mine. *Oh, it's so addicting.*

I want more, but Ryker slows down his pace and his lips pull away from mine all too soon. My eyes slowly open and I see Ryker, who is wide-eyed. Like he made a mistake. *But, that can't be possible, can it?*

Confused as to why he stopped, I inch closer to him for another kiss, but he steps back.

"What's wrong?" I ask, furrowing my eyebrows, trying to figure out how the passion has turned cold so quickly. I instantly feel the wind chill around me again, sending shivers throughout my body. I take a step back from Ryker and cross my arms around myself, trying to keep the warmth in.

I watch as his eyes quickly look up and down at me, as if to gauge his mistake. His mistake of pulling back too soon. Or maybe his mistake of letting me go.

As he quickly closes the distance between us, I ignore the awkward moment that just occurred and enjoy his arms around me once again. Laying my head against his chest, I feel my body quickly warm up. Back to how I was feeling before. When our lips were tied to one another.

"Nothing. Nothing at all, beautiful." He finally answers, after what feels like minutes standing there. "It's just getting a bit late, is all." Ryker pulls back slightly and looks at me in my eyes, before saying, "Come on, I'll walk you back."

"Okay." I say, letting him lead me back through the double doors to the elevator. I follow, staying silent as we ride the elevator down to my floor. I look up at him a few times as the elevator dings through each floor, but he stares ahead, not looking down. *Did I do something wrong?*

The man that I had been envisioning in my mind since Nashville was finally here, next to me. I had manifested how the rest of the night would play out in my head during dinner, but I did not expect for him to stop it from happening. Stop *us* from happening. Why would he end it? Was he not feeling the attraction between us? Did he not want more?

I look down at my heels against the floor. The kiss we shared would settle into my deepest thoughts and I knew I would replay it in my head over and over again after he left. I mean, how could I not?

I look back up at Ryker, stoic as he stands looking forward. I want to feel it again. His lips against mine. I want it to happen now. *Please.*

As we arrive at my floor, I step out, expecting him to follow, but he doesn't as he stays standing in the elevator. *Shit.* The door begins to shut, but he holds his hand out stopping it, locking eyes with me.

"Do you want to come in?" I tentatively ask, already knowing he won't as the elevator doorway separates us. A silent divider.

"Not tonight." Ryker quickly answers. My eyes scan back and forth on his face and as if he can tell I'm slightly disappointed, he gives me a quick smile. "But I'd like to see you again soon."

"Me too." I say, before quickly adding, "Let me give you my number now!" I quickly grab my purse that's hanging off my shoulder and pull my phone out to hand it to him.

"Don't worry about that." Ryker says, putting his hand up. "I don't think it'll be too hard to find you." He teases.

"Oh, of course." I chuckle, putting my phone back into my purse.

"See you soon, beautiful." Ryker takes his hand off the doorway and the elevator doors start closing immediately. As they are about to close, Ryker winks and my eyes immediately widen and I catch myself taking a breath in as the doors shut.

For the first time in years, I was looking forward to dating. Apart from tonight, it had been months since I had gone on a date at all and yet, by chance, he showed up. In all places. He showed up at the same restaurant I was at. I could care less who my blind date tonight was supposed to be because I got to have a night with the one person I had hoped to see. The man that I get to see again. *And hopefully soon.* The man that took my breath away the first night I saw him at that bar in Nashville. The man that fell back into my life, as if by chance. The one person that I couldn't stop thinking about and that I felt drawn to. *Ryker Blackwell.*

Chapter Eight

Paige

The following morning, I needed to see Lily. I pick up my phone and text her.

Hi, meet at Hanleys in 20?

Within a few seconds, Lily replies.

Obviously! I need to hear about your date!

Oh yeah, the date that never showed. I take a quick look outside, then walk over to my closet. I put on a pair of jeans, throw on a striped knit pullover sweater and head for the door, where I slip on a pair of sneakers. I look in the mirror hanging on the wall before leaving and I'm reminded of the outfit, which made me feel underdressed, that I wore over to Lily's new apartment - jeans and t-shirt. Honestly though, today's outfit would have been a better option for going over to her place, as it's more elevated than what I had on then. *Oh well.*

As I grab the doorknob and walk out of my apartment, I start to close the door behind me and I'm reminded of how Lily kicked me out of her apartment so suddenly. *The favor.* I lock the door and grab my phone out of my purse as I head toward the elevator.

Remember, you owe me a favor! I'll take a large coffee!

I grin as I write the text.

A ding chimes from my phone as I walk into the elevator. I click the elevator button for the ground floor before checking it.

Fine! Heading there now!

See you soon!

See ya!

I put my phone back into my purse, as I step out of the elevator and walk out of the building, turning toward Hanleys. As I start to walk, I stop and turn to the park across the street - the one Ryker showed me from above the night before. *So much more beautiful in the daytime.* I watch as the light breeze rustles the trees and some orange and yellow leaves slowly fall to the ground, which instinctively makes me tilt my head. *Has it always looked this nice?*

Before I know it, I'm standing in front of Hanleys, where I can see Lily sitting at our signature corner table. I walk inside, around a group of people, and head over to her. Lily stands up, smiling, and hands me a large coffee.

"Just how you like it!" Lily says, sitting back down in her seat.

"Thank you! I needed it!" I say, sitting down across from her. I take a sip of coffee and look around the coffee shop, which is bustling with people. Each table has one or two people sitting down at it and the line to order is almost out the door. Placing my cup back on the table, I look back at Lily.

"Pretty busy, huh?"

"I know! It's kind of weird, right?" Lily chuckles, looking around the room. "I guess I always forget that people get coffee on the weekends too, not just Mondays."

"Well, I guess we broke tradition today." I say, as a small yawn comes out through my chuckle.

The events of the night before kept me awake most of the night, replaying in my head over and over again. Ryker's arms around my body keeping me warm. Ryker's hands holding my face. My breasts pressed against his chest. Ryker's soft lips devouring mine. Every image that replayed only made me want him more.

"So, how was last night?" Lily asks, snapping me out of my vivid, divulging memories. I watch as she takes a sip of her coffee, then lowering the cup, she raises an eyebrow at me.

"Honestly, one of the best nights I've had in a long time." I say, before reaching for my coffee on the table between us. I take a sip.

"Oh! Well that's a first!" Lily says wide-eyed. I smile back, keeping quiet. "So I guess that means I'm a blind date expert now!" Lily laughs.

I look up at her, shaking my head. "Erm, no, I don't think that makes you an expert."

"What!" Lily almost yells. She looks around the coffee shop, where other people are looking at her. She shakes her head and turns back to me. "Whatever."

I chuckle. "You still have yet to pick a good one."

"What do you mean!" Lily demands. "You just said you had one of the best nights!"

"Well, this date of yours," I put air quotes up. "Didn't even show up." I grab my coffee and take another sip.

"Ryker never showed up?" Lily frustratingly says. *What did she just say?*

The coffee in my mouth nearly makes me choke and I start coughing. My eyes start watering as I try to catch my breath between each cough.

"Are you okay?" Lily's frustration quickly turns to concern.

When I'm able to control myself, my eyes widen.

"Did you just say Ryker?" My mouth stays open as the words fall out.

"Yeah, Ryker Blackwell. Are you seriously telling me he didn't show up?" Lily grabs her phone, which was face down on the table, and I watch as her fingers start frantically typing.

I quickly blink, trying to understand Lily. "Wait, the blind date was with Ryker?"

Lily doesn't look up from her phone as she keeps texting. Frustrated, she says, "He has half a nerve to not show up for the date. I can't even believe he would do something like-."

I quickly interrupt Lily, hoping to calm her down for just a moment.

"Wait, wait, wait." I hold my hand up in front of me. Lily stops typing for a moment and looks up at me, her face filled with annoyance. "Ryker was there."

Lily's face almost immediately relaxes and she quickly locks her phone and nearly slams it back on the table in front of us.

"So, he was there?" Lily raises both eyebrows and smiles.

"Well, yes, he was there." I say. "It's just-"

"Oh, well that's good!" Lily smiles then takes another sip of her coffee, as if she was never phased by my words.

"I mean, yes, but that wasn't supposed to happen." I lean my head toward her. "I was waiting there for quite some time, but your blind date never showed up. I was just about to leave until I ran into Ryker."

Lily gives me a confused look, then bursts into laughter. *What's going on?* I watch as the people around us in the quiet coffee shop look up from their phones and computers to stare once again at Lily. Looking around at their annoyed faces, I quickly mouth around the room "sorry" and hold my hands up in front of me. Once Lily settles down after her spell of laughter, I turn to stare at her, a bit confused.

"What's so funny?" I raise my eyebrows at her. Lily lets out one last chuckle.

"Paige!" Lily says, a bit loudly once again. "The blind date was with Ryker." *What?* I stare at Lily for a moment, before the words register.

"Ryker was my blind date?" I ask, staring at Lily in disbelief.

When I arrived at the restaurant, Ryker had already been sitting at the bar before I arrived. He must have been waiting for me to walk through the doors, but didn't catch me coming in. Did he also pick the restaurant as well? *Of course. He must've.* Who wouldn't want to take someone to Forrester's? So he was just playing coy the entire time, pretending that my blind date hadn't shown up, when he knew they wouldn't. *How charming.* I let out a small laugh.

"Did he give you the impression that you just ran into one another?" Lily asks.

"I mean," I pause. "Kind of!" I let out a chuckle. "It's honestly kind of funny though. I've been thinking I would run into him since Nashville, so I completely believed it." Lily laughs.

"Wait, wait, wait, how did you even find him?" I say, tilting my head to Lily and leaning forward, eager to hear more.

"Honestly, it wasn't hard. He actually found me!" Lily smiles and I raise both of my eyebrows. Now, I'm even more confused.

"Well, not in that way. When Mason and I agreed to get a new apartment, he told me his friend could help us out. So his friend called me and he was able to set us up with a new place almost immediately. It wasn't until I saw his name on your phone at my dress fitting that I realized that the Ryker I knew was the same one you did." Lily takes a sip of her coffee, catches her breath and quickly raises her eyebrows.

I lean back in my chair in disbelief, then lean forward once more, waiting to hear the rest.

"Oh!" Lily puts the coffee back down on the table. "So I immediately called him that day and told him we wanted to invite him over for dinner to show our appreciation to him."

"Okay." I say slowly.

"And that's when I told him he was going on a blind date with you." Lily lets out a small chuckle.

"Wait." I put my hand up between us to stop Lily from saying more. "You told me I had a blind date before you even confirmed that he would be there?" I press my hands against my temples.

"Oh my gosh Lily. What if he had said no?" I glare at Lily.

"It wasn't hard to convince him, even though I had no doubt I could, but I could tell he was eager to see you again. A girl just knows." Lily smiles before taking another sip from her coffee. She sets it back down on the table and puts her hands together in front of her. "And look, it worked out didn't it?" She raises one eyebrow toward me.

"I mean, yes, but it may not have." I say, rolling my eyes.

"But it did, so you don't have anything to worry about!" Lily says, smiling. I lean into my chair again, taking it all in. "And was the date everything you expected?"

I laugh. "I expected a random person to be my blind date, not him." I roll my eyes. "So, yes, it was better than I could have imagined!"

"So," Lily says, lengthening the word. "When are you seeing him again?"

I blink quickly, then grab my phone off the table and look at the time. *11:23*. Despite not having my number, I hoped he would somehow get it and text me, but he hadn't yet. He said he wanted to see me again, but the way he brushed off our kiss and my question for him to stay the night only peaks my anxiety.

"Did he text you?" Lily peers over the table looking down at my phone. I set it back down on the table.

"No, he doesn't have my number."

"Seriously? Even after your date last night? He still doesn't have it?" Lily rolls her eyes.

"Well, I mean," I sit up in my chair. "There's a good reason for that." Lily tilts her head. "You won't believe this, but he owns our apartment complex."

"Like, he owns an apartment in it?" Lily furrows her brows.

"No, like he owns the entire complex. Every apartment, including ours." I look at Lily wide-eyed, waiting for her reaction.

Lily grabs her coffee and takes another sip. "Honestly, I wouldn't doubt it. He owns so many places here in the city. When did he buy it? Do you know?"

"Well, that's the thing," I start. "He bought it right before we moved in after college."

"Oh wow! That's ironic! Did you mention how we were thrilled with the low rental price?" Lily asks.

"Well," I scratch my neck. "He didn't really say much about that when I asked. Maybe it was a mistake and he just let it slide?"

"Possibly, but I was just happy we could afford such a nice place!" Lily says, letting out a laugh. "So, did he just not ask for your number since he knows where you live already?"

"I mean, basically." I grab my coffee off the table and take a sip, wincing at the sudden coldness against my lips. *Damn.* "Coffee is cold." I udder under my breath.

"Well, are you just going to wait for him to show up at your door unannounced?" Lily laughs, then looks up to the ceiling, as if to think. She looks back down and grabs her phone off the table. "I'm just going to send him your number."

"Wait, what?" I quickly lean over the table, trying to grab the phone from Lily, who is now leaning back against her chair, typing away on her phone.

"Sent!" Lily looks up from her phone and smiles.

"Ugh, Lily!" I press my hand into my forehead. "What did you even say?"

Lily smiles. "I just sent him your number and told him he should text you."

"What!" I basically yell. The people around us once again stare over at our table. I ignore them and look back at Lily, who has a wide grin on her face. "Now, how will I know if he actually wants to see me or if it was just because you told him to text me?" I shake my head.

"Paige!" Lily says through a laugh. "You should have seen the look on his face when I told him he was going on a date with you! He definitely will want to see you again!"

"Great." I say sarcastically.

As I give Lily another annoyed look, a ding comes from my phone on the table. Lily's eyes widen as she gestures with a head nod toward my phone. I roll my eyes at her before grabbing my phone off the table and opening it. A text from a random number reads:

Hey beautiful, seems like I finally got your number.

I look slightly up at Lily, who is eager to know who it is, but by the words "beautiful," I knew instantly it was him. I roll my eyes at her before looking back down and replying.

You know, you could have gotten it last night when I offered.

> **True, but then I wouldn't have known you were talking about me.**

I blush at the thought and I can only imagine him smirking down at his phone.

> **We weren't.**

> **We? Hmm. Must be a coincidence then that Lily demanded I should text you at this very moment.**

If Lily hadn't texted him my number, then he wouldn't have known we were talking about the date, but then again, I kind of like the fact that he mentioned it. *Maybe he had been thinking of me too?* I give Lily an annoyed look, but she doesn't see it as she stares down at her own phone. Another ding comes from my phone and I look down.

> **When can I see you?**

> **Depends. Will you "accidentally" run into me again?**

Lily told you?

Yes, but I'll let it slide just this once.

Ha, well I'll pick you up tomorrow, that way you'll know your date is with me.

My blush that had faded, returns to my face. I look up at Lily, who quickly glances up from her phone. When she notices my red cheeks, she taps her cheek with her finger and gives me a smirk before looking back down at her phone.

Wait, you don't even know if I'm free?

I have a hunch. 5pm tomorrow? Wear warm clothes.

What are we doing?

You'll see. See you tomorrow, Beautiful.

I set my phone back down on the table and Lily looks up from her phone. A smile slowly starts growing on her face.

"So, are you seeing him again?" Lily quickly asks, raising her eyebrows.

"Yes, but it wasn't because of you, okay?" I say through a laugh. "So don't act like you were the mastermind behind it all."

"What! I didn't say anything!" Lily scoffs. "But you have to promise to tell me about it!" Lily takes one last sip of her coffee, tilting the cup into the air to empty it fully.

"Of course I will, you know that." I say sarcastically.

Lily stands up from her chair. "Mason and I have to finalize some wedding details, so I have to head out, but don't forget to ask Ryker to be your date to the wedding!"

"What! I can't ask him that?" I grab Lily's hand as she reaches for her phone on the table.

"I can tell him he has to?" Lily chuckles.

"No, no demands!" I say, glaring at Lily. "I can't invite him. I've been on one date with him." I let go of Lily's hand. She picks up her phone and puts it into her bag.

"Paige," Lily says. "Considering he will already be at the wedding, I can't imagine he'd say no." Lily smiles before turning and walking toward the door.

"He's coming to your wedding?" I whisper under my breath. I let out a quiet sigh of relief.

Lily gives a quick wave before I watch her step outside and slide into a black town car that was waiting for her outside.

Standing up from my chair, I put my phone into my back pocket and throw away both our coffee cups into the trash can. Walking out the door, I turn and head back to my apartment.

I should have known that Lily already had someone in mind when she told me I needed a wedding date. She always had a plan. And honestly, if I had known better, she would have thrown someone random at me the week before, so I guess I should be lucky? I mean, at least it was Ryker she threw at me. It can't be that hard to ask him to be my date then, right? *I hope not.*

Chapter Nine

It's exactly five o'clock as I sit down on the steps that lead up to my apartment complex. The air outside is cool, but not cold and I'm happy knowing I dressed warm enough for the evening, as Ryker suggested.

I look down at my feet, happy to be wearing boots this time rather than heels. *I dreaded that*. My tight black jeans are tucked into my boots and as a slight breeze flies by from a passing car, my, at first questionable, choice in wearing thicker socks gets confirmed. My eyes glance from my boots up to my hands resting on my knees and I quickly pull my sleeves from my blue wool sweater over my exposed fingers. The sweater is similar to one I had as a child and when I wear it, I always think of my dad. Earlier when I put the sweater on and looked in the mirror, I couldn't help but smile thinking of what my dad would say. How my sweater would make my eyes stand out.

Each passing car, I study, trying to see who is driving. An old man with a gray beard in a suit. A woman talking on her cell phone with one hand on the wheel. Several taxis pass as well. With each car, I hope it will be Ryker. *5:08. Where is that man?*

I look up from my phone just as a black town car rolls up and stops in front of me. Something similar to what Lily is always picked up in. I look around, trying to see who is driving through the tinted windows, but I'm unable to see.

On the driver's side, the back door opens up and I see the back of Ryker's head as he smoothly exits the towncar. Instantly, I feel my heart race. As Ryker turns around toward me, he gives me a quick smirk before walking around to the other side of the car, where I'm still sitting down on the steps.

As he stands in front of me, I'm taken back by his casualness. His facial hair has started coming in and his chiseled jaw is covered by a 5 o'clock shadow. Unlike his polished look from Friday night, he is wearing a gray knit sweater that has a simple knitted design around the chest. If I hadn't known already, it would have been hard for me to tell how muscular he was under all the material. He is also wearing a pair of dark blue jeans and brown chelsea boots. A complete opposite of the two other times I was with him. Yet, every time I see him, no matter what he is wearing, I always think he is handsome.

As I study his outfit, my eyes go up his body and back to his green eyes looking down on me. By his facial expression, he must have thought I was checking him out because he quickly raises an eyebrow above his smirk. *I mean I was, but he didn't need to know.*

"You look different." I say, cocking my head to the side.

"Good different or bad different?" Ryker asks with a slight chuckle.

"Good." I say, standing up. "I mean, you always look good."

My eyes widen as he lets out a quick chuckle between his wide grin. *What did I just say?* Quickly changing the subject I blurt out, "You're late again."

"Am I? I hadn't realized." Ryker says, with apologetic eyes. "Wait, again?" His eyes blink quickly.

"Yeah, you were late on Friday." I say, almost arrogantly.

Ryker swiftly walks over to me until we are inches apart. Looking down into my eyes, he says, "Technically I was there early, I just didn't notice you had shown up."

I break our eye contact and look off to the side trying to think. "Okay fine. You win." I laugh.

Ryker laughs before grabbing my hand that's resting on the side of my body and he intertwines our fingers. Against his warm hands, I hadn't realized how cold my fingers truly were until now. I look back at him and our eyes meet once again. His green eyes studying my own.

"Your eyes look even more beautiful with that sweater." Ryker says, rubbing his thumb along the top of my hand. "Come on, Beautiful. Let's get going before it gets too late." Ryker pulls my arm toward the car and I willingly follow.

When we reach the car, Ryker uses his other hand to open the door before gesturing for me to get in. I let go of his hand as I slid inside of the black town car. As I sit, I expect the seats, which are leather, to be cold under my legs, but I'm immediately welcomed by warmth. *Ah, seat warmers.*

Back in my childhood, I remember the car we drove. *A 90's Land Cruiser.* That car was the one we drove everywhere around town and for the rare moments we went on vacation. I remember each winter always being thankful that we had fabric seats because we weren't able to afford a car nice enough to have seat warmers. I remember the SUV's that the neighborhood kids' parents drove and I had no doubt they all had seat warmers. Each one looked brand new and seemed to have all the bells and whistles. I mean, I assumed at least. I was never close enough with any of them to actually get into their cars, but I just had a feeling. I imagine though that within another month or two, we would have had a brand new car, especially considering how well my dad was doing at work. *I'll never know.* Unfortunately, we lost that car in the accident and never got a new one. Once we moved to the city, driving a car was rare and we resorted to public transportation.

"You okay, Beautiful?" Ryker says from the seat next me. I look up at him to see his eyes full of worry. I hadn't even realized we had started driving until I looked around us.

"Yeah, I'm good. Sorry!" I quickly say, giving him a small smile.

"What are you thinking about?" Ryker asks.

I don't want to tell him I was thinking of my childhood because I know it could be a deep dive into a part of me that I don't want to bring up, so instead I just bend the truth a bit.

"Seat warmers." I bluntly say. I quickly realize how weird that sounds and shoot my eyes down toward the car floor and away from him.

"Seat warmers?" Ryker asks, letting out a laugh. "That's a new one."

"Yup!" I try to confidently say to avoid sounding weirder. *Let's change the subject.* "Where are we going?"

I look outside the window to see if I recognize the area and realize we are about fifteen blocks from my apartment complex near the largest park in the city.

"I think you'll be pleasantly surprised." Ryker says, putting his hand over mine, which is resting on the seat between us. I look up at him and smile.

The car pulls to a stop on the side of the road and the driver, a young, blonde-haired man dressed in a black suit, gets out of the car. Ryker quickly swings his door open and slides out of the car before I even realize he is gone. As the driver walks around, inching closer to my door, Ryker stops him and gives the driver a firm handshake. They exchange a few words before Ryker turns around and smiles at me through the door. The driver turns around and walks around to the front of the car. I turn to look back at Ryker and he opens my door, holding his hand out for me to grab.

"Come on, beautiful." Ryker says, as I grab his hand and he pulls me out of the town car.

I eagerly follow as he leads me across the street and through a large metal archway into the park. I haven't been to this park during the fall, but I'm pleasantly surprised. The light breeze blows the leaves, one of every fall color, across our path. We take our time as we walk down a winding sidewalk through the park and Ryker, still holding my hand, leads me.

We cross under a stone bridge and when we slightly emerge through the other side, I catch sight of someone sitting on a bench, with an easel and canvas in front of him. I squint, trying to make out what he is painting as we inch closer. I fully expect Ryker to walk us past the man on the bench, but instead, I feel him grip my hand slightly tighter and lead me off the path for us to walk behind the man.

As we get closer to the man, he quickly looks up at us walking toward him and smiles, before turning back to his canvas. He appears to be older, maybe in his 50's or 60's, but still has quite a few wrinkles around his mouth and on his forehead. *My dad would be around the same age if he was still here.*

We stop behind him, just as he adds tiny dabbing brush strokes of orange to his canvas. His painting, a portrait of the bridge we just crossed under, is surrounded by the autumn trees. I look closely at the canvas and I'm surprised when I see buildings above the bridge. I look away from the canvas and I'm more surprised to see a small view of the skyscrapers in the distance. I hadn't realized we would be able to see the buildings surrounding us through the thick trees, yet here we could. Everything about the painting reminds me of what I used to paint when I was younger. Yet, this man definitely had talent. I don't know if six-year-old me could have competed.

Ryker puts his arm around my shoulders and I look up at him. I wonder what he is thinking. *Does he see the beauty of this painting that I'm seeing?*

"This is amazing." I say, looking away from Ryker and back down at the man painting. The man does not respond as he dabs another color onto the canvas.

I take a deep breath in and out, as if to take in the sight. Ryker squeezes my shoulder slightly and we turn away from the man painting and move back onto the path.

"My dad used to love to paint." I say to Ryker, keeping my eyes straight ahead of me.

"Did he?" Ryker asks.

"Yeah, he was the one who taught me how to paint." I say, watching my footing as the path slightly steepens.

"And how to draw too." He states quietly, not phrasing it in a question.

"Yeah, he did actually." I say, tilting my head.

"You are an extremely talented artist." Ryker says, looking down at me with a smile.

"But I haven't shown you any of my work." I furrow my brows. A moment passes and Ryker blinks quickly before answering.

"Well, Lily showed me a bit." He scoffs.

When Lily and I lived together, she would always give me suggestions on what to paint so she could display them proudly in her room. She always said it was fun having a "Paige original." When I went over to her new apartment, I knew I had seen my paintings somewhere, but I was too distracted by the view to really notice. *Of course, that must have been it.*

"When you three had dinner?" I ask, not realizing I had stopped walking.

"Yes and they were beautiful." Ryker smiles again, squeezing my hand.

Before I have a chance to reply, he pulls me back into a walk and we continue down the path. Within a minute, we arrive at the top of a small hill that leads down to an ice skating rink. Ryker tries to pull me down the steep path toward the arena, but I pull back, stopping him.

"Are you okay?" Ryker steps forward, with concern in his eyes.

I stare down at the ice arena, ignoring Ryker now standing next to me. Flashbacks of my childhood rush back to me from some of my deepest memories.

Every winter, my dad and I had this tradition. When the snow started falling, we would patiently wait for the pond down the street from us to freeze over. It was definitely a waiting game, but when it finally dropped down to a cold enough temperature, we knew it was time. The pond was located in a small park that was mostly used during the other seasons for basketball and small get-togethers, but we saw an opportunity with the small pond each winter. My dad would help me get dressed in my warmest clothes, he would grab the snow shovel from our garage and we would drive down the street to the pond. He would slowly start to scrape the snow off the top of the frozen pond, row after row, meticulously clearing it to the sides. I would always sit on one of the park benches, just watching him. When he finished, he would grab the buckets of water sitting in the back of our Land Cruiser and carry each over, spreading the water over the pond to smooth it out. It was definitely a long process to get the pond ready, but my dad knew how much I loved the tradition we started and I knew he was just happy to see me smile.

When he was finished, I'd grab my ice skates from the back seat of the car and carry them over to the side of the frozen pond. Pulling on each skate, I'd carefully stand up and take my first glide across the ice. A little wobbly at first, but within a few minutes, I would be gliding across the ice with ease. My dad always sat on the bench, watching me as I skated and he drank his coffee that had been sitting in the car. He didn't skate himself, but I could tell he enjoyed watching me from the sidelines.

I shake my head. "I just," I pause. "I haven't skated since before my dad passed."

Ryker quickly pulls me in for a hug, his arms surrounding me. I bury my face into his sweater, soft against my face.

"I'm sorry, I shouldn't have brought you here." Ryker pauses. "I just thought you might like it."

I pull back and look up at Ryker. Although he doesn't know much about my childhood, I had tried to tell him about the happy times I had when I was younger. Weeks ago, I would have hated going ice skating or being surrounded by the changes that came with fall, but since meeting Ryker, I've started to see it all in a different light. *A good light.* And, the ice rink at this park had just opened up. We couldn't pass up on it.

"I do like it." I piece together a quick smile.

Ryker's eyes turn from concern to happiness and he places his hand on my jaw, rubbing his thumb against my cheek.

"Okay, Beautiful."

"Okay." I say.

Ryker pulls his hand off of my cheek and grabs my hand once again, leading me down the hill to the ice skating rink. As we get closer to the rink, I notice the amount of people or lack thereof. *It's just the two of us.*

"Size twelve and size?" Ryker looks at me as he talks to the attendant.

"Size eight." I chime in, looking around for anyone else.

The attendant turns around and grabs the skates from the cubbies then places them on the table in front of us.

"Here you are, Mr. Blackwell." The attendant says.

Ryker quickly grabs the skates and walks them over to a small bench next to the rink. I continue to stand there, looking at the attendant. *Do they know one another?* I quickly turn around and jog over to Ryker.

"What?" I scoff. "Do you own the ice rink too?"

Ryker lets out a deep snicker then smirks as he sits down on the bench. He looks down and I stand there watching him as he takes off his shoes and laces up his skates, ignoring my question.

"No, seriously. Do you? Where is everyone?" I say anxiously. I put my hands up and look around, trying to show him what's obviously not in front of him: other people.

Ryker lets out a chuckle, then looks up at me. "I don't own everything you know."

"Well, of course not, but." I pause, tilting my head. I furrow my brows. *Could he actually own this rink though? I mean, how else would-?*

"I know a guy." Ryker finally says. "He owed me a favor." So he only owns *almost* everything.

I sit down next to him and take each of my boots off. As I'm about to grab my ice skates off the ground, Ryker swiftly gets up and kneels down in front of me. He looks up at me and our eyes lock. A slight smile grows on his face. *What is he doing?* In a million years, I never expected a man to be kneeling down in front of me on our second date. My eyes widen. *This is not happening. This can't be.*

"What are you doing?" I can hear my own fear in my words.

"Giving you a hand." Ryker calmly says. He grabs my skate and slides it onto my foot, without a second thought.

"Oh," I say, pausing. I shake my head. "Thank you." *Too many damn romance movies making me question everything.* Ryker finishes lacing up my one skate.

"Anything for you, Beautiful."

Ryker puts on my other skate and starts lacing it up. I suddenly realize my heart has been beating out of my chest and I feel my mind slowly coming to ease. *Phew.* That would be quite the story to tell the next time I saw Lily.

I let out a quiet chuckle before Ryker stands up with poise, despite wearing skates. He holds out his hand and I grab it, pulling myself up from the bench and into his arms.

Surprisingly Ryker is better than I had expected as we get out on the ice. He definitely knows how to skate. My guess is that he played hockey when he was younger. I can't tell for sure though because Ryker hasn't told me much about his childhood. He mentioned it wasn't something he liked to talk about, so I didn't press for more. I, on the other hand, am a bit wobbly. I guess that'll happen after 20 or so years of not skating.

"You aren't bad!" I say to Ryker, my shock coming out through my voice.

I look over to Ryker as I hesitantly try to glide next to him and keep his pace and I see him smile and nod. In that moment, I wobble and nearly fall down, but he quickly catches my other arm and holds me up.

"I've got you." Ryker looks at me, smirking.

As if in a swift dance move, he pulls me back up and I'm suddenly against him with my hands pressed against his chest. The ice dance suddenly reminds me of a question that Lily told me to ask. *The wedding.*

"So," I look into Ryker's eyes, keeping my word. "I heard you'll be at Lily's wedding."

"Yes?" Ryker raises his eyebrows.

"And I was wondering," I pause.

"Uh huh." Ryker nods his head. He definitely knows what I'm trying to ask. *Do I really have to say it?*

"Since we'll both be at the wedding," I pause again.

"Of course, I'll be your date." Ryker says, smiling.

"Oh," I say, almost surprised. "Good!" I smile back. *Thank goodness he said it first.*

"If the way you skate says anything about how you are on the dance floor, you'll definitely need my help though." Ryker says, his grin reappearing. I roll my eyes.

"I'm not that bad!" I argue through a laugh. "It's just been a while."

"I know, Beautiful." Ryker says, pulling back from me and grabbing my hand once again. "Let's skate." I begin to get my footing and follow him.

We skate for an hour. The same time I would have spent out on that frozen pond as a child. Different than I would have imagined, but the memory feels closer to me somehow. Could it be because I have Ryker next to me? These memories would have broken me down before, but now I see the happiness in them. I see the happiness that Ryker brings out in me.

As we return our skates, Ryker puts his phone to his ear, speaking to his driver. "Hey." He pauses. "Yeah."

"Let's walk back." I say, remembering the short drive from my apartment complex.

"Actually," Ryker pauses and gives me a quick look. I take a quick breath in and press my lips together. "No need. I'll call you if we need you." Ryker says.

He brings his phone down from his ear and slips it into his pocket before brushing his hand through his hair.

"Lead the way then, Beautiful."

I reach down and hold out my hand, which Ryker immediately holds onto, interlocking our fingers. I think back to how nervous he made me when our hands first touched. That night in Nashville. I felt my entire body tense up, trying to contain the sensations I was feeling. And now, I couldn't get enough. I wanted his hand in mine as much as possible.

"I think I definitely did better by the end of it." I chuckle, gesturing my head toward the ice rink.

"Definitely, Beautiful and-" Ryker pauses to look down at his watch. "It only took an hour." He chuckles and I roll my eyes through a smile. We walk out of the park and head toward my apartment complex.

It's only a few minutes later that I feel shivers throughout my body from my neck down to my toes. I feel my breath slowly come out of my mouth and I watch as I see it disperse into the air. *It's cold.*

I look at Ryker walking next to my side, then look up to the sky. Darkness glooms above us. Before I can think of what to do, a single drop of water falls from the sky and lands on my forehead. I stop walking and press my finger against the wet spot, then look down at my finger, studying it. Ryker turns and looks at me, furrowing his brows. I look back up at the dark clouds above me and Ryker follows suit.

Within a moment, several other drops fall from the sky and our faces are covered with wet spots. Our heads turn and look at one another and as if we can read each other's minds, large grins grow across each of our faces. We momentarily ignore what's happening around us, we stare at one another as the drops start coming down faster and faster. It isn't long before Ryker and I are running down the street, hand in hand, toward the apartment complex as we to escape the rain falling from above.

On our first date, I felt compelled to invite Ryker into my apartment. I never expected to be that kind of person, yet after our instant bond on the first date, it was a no brainer. I wanted him to come inside my home. I wanted him closer to me. To touch every inch of me.

From the moment I met him in Nashville, I've felt this pull toward him that was unexplainable. Not only have I felt more like myself in years, but the confident person I used to be has come back out. He's made me rethink what I imagine and desire for my future. What I want to do with my life. I don't want to be cooped up and thinking about the past. I want to be living in the moment every single day. With him. *And all thanks to him.*

It was hard to see him leave when the elevator doors shut that night, so I couldn't imagine it happening again. Not this time. It was raining and we were soaking wet. We'd have to get dry somehow and I knew these sweaters of ours weren't going to dry quickly.

I catch myself and wipe the grin growing on my face as we continue running. With each step down the wet sidewalk, I find moments to glance over at Ryker running next to me. His soaking wet hair pushed back on his head. *I want to run my fingers through it.* Drops of rain falling from his chiseled chin. *I want to grab his cheek and pull him in for a kiss.* His soaking wet sweater pressed against his muscular shoulders. *I want to feel his bare muscles holding me close.* My eyes move back up to Ryker's face and his eyes lock with mine.

Ryker slows down into a walk and my body matches his pace. My breath finally catches up to me and I take a deep inhale. I can feel my heart beating faster and faster, unaware if it's from running or the possibilities of what could happen tonight.

As we stand there on the sidewalk completely disregarding the weather around us, I watch Ryker take a deep breath. The green in his eyes barely visible as the water droplets slowly trickle down from his forehead and over his eyebrows. I watch the droplets slide down his face and over his mouth, which slightly opens. We take another deep breath in unison, then his lips press together and the corner of his mouth slightly raises.

Before I'm able to look back up at his eyes, he pulls me off of the sidewalk and out of the rain. It's a quick movement, but it catches me off guard as I feel my back press against the side of a building. Ryker's one hand is still holding mine and I glance up, noticing his other arm is pressed against the wall above my shoulder. I move my eyes down his arm until our eyes are once again locked onto one another's. His eyes darken and I sip a small breath in, waiting for him to kiss me. To devour my lips like before. Instead, Ryker leans in and presses his forehead against my own and I feel the heat coming off of his body. Almost steaming from the heat between us under the cold rain. I instinctively get chills down my body and feel a wetness between my legs, but I'm unable to tell if it was created by me or the storm.

"Let's get inside." Ryker slowly says, pulling back to look up at the building.

I blink quickly as he pulls back from our close contact and I quickly look around to see what he's looking at. *My apartment complex.* I can only imagine I have a puzzled look on my face, but Ryker appears to be holding back his thoughts as he presses his lips together. I'm not sure if I'm more surprised by how quickly we ran here or that he is actually wanting to come in. Ryker runs his hand through his hair, pulling water out of it as he takes a step back from me. *Please don't leave this time.*

I turn and quickly enter the code for the building as Ryker grabs the door and holds it open for me, gesturing for us to go inside. As we step onto the tile, the water dripping from our clothes echoes throughout the room. Each step toward the elevator echoes louder and louder and sloshes against the floor. Ryker quickens his pace and clicks the elevator button before I can, and the doors immediately open. *Does he want me as badly as I want him?*

We step inside and Ryker clicks the button for my floor. Floor 5. *He remembers.*

As the doors close, I look down at my feet, which are sitting in a puddle of water that's grown around me. I glance over at Ryker's feet on the tiled elevator floor and see a similar puddle. *Ding.* My eyes move up his body, up his jeans to the bottom of his sweater. *Ding.* I glance at his hands, resting at the side of his body, relaxed and open and my eyes start to move up his arms. *Ding.* My eyes stop at his chest, each muscle outlined by his wet sweater. His chest rising and falling ever so slightly. *Ding*. My eyes move up his neck, across his lips and nose, finally landing on his eyes, now visible thanks to the elevator light. *Ding*.

I turn my head as the elevator doors open and before I can see what Ryker does, I quickly walk over to my apartment door, five steps from the elevator. *Is he following? Is he still in the elevator?*

Without turning around, I grab my key from my pocket. As I lift the key up to my doorknob, I feel Ryker's body behind me. I hear a slight buzzing sound and then his chest presses up against my back. A slight feeling of déjà vu, but this time, I can't ruin it with a pair of cocktail drinks.

I feel his hand reach around my body and tighten on my hip. His other hand mimics the movement on the opposite side. I sip a breath in and close my eyes, wanting to feel every second of his hands against me. I feel Ryker's head press against the side of mine and move down to the top of my shoulders. I push the key into the lock. Slowly, Ryker pulls his hand off of my hip and carefully slides my hair away from my neck, exposing it to his warm breath. I quietly release my breath I've been holding in, careful not to ruin the satisfying tension between us. Ryker's breath inches closer and I can feel the light stubble of his chin hairs against me, just as his soft lips press deeply into my neck. I take another breath in. I feel his lips slowly inch down, meticulously placing a kiss down to the base of my neck and onto my collarbone. My eyes widen and every tingle throughout my body urges me to turn around to face him.

With no time to react on my own, Ryker pulls his arm around my body and turns me toward him, his eyes locking onto mine as my back presses against my door. We study one another's face in the brief moment we are turned toward one another.

"Kiss me." I say, demandingly, but I realize I shouldn't have said a word. I shouldn't have said anything that would possibly end this moment. My eyes search his face to see how he reacts and I see a brief surprised look in his eyes. I immediately suck in my breath. *Oh no, please don't let this ruin the moment.*

Ryker's eyes relax and a smirk grows on his face. Before I can say another word, his lips are pressed against mine. Deeply, he kisses my lips pulling our bodies against one another until there is no space inbetween. I lift myself up on my tippy toes to get closer. To get more of him somehow. The sweet taste of him in my mouth warms me from the inside. Briefly making me forget about our soaking wet clothes. *I just want more. I want more of him.*

His hands slide around me and I'm lifted up from behind. Instinctively, I throw my arms behind his neck and lock my legs around his body, barely able to hold on. His arms wrap around me as another quick buzz from his body distracts me for a brief moment. I brush it off. I savor his lips against my own. The one thing I had longed for all night. I feel his tongue swirl in my mouth and a brief moan escapes between my lips accidentally, but I don't care. I want him to know how good it feels. How good it is to have him kissing me. To have him wanting me.

From behind me, I feel my apartment door get pushed open as Ryker carries me inside, still fully focusing on each kiss while also carefully watching his steps as he goes inside. I hear the door close behind us while Ryker steps further into the room. *He's not leaving this time.*

I feel one of his hands slowly move down my back and slide under my sweater. As it touches my skin, I pull my lips back from Ryker momentarily, expecting his hand to be cold, but I'm relieved when it isn't. It's warm and comforting against my wet skin, which I should have expected coming from this perfection of a man. I slide down from Ryker and land my feet back on the ground, while our bodies are still pressed together and we lean in to kiss once more.

I hear another buzz, but this time I'm able to feel it coming from Ryker's pants pressed against my body. This time, it's hard to ignore.

I pull back from Ryker's lips, despite not wanting to whatsoever, and look him in the eyes. *Does he notice it too or is he ignoring it?* I scan his eyes, right to left, as I wait for him to say something, but I pull back slightly, hoping he'll take the hint. He takes a breath in and then moves his hand out from under my shirt, even though I would have loved for it to have stayed there.

"Go ahead, you can answer it." I say, slowly backing up more.

I give Ryker a seductive smile as I take careful steps backward, not losing our eye contact even for a second. His eyebrows quickly raise as I reach the edge of my couch and sit down. Ryker's eyes darken and he glares at me as I lean down and remove each one of my boots.

A momentary break in our eye contact, Ryker looks down, as I hear a muffled buzzing sound once more. He reaches his hand into his pocket and pulls his phone out, looking at the screen. He furrows his brows then looks back up at me, as if to ask for reassurance to answer the call. Even though I slightly hope he will ignore it and walk over to continue what we started, I decide that having him here in my apartment is already moving us forward. *It wouldn't take too long, right?* I nod and give him an approving nod.

Ryker takes another deep breath and puts the phone up to his ear.

"Hello? This is Ryker Blackwell." He confidently says through the phone.

As I remove my socks, which are partially wet from the water seeping into my boots, my mind immediately starts thinking of what Ryker will do next. I'm already freezing from my wet clothes and I imagine he has to be too, which can only lead to one of two things. I look down at his clothes, picturing what his naked body would look like in front of me and I'd gladly let him remove every single thing I'm wearing if that meant we could take a shower to warm up. But, he's distracted. He's on the phone. So, I have to be the one to make the daring first move.

I tilt my head toward Ryker and quickly squint my eyes, thinking of how to distract him. How to grab his attention toward me. He teased me on our first date when he lied about not being my blind date, so I might as well tease him this time.

I quickly raise my eyebrows at Ryker, then slowly grab the bottom of my wet sweater and lift it up over my head. My eyes lose sight of Ryker for a second beneath the material, then meet his again as I drop my sweater to the floor. My breasts, held up in a black lace bra, fall to my chest and I watch as his eyes widen, staring down at them. His eyes quickly shoot back up to my own, as if embarrassed to be seeing me partially naked in front of him. The corner of my lip raises as I stand up from the couch edge.

I hear him continue to talk to the person on the phone, but his voice is quiet as I focus on distracting him. *Okay, next move.* I watch as his eyes follow my hands down the sides of my torso as I grab the tops of my jeans. I move my hands slowly down my thighs as I bend over, bringing my pants down to my ankles. As I straight myself back up, I take each leg and step out of my pants that are lying on the ground. I watch as Ryker's eyes become magnetic to my body. Glued to me. Focusing on each curve that was hidden beneath my clothing. I watch as his eyes move up from the floor and slowly up my legs. Up to my waist.

Back onto my breasts and finally meeting my eyes again.

This time when our eyes meet, I can tell he is no longer embarrassed to look. He understands this show is for him. And only him. His lips press together and I smirk at him. I can tell he craves my body and all I want is for his hands to be all over me.

I see his mouth move once again as he continues talking on the phone, but once again, I hear no words as I stay entranced in this game of mine. This game that keeps him wanting me. This game that'll make me irresistible to his temptations.

I lean my butt back against the edge of the couch and reach my hands behind my back to unhook my bra. Before I can reach it though, I can't help but notice the change in Ryker's face. When I should expect him to be looking at me with lust, it's the opposite. His face appears disturbed. *Did I do something wrong?*

He presses his lips together and furrows his brows, then I'm reminded that he's been on the phone this entire time. *I really should have been paying attention to what he was saying to the person on the other line.* As his voice fades back into my own ears, I'm finally able to make out the words coming from his mouth, but it's too late as I hear him say, "I'll be there soon." *He means tomorrow, right?*

I drop my hands from behind my back and quickly turn around, reaching for the blanket sitting on the couch behind me. I pull the blanket around my almost naked body and hold it closely in front of me, covering myself up.

My eyes quickly scan his face, trying to get some information out of his reaction. *Something is definitely not right.*

Ryker brings his hand down and holds his phone at the side of his body. I press my lips together as we stare at one another, waiting for the other to speak.

"What's going on?" I finally say as I stand up with the blanket hanging down to the ground. Ryker stays quiet, breathing in deeply. "Ryker?" I anxiously ask.

"I'm sorry." He quietly says. *Sorry? For what?* I look at him with worry, unsure of what he is apologizing for.

"I have to go take care of some-." Ryker pauses, pressing his lips together as if he doesn't want to say the word. "Something."

"Is everything alright?" I cautiously ask, as I carefully take steps toward him.

Ryker puts his phone into his pocket and looks down to the ground, just as my feet stop in front of him. I look down at the water droplets sprinkled around our feet, then look up at him from below.

"What happened?" I ask, trying to get information out of him.

I watch as his eyes, still glued to the floor, search the floor, as if he is trying to think of what to say. Finally, he lifts his head up and looks me in the eyes, before placing his hand on my cheek. It's at that moment that I see it. The dreaded look of regret. And I know that it can only mean one thing. He's leaving.

"I need to take care of something, but I promise I'll make it up to you." Ryker says, leaning down and kissing my forehead. I instinctively close my eyes as he pulls away all too soon.

As I hear the door open, I try to keep my eyes closed, but I can't. I know I have to see him leave or I'll regret it. I feel my body scream from inside and my eyes shoot open just as I see Ryker standing in the open doorway.

I want to run after him and stop him from leaving, but I feel a tightening around my body. An invisible rope keeping me back. I know I can't stop him. Something happened and he needs to leave. Something he has to deal with. I have to let him leave once again.

Turning his head enough for me to see one side of his face, Ryker gives me a quick smile, which feels forced, but it's one piece of reassurance. The only piece of hope that he will return. But then, as if he knows another moment to linger in front of me would prevent him from leaving, he closes the door and I'm left standing alone in my apartment. Once again hoping this won't be the last time I see him.

Chapter Ten

Every ounce of me wants to turn around and walk back through that door. To walk over to Paige, hold her in my arms and apologize for leaving her, not once, but twice. But I can't. I know I can't.

I don't get upset often, but that call was a trigger that went off in my head. An anger that lingered inside me that was waiting to come out. I couldn't show that side to Paige. I just couldn't.

No matter how much I wanted to stay with Paige, touch every part of her body as she undressed in front of me, and kiss every inch of her, that call was something I couldn't ignore.

I hadn't recognized the number when I answered the call, but immediately when I heard the voice on the other end mention that name, the night had already been ruined in my mind. I had to take care of it - or rather - him. The person I've been dreading to hear about for so many years.

I can't imagine standing in front of Paige's door while I wait for the elevator to arrive, so I quickly run down the stairs, calling Turner, my driver, on the way. By the time I'm on the ground floor, I see him parked out front, standing there with the door open. After I had let him know Paige and I would be walking home, I imagined he stayed close, just in case. Always ready at a moment's notice.

As I approach Turner, he quickly holds out his umbrella for me before giving me a quick glance up and down. His face meets my eyes again with a friendly smile, but I can tell he noticed something I didn't. I quickly look down at myself, remembering that my clothes are damp from the rain, then look back up and nod at him as I step into the open car door.

As Turner walks around to the driver's side, I notice a bag hanging on the hook above the seat next to me. I unzip the bag to see a freshly pressed navy suit and a tie. My eyes glance down at the seat next to me and I see a pair of dress shoes and socks laid out as well. I quickly pull the damp sweater off over my head and place it on the floor in front of me.

"Where to, sir?" Turner asks, as he sits down in the driver's seat.

"Parker Memorial." I say, leaning over and pulling each of my damp shoes off. Drops of water fall from out of each shoe as I set each one on the floor. With a click of a button next to me, a privacy screen rolls up between us.

Ten minutes go by and we arrive outside of the hospital. Turner parks the car under a covered entrance, blocking the rain. He walks around the car and opens my door.

"Sir." Turner says, standing up straight as he holds the door open. I slide out of the car.

"Thank you, Turner." I say.

I give him a quick nod and turn toward the front of the car, positioning the mirror up. I look at myself and notice my hair is still damp. With my hand, I brush it back, with the dampness working in my favor. I fix the mirror and straighten myself up, buttoning the middle button on my suit jacket. I take a deep breath and walk toward the entrance and through the automatic doors.

Looking around, it's quieter than I expected for a Sunday. I see only a few people sitting in the waiting room, as I hear the rain quietly fade as the doors close behind me.

I place my hand on the counter in front of a woman typing on a computer.

"Hello, I'm-" I say. The woman looks up before I can finish.

"Mr. Blackwell." She says wide-eyed as she quickly stands up. "We've taken care of everything you've requested. Down the hall behind me. Room thirteen."

I peer around her to the hallway, then look back at her.

"Thank you." I say. I walk around the desk, but I stop as I reach the hallway.

When I spoke to the nurse on the phone, I needed assurance that everything was kept private. I had gone through my entire career without him showing up to somehow ruin it and I wanted to keep it that way. There had been times in the past that I thought he had found his way back in my life, but he hadn't. Just a few imposters here and there, pretending to be someone they weren't. Maybe to wedge their way into my life? Maybe for power or money? I'll never know. This time, when the woman on the other line mentioned a gunshot wound, I just knew it was him. There wasn't a doubt in my mind.

I wanted to keep him out of my life and I had been successful for the past twelve years, but now he finally came back and this time it wasn't a fake. I hadn't seen him since my mom passed away when I was eighteen and I had found out the truth of what had happened in our past. I wasn't going to let him come back into my life after all these years and ruin it. Not again. Especially not now.

I always thought about what I would say to him if I ever saw him. What I would do to ensure he never came back into my life again. I wasn't a violent person in any regard, but when it came to him, a rage would always fire up within me. To think of all the lies and deceit he put us through. All the trouble I had to put behind me in order to start a new life for myself. I didn't want him in it. Not at all. No matter how far away I got from him, I always had this feeling that he would find his way back into my life and I didn't want today to be the day. And certainly not while I have Paige in my life. I can't let anything happen to her. I have to keep her safe. I have to make sure no danger comes to her. And I can't be sure of that unless he is gone for good.

I take a deep breath in as I take a step into the hallway and start walking down it. With each step, the words I had planned to say to him get diminished in the back of my mind. I had been planning these words for twelve years, yet now they are gone. Jumbled up in my head. I stop.

I turn and face the plain door that reads "Room 13" in capital letters. I take another breath in as I reach for the door knob. As I turn the knob, I slowly release my breath as the door begins to open. Through the small opening in the door, the bright light from inside seeps out. As my eyes adjust, I look inside the white room to see a turquoise curtain hanging from the ceiling. A quick beep goes off. *I can't see him yet.*

I open the door wider and step inside, keeping my eyes straight as I slowly close the door behind me, trying not to let it slam against the frame. A click from the door behind me and I look around the room. Anger quietly fueling me inside as my body tenses up. I haven't even seen him yet, but I know he's here. Just on the other side of the curtain.

I look to my left and see a small television against the wall that's turned off. I squint my eyes for a moment at the black screen as I focus on the reflection against it. The image of a man lying in a hospital bed with his head turned to the side. The curtain still separating us.

I hear several beeps from the machines within the room. I take a few steps forward, carefully watching where my feet land on the floor as I try to delay the unavoidable. Just for a moment at least. I stop and peer my head around the end of the curtain and quietly suck a breath in. *It's him.*

Expecting my anger to seep out, I blink several times, taking in the sight before me. It's him, but different than I had expected. The man I cut out of my life was frightening. Someone that was a force to be reckoned with. A danger to those around him. But this man? He was weak. He was frail. He was dying.

"Mr. Blackwell?" A woman's voice whispers from behind me.

I turn around to see a brown-haired woman wearing a white coat peeking into the doorway. Different from the nurse I saw at the desk. I hadn't even heard the door open. I blink a few times, then straighten myself up as I walk over to the doorway. She steps back into the hallway and I open the door slightly wider as I step into the hallway with her, closing the door quietly behind me.

"Yes?" I say, confused as to why I was being interrupted. I had no intention of staying long with him, but I needed to make sure he wouldn't be in my life again. But, just moments ago, I hadn't expected to see this. To see him already deteriorating in front of me.

"Did anyone explain to you what happened?" The woman asks, trying to be sympathetic, but unaware that this man doesn't deserve a single ounce of sympathy from me whatsoever. I look down at her nametag on her white coat that reads, "Dr. Farrow."

"I was told it was a gunshot." I say coldly. It was the only thing that I knew would bite him back in this dreadful life he created for himself. It was inevitable.

"Yes, that's correct." Dr. Farrow takes a deep breath. "When he arrived, it was bad. He had no identification on him and he was barely able to speak due to the pain." *Well, you would be shocked if you knew who he really was. What he really did.* I raise my eyebrows.

Dr. Farrow continues, "He mentioned your name though. Said he was your father. We tried to contact you, but couldn't get through, so we had to make the choice to take him into surgery." She pauses. "For his best interest. In order to save him." *Should have just left him for dead.*

I unbutton my suit jacket and cross my arms in front of me, my sleeves tightening around my muscles.

All I can say is, "Okay" without sounding too disappointed.

"We were able to remove most of the bullets, but several fragments lodged themselves into his lungs. X-rays also showed fragments from past injuries that still remained, which we believe have been contributing to his decline, due to lead exposure." Dr. Farrow pauses, looks down at the ground, then back up to me, furrowing her eyebrows as she shakes her head. "He doesn't have much time left." *The only news I wanted to hear.*

"Thank you." I say, uncrossing my arms.

"I'll give you some time to say your goodbyes." Dr. Furrow says, putting her hand on my arm.

She gives me a small nod, then walks around me. I hear her footsteps against the tile as she continues down the hallway. I quietly scoff to myself, button my suit jacket once more and step back into the room. This time, I know it's him and I don't care if he hears me come in.

I walk over to the curtain and pull it aside, exposing him to the rest of the room. The monitors beep once again and I watch as the lines drop and fall on the heart rate monitor. *68.* I see his chest slowly rise up and down with each breath he takes using the machine. *He'll be good as dead soon enough.*

I step over to the end of his bed and walk back and forth for a few moments. What do I say to this man I hate? The man that's ruined everything good in my life? I stop and turn toward him, resting my hands on the end of the hospital bed rail. *He needs to hear what I have to say. How much I hate him.*

"Hm." I say, giving a slight smirk as I look down at his frail body. "I'm glad karma has finally bitten you back ole' man."

I pause and take a breath in. "I didn't expect to see you here of all places. I always imagined you'd die somewhere on the side of the road where nobody cared about you. But, this is basically the same. You, here, in a place where nobody cares about you."

I pause again as I hear the monitor beeps slowing down. *51.* The doctor made it seem like he wasn't going to be waking up, but oh, I wish he did.

Just for him to see that the person who hated him most, got to see him on his deathbed.

"You know, I've always thought about what I'd say to you if you wandered back into my life." I pause. "Into our lives." I let out a quiet chuckle. "What I'd do to you."

I straighten myself up and let go of the bed rail. "But you've done it to yourself. This was always going to be your demise. Your ending. I didn't have to be around to have guessed that."

I look at his closed eyes, his eyelashes slightly flickering. Another beep from the machine forces me to look up at the monitor again. *39. Almost time.*

"But you've already been dead to me."

I turn and take a step toward the door as the beeps from the machine fade out with each step. I grab the door knob and open the door slightly, before stopping in my place. I look down at the ground, then slightly turn my head to the side toward the hospital bed behind me, unable to actually see it. At that moment, I hear a single, long beep come from the machine.

"Enjoy hell, ole' man." I say, before turning my head back around, looking straight ahead and walking out the door. *Good riddance.*

Chapter Eleven

I watch as the raindrops slowly sink down the window, lower and lower. Every so often, two raindrops race as the rain picks up outside. I turn away from the window and stare down at my blank sketchbook page open on the table. *I can't.* I turn back to the window. I can't help but distract myself from my work as I find ways to avoid the biggest thought in my head that keeps trying to push its way forward.

My phone dings from its spot behind me and for a moment, my heart races. A smile grows on my face as I whip my chair around to check my phone, but as I pick it up, my smile slowly vanishes. Not because it's Lily who texted me, I mean, she's my best friend, but because I was only hoping to hear from one person today and it wasn't him. I open my phone to read the text.

Hi! How was your date last night?

I take a breath in. Where do I even start? Do I tell her about the part where we had the most amazing evening? How we ran through the rain like in one of those cliché romance movies she loves? Do I tell her we went upstairs to my apartment and how-.

My thoughts pause and the one thing I've been trying to forget about comes rolling back to the front of my mind. *He left.* Do I tell her that? How he was there one minute and the entire night that played out in my head was about to happen, but then it didn't? How he just sprinted out of my apartment with a look I didn't imagine I'd ever see on him? How I still haven't heard back from him?

I glance up at the time on my phone. *10:12.* I know it hasn't been *that* long, but I haven't even gotten a single call or text from him. Even just something along the lines of "Hey, sorry I ran out last night." Something would be better than nothing, but then again, does he really need to apologize?

By the look on his face, it was a surprise to both of us that he got the phone call. I highly doubt he wanted to leave. He definitely didn't. *He wanted to stay, right?*

I take a deep breath and start typing back to Lily, but after typing out a message and deleting it several times, I finally reply.

I'll give you the details later!

A simple reply that won't give anything away, but will ensure Lily won't ask me more about it today. She quickly replies.

Okay! I can't wait to hear about it!

I lock my phone and put it face down on the table. Resting my elbows on the desk, I burrow my face into my hands, rubbing my eyebrows with my fingertips. I take several deep breaths, hoping I can somehow get myself into work-mode and knock out at least one page of my project before the end of the day. Just because someone let me down, doesn't mean I can forget about everything else I need to take care of. I'm an adult. I have responsibilities. But, why is it that I can't think of a single thing to draw at this moment?

With my eyes still closed, I rest my hands on my cheeks, holding my head.

"Paige Palmer?" I hear a shrill voice ask from above me.

I quickly pull my hands away from my face and sit up, looking at our intern standing behind the divider of my cubicle. I quickly blink to help my eyes adjust to the harsh office light and tilt my head to the side.

The intern, whose name I can't remember, raises his eyebrows then brings his fist up to his mouth as he lets out a light cough to clear his throat.

"Paige Palmer?" He asks again, with an awkward side smile forming on his face. I blink once again before realizing that I never answered him.

"Yeah?" I ask, confused as to why he doesn't know my name yet despite bringing everyone's mail to them twice a week. I purse my lips together, holding back a laugh. I should be the one to talk, since I still don't remember his name, but then again, I've never been good with names to begin with. My dad always said it was because I had a better photographic memory. *An artistic eye.*

"These are for you." He says, lifting up a bouquet from behind the cubicle divider. My eyes quickly grow wide.

The bouquet is filled with at least four dozen red roses surrounded by little bits of baby's breath, which I only know because of Lily. She had explained to me a few weeks ago exactly what was in the wedding bouquets she had picked out and that included this small white flower.

As the intern sets down the roses on my desk, I take a deep breath in, smelling how fresh and pleasant they are. A slight and cheerful "Hm" slips out of my throat and I am almost shocked at myself for the turn in my mood.

The only time I had ever received flowers in my life was after my dad had passed. We had so many bouquets from the funeral that they filled our entire living room to the brim. Bouquets of every color and every size. Even more than I could have imagined. Every table was practically overflowing with flowers. which was a little overwhelming at the time, but it made me think of how many people truly cared about my dad and were impacted by his passing.

Having those flowers around, even in some way, felt like his memory was being kept alive. Unfortunately, from what I remember, every bouquet I smelled gave off an unpleasant odor. My mom said I was imagining it, but it didn't matter, the florals gave an unmistakable aroma. The smell of death. Something that I couldn't escape.

Yet, this bouquet is different. It's a surprisingly strong, sweet and earthy scent. A pleasant, addicting smell.

I smile down at the flowers on my desk before looking up, hoping to say thank you to the intern whose name I still don't know, but he has already left. As I study the bouquet, slowly turning the expensive looking crystal vase on my desk, a white piece of paper hidden among the roses catches my eye. I quickly grab the white paper and pull it out from the bouquet.

I slowly unfold the card and before I can see what's written on the inside, his name at the bottom catches my eye. *Ryker*. My head lifts up slightly as my smile turns into a glowing grin. I quickly unfold the rest of the card and read what it says:

> *Hi Beautiful,*
>
> *You deserve every apology from me. I truly didn't want to leave you last night, but I had some urgent business to attend to. I will make it up to you. I promise. See you on the dance floor.*
>
> *Yours, Ryker.*

The last two words strike out at me. Despite the instant change in mood knowing that he reached out and apologized, and he really didn't need to, I can't help but smile as I read the words again. *Yours, Ryker.* Those two words are the only things I can focus on from the note. *Is he saying he's mine? This has to be crazy, right?* I've only known him for a short period of time. I mean, we only went on two dates. But then again, I've felt like I've known him for years. This invisible pull between us is undeniable. I mean, I guess I shouldn't read too much into it, right? At least I know he isn't some psycho since he is close with Mason and Lily. *At least I hope.* I don't know if I trust Lily's judgment in men, but I have to trust Mason's. *Right?*

I quickly blink and turn back to the window. The rain has picked up outside and the droplets on the window are racing faster than before. I take a breath in and my lips stay parted as I breath out. I'm definitely reading too far into this. *It's just a note.* I let out a small chuckle.

"What's so funny?" I hear a woman's voice from behind me.

Startled out of my thoughts, my grip tightens around the note, crushing the paper between my fingers. I quickly turn my chair to see my team lead, Anna, standing behind me.

I quickly grab my sketchbook off of the desk and hold it against my chest, closing it shut.

"Oh, nothing!" I lie.

I pull the sketchbook back from my chest and glance down at it, careful to not let Anna see the blank page that was open.

"I just had a cute idea to add to my sketches and it made me laugh." I lie again.

"Well, if they are anything like the pages you sent me last week, I have no doubt I'll find them amusing as well." Anna says smiling as she clicks the top of the pen in her hand.

"I know you'll love them!" I quickly reply, giving her a whimsical smile.

"Looking forward to it." Anna says, nodding as she turns to walk away.

I slowly pull the sketchbook away from my chest just as Anna steps back again and next to my cubicle. With a jerk reaction, I flop my sketchbook onto the desk facing down and look back up at Anna.

"Also, what lovely flowers." Anna raises an eyebrow and smirks. "Seems like he's a charmer."

With a turn of a heel, Anna is walking away once again before I can reply.

I slowly open my hand to reveal the small wrinkled piece of paper expanding as my fingers curl away from it. *Damnit.* I quickly grab the corners of the note and scrape it across the edge of my desk, hoping to remove the wrinkles. Once most are removed, I quickly read the note once again.

See you on the dance floor. With everything that happened last night, I had completely forgotten that I had invited Ryker to Lily's wedding. Better yet, he said yes. While every ounce of me wants to see him before then, I have to be patient. He said he had urgent business. I don't know what that entails, but I can only assume he will need some time to sort things out.

I look down at my sketchbook sitting on the desk. I mean, I'll be pretty occupied this week too catching up on unfinished work. But, before I know it, it'll be Lily's wedding.

I look up at the flowers in front of me, then back down at the note, as I feel a wide smile grow on my face. *I'll see you there Ryker.*

Chapter Twelve

Today is Lily's wedding day and I couldn't be more excited for her. The days leading up to this were so chaotic and crazy that despite Ryker being at the top of my mind at the beginning of the week, I quickly became focused on Lily. I knew though once the day had settled, Ryker would be right back to the top of my mind in a moment's notice. *See you on the dance floor.* I was looking forward to something at the end of the night that couldn't come soon enough.

When Lily and Mason were picking out their venue last year, I fully expected them to tell me they would be getting married by Lake Como in Italy or at some French chateau in the countryside. I mean, Mason came from old money and Lily always liked the nicest things so there wasn't a doubt in my mind. *Boy, was I wrong.*

Lily and Mason managed to find a location not only that gave them that European feel, but it was only 50 miles outside of the city, which I would have never guessed.

The venue, Arthur Estates, was an 100-acre property nestled between large trees and green hills, that sat on its own private lake. The estate just oozed luxury. The main building that sat in the middle of the property at three stories tall, was inspired by a French estate outside of Paris, from what I've been told, but with everything you'd expect an Italian estate to have: fountains, long pebble walkways and a well-manicured garden leading to the lake. On each side of the main building were one story buildings that stretched out and slightly wrapped around the front of the garden.

Following the reception, Lily and Mason would be staying in the main building, however, the property included onsite accommodations for family and friends in luxury cottages nestled behind the building between the trees. When Lily mentioned that this morning as I arrived, Ryker all of a sudden jumped back into my mind once again. *Will he be in one too? Or maybe in mine?*

I grab my bag and one of the estate attendees helps me navigate over to the cottages. As we walk over, I look around, entranced by the vast amount of trees that surround us. While I expected the trees to mimic the city with their fall colors, I'm surprised to see only green trees, an image that I wouldn't think of when it came to this time of year. For a moment, I'm almost disappointed the trees aren't shades of orange and yellow.

After a short three minute walk, he gives me the option to pick out which cottage I'd like to stay in, considering I am the first to arrive. To try to not be on the spot for too long, I quickly point to the cottage off to the left. It isn't right in front, but still feels close enough to access quickly in case I need to grab something from my bag throughout the day. *Or in order to bring Ryker back quickly.* I let the attendee know I can handle it from here and he hands me the key before heading back to the main building.

I walk over to the luxury cottage, which might as well be a house considering its size and place my bags at the bottom of the small set of steps. Looking up at the cottage, it resembles the main building with its French style, but it still has the feel of a secluded forest home.

I walk up the steps and unlock the door, as I feel a buzz from my phone in my back pocket. I slightly open the door, not enough to get a look inside and I pull my phone out to read the text.

Come meet me in the bridal room for hair and makeup when you're done!

I grab my bag at the bottom of the steps and pull it through the front door.

I know how much work it takes to get everyone ready for a wedding, so I quickly close the door behind me without even taking a peek into the luxury cottage. *Later.*

I grab the key from the door and hurry back to the main building, where the bridal room is located.

While Lily had every team at her disposal, especially her grandiose planning team, she insisted that I be there every step of the way to ensure it all ran smoothly. And I didn't mind honestly. I wanted everything to be perfect for her wedding day and I felt it was my duty to ensure that.

I was just thankful that Lily was so calm and at ease with all the craziness circling around us. Not that I thought she would be a bridezilla before, but I did expect her to be more nitpicky with all the details, especially since this was the biggest day of her life. *Right? That's what all wedding days are?* However, it was surprising to see her really let go and let her team make her day perfect, with only a little oversight from me at her request. She had to have someone watch her back, so who better than her maid of honor?

The ceremony had just finished getting set up near the lake at the edge of the garden when I went outside to see if anything was missing or still needed to be put together. Luckily, it was absolute perfection.

The pebble pathway leading to the seating area is layered in white rose petals meticulously placed down the path that wraps around a wide, round fountain that sits in the middle of the aisle. On the outside of the path are beautiful rose and boxwood bushes newly landscaped and shaped. As I walk around the fountain, carefully ensuring I don't step on the petals, and down the path a few steps more, I see the ceremony setup. Rows and rows of clear, see-through folding chairs on top of a grassy area line the sides of the pathway. At the end of each row next to the aisle are white flowers and roses tucked between strands of greenery. Each one wrapped with a white bow to hold it all together and they sit in large, white square vases. Between them are round, cylinder vases filled with sand and small candles. At the end of the aisle, where Lily and Mason will exchange their vows, stands a large square archway covered in florals, similar to the florals sitting along the aisle. It's a beautiful set up and one that I can only imagine for my own wedding. It is even more stunning to see the large, private lake sitting in the background surrounded by big, beautiful trees.

As I walk back toward the main building, I catch a glimpse of the four-tiered cake being carried through the front entrance and over to the reception space.

The reception space is located on the west side of the main building. As I walk over to take a look at what will soon be the dance floor I will meet Ryker on, I'm once again interrupted by a buzz. I stop in place as I take my phone out of my pocket. *Lily.*

Hey, is everything looking good?

Yes, it looks so beautiful!

Yay! We are about to start taking photos. Where are you?

I glance up at the time on my phone. *1:05.* The ceremony starts at three o'clock and I'm still not dressed. On top of that, I have a feeling that I'll need a quick touch up on my hair and makeup, considering how crazy it's been for me this morning. I quickly text her back.

Heading back now!

For what felt like hours running around to double check everything with the wedding planners in order to make sure it was set up to perfection, I'm shocked how quickly the time has snuck up on me.

As I push my way through the busy hallway, I get a quick glance at myself in a mirror. *Wait.* I backtrack until I can see myself once again in the hallway mirror and my eyes widen. I had gotten my hair and makeup done around eight o'clock this morning, and to my surprise, it had held up better than I expected. Both my hair and makeup really did hold in place like glue! Now I understand how every wedding photo I've seen online, the bridal party always looks amazing even at the end of the night. I smile at myself in the mirror and continue back to the bridal room, this time walking at my normal pace.

As I open the bridal room door, I stop in place as I spot Lily standing in front of a full length mirror across the room. Staring at herself in the reflection of the mirror, she doesn't notice I've opened the door and continues looking up and down at her reflection. I admire her as I watch from afar.

Despite seeing Lily this morning when she got her makeup done and had her hair pinned up into a perfectly manicured, yet meticulously messy bun, it was different seeing her finally in her dress. I had seen the dress on her several occasions before, but just seeing her all put together for the first time, it was hard not to get emotional. My best friend, who in just a couple short hours, will be marrying Mason. I couldn't be more excited and proud of her. To me, she is practically my sister. The person I grew up with here in the city. The person who has been through just about everything with me.

As my eyes slowly fall down from her hair to the back of her dress, studying every detail in order to remember this memory, I loudly hear my name being excitedly called in a familiar voice. My eyes shoot back up to Lily's face in the mirror, where she is gleaming with a smile as she stares back at me through the reflection. Finally taking a step into the room as the door closes behind me, I smile widely back at her as I walk over.

When I reach Lily, she turns around and gives me a hug, careful to avoid our faces touching to prevent our makeup from getting damaged.

"It's almost time!" I say, as Lily pulls back from our hug.

"I know!" Lily turns back toward the mirror to look at herself. She grabs the sides of her dress and gives it a small twirl back and forth. "Can you believe it?"

"It'll be beautiful." I say, looking down at the dress. My eyes shoot back up to hers in the reflection of the mirror. "You look beautiful." I smile.

"I'm so nervous!" Lily turns back to face me. "I have no idea why!" She lets out a small chuckle.

"What?" I say, almost shocked. "You're never nervous!"

"I know!" Lily takes a quick breath. "Who am I?" She says loudly, while chuckling again.

"Well, don't be." I calmly say. "This is your day and it'll be exactly what you've been looking forward to since we were kids!"

I smile, taking a quick breath in, just as a quick thought races through my head. *My own wedding.* Lily is the one getting married, but I never thought about what my own wedding would be like. Would it be close to home? Would it be as grand as Lily's? Who would my husband be at the end of the aisle? I shake off the thoughts and look back at Lily.

"Did you hear me?" Lily asks, a small look of confusion on her face.

"Oh no, sorry! What did you say?" My eyes flicker for a moment before I make eye contact with her again.

"Is it all perfect?" Lily locks her hands together in front of her dress and moves them up in front of her chin, pursing her lips together.

"What?" I ask, feeling like I misheard something else she said.

"Outside."

Lily walks over to the large window and takes a quick peek around the tall floor to ceiling curtains hanging on the wall.

"Is it all perfect?"

Still holding the curtain, she looks back at me, waiting for my response. I quickly step over to her and put my hands on the sides of her arms, giving a quick squeeze for assurance.

"It's all set, ready to go and looking like it's out of a dream." I confidently say, thinking back to the rose petals lining the stone pathway and the floral archway that I can envision Lily and Mason standing in front of at the end of the aisle.

"Oh, good!" Lily excitedly says before turning back to the window.

As I go to peer out the window with her, the door to the bridal room startles me and I turn on my heel to see who is coming in. My first concern is that it's Mason, despite knowing he is on the opposite end of the building. I couldn't imagine anything more unlucky than a groom seeing his bride before she walks down the aisle.

A sigh of relief escapes me as I see the photographer peeking out from behind the doorway. A quiet scoff exits my nose. *When did I become the superstitious type?*

"Hey, Lily?" The photographer asks, opening the door a bit wider. "Oh!" Her eyes quickly turn to me. "Glad to see you are back!"

I look at Lily and then back to the photographer.

"I have the other bridesmaids in place for photos and now that Paige is here, let's get the ball rolling!" She says, almost demanding.

Lily pulls my arm, nearly making me fall backward and pulls me toward the door. *Another subtle reminder of Lily being Lily.*

"Okay! We're ready!" She says, looking at me with a smile until I mimic hers.

The photographer peers outside the bridal room and looks both directions down the busy hallway, then back to us.

"Coast is clear! Let's go quickly!" She says.

I quickly follow Lily's pace, careful not to step on the side of her dress while standing close to her, as we head out of the bridal room and down the hallway.

Chapter Thirteen

Paige

It's nearly three o'clock when I begin to hear the harpist play softly from behind the large, wooden double doors that exit the main building. In front of me stands the other four bridesmaids next to Mason's groomsmen, which I am a little disappointed to see Ryker isn't a part of. Then again, I knew Mason and Ryker had known each other well, but maybe not as well as I had thought. Lily tends to over exaggerate how well she knows someone, which I found out from that first blind date she sent me on. She *clearly* didn't know him as well as she said she did. Nonetheless, I knew Ryker would be sitting out there somewhere in the crowd. I just had to spot him.

I turn back to look at Lily, who now appears calm as a clam, a complete turn around from just a few hours before when she acted so nervous and unlike herself. But now, Lily was back to herself and I could see in her eyes, she was confident and she was ready to get married.

Her dad steps out from behind her and stands next to her, holding his elbow out for her to interlock her arm with. She looks at him and pulls her arm into his, just as he carefully places a kiss on the top of her head. Lily turns to smile at him as he pulls away, straightening himself up next to her. *Something I'll never have.* A brief moment of sadness echoes through my head, but it's cut short as I hear the double doors open from behind me, distracting me from my thoughts. I quickly turn away and face forward, looking at the back of the bridal party standing within the open doors.

I watch as each pair steps out and walks down the pathway. *It's time.* I feel a tug on my arm and I'm reminded that I have my arm interlocked with Mason's brother, Miles. I follow Miles' pace as we walk through the double doors and down the three steps onto the pathway. It takes about thirty seconds of the song for us to reach the part of the pathway that is draped with the white rose petals. As we walk around the fountain and between the rows of chairs filled with the hundreds of guests, I keep my eyes straight ahead as the photographer, who is standing near the arch, snaps photos of us walking. If it weren't for her standing at the end of the aisle, my head would surely be turning in all directions to look for *you know who* in the crowd.

As we reach the end of the aisle, Miles unlocks his arm from mine and steps off to the right to stand at the front of the groomsmen line along the side of the archway. Mason is already waiting there next to him and I quickly give Mason a full-faced grin. *It's almost time!* I quickly scurry over to the left to stand in my place in line closest to the archway.

As I turn around to face the crowd, the harpist swiftly changes up the song to a slower beat and before I can focus on anyone's faces, the guests quickly turn around to face Lily, who is now walking through the double doors and toward the pathway. *Missed my chance.* Instead, I focus my attention on Lily, the only person I can clearly see. *She really looks so happy and beautiful.*

Wearing her stunning dress that I can only imagine cost a pretty penny, I watch her meticulously take steps closer to us, careful not to trip over her dress as she walks down the rose petal covered pathway. The carefully-placed pearls attached from the shoulders of her dress down to the floor have a slight sparkle to them as the light reflects off her dress as she walks. I look back up to Lily's face, whose attention I imagine is only focused on one thing in front of her. *Mason.*

As she and her father walk around the fountain in the center of the aisle, I turn my attention to the only other person's reaction I hope to see: Mason's. In all the romance movies that Lily forced me to watch growing up, I always remembered the one thing they all had in common. During a wedding scene, the camera always panned over to show the look on the groom's face as his bride walked down the aisle and I'm not going to miss this real-life moment. As I look at Mason, his face surely says it all.

Despite not knowing Mason long, he was always hard to read. I tried my best to get to know him as well as one could, but I never felt like we formed a solid connection. I could ask him a question and he would always give me short answers, despite what I asked, and when I tried to invite him out with Lily and I, he always seemed preoccupied with something business related. So when Lily assured me after they got engaged that he was a heartfelt and caring man, I had to believe her. I mean, I wasn't going to tell her to call it off or anything. It wasn't my place. Yet here on their wedding day, I'm able to see a side of Mason I hadn't ever seen before. *A softer side.*

A single strand of blond hair falls over Mason's forehead and he quickly runs his hand through his hair and out of his face. As he does, he slightly turns toward my direction and I can see tears filling in the wells around his blue eyes. With a quick glance toward Lily, who is now about halfway down the aisle, I look back at Mason just as he brings his hand up to his cheek to wipe away his tears. *I guess he really is an emotional guy.* As he brings his hand back down to his side, the quick tears dissipate and a large, uncontrollable grin brightens up on Mason's face. It's at that same moment that Lily reaches the end of the aisle. Her dad kisses her cheek and she reaches out to grab Mason's held out hand. Once they are next to one another, the officiant promptly starts talking.

Unaware of the impact their wedding is already having on me, I suddenly notice a slight wetness against my cheek. Pulling my hand up to my face, I wipe away a single tear that's escaped my eyes and glance down at the wetness against my finger. For a second, I'm caught off guard. Almost surprised actually. I pictured crying as a sad gesture, with little connection to happy moments like this because my dad's passing affected me so harshly. This wasn't a sad moment though. It was a happy one. A wedding!

As a grin slowly grows on my face, I push down the grief stricken moments of the past and embrace this moment, a happy moment and I consider other future moments like this.

I watch as the officiant continues to talk between the happy couple, bringing up past memories that Mason and Lily shared together as well as talks of future hopes and dreams. All the mushy stuff that I just knew would bring more cheerful tears to my eyes. They exchange rings and read each other the generic "till death do us part" vows, even though I know they have personal vows written to be read to one another tonight. Then when the time arrives, Mason and Lily kiss and officially become husband and wife. Another tear escapes my cheek and ignoring it, I start clapping along with the crowd for my best friend, as my large grin never vanishes from my face.

As Lily and Mason start walking down the aisle back toward the main building, I look at Miles who meets me halfway to link our arms together once again. With the crowd turned and facing toward the couple walking away, we start down the path again following suit.

It isn't until we are walking around the fountain on the path that something catches the corner of my eye. *Red roses.* The bushes along the pathway strike my memory and I'm quickly reminded of what I was looking for when the ceremony started, or better yet *who.* A quick look over my shoulder and I see the crowd dispersing as the rest of the bridal party walks closely behind us on the path. With the rapid movement of the crowd and the distance not doing any favors, I let out a quiet sigh, disappointed I was never able to catch a glimpse of Ryker. *Was he even there?*

When we reach the main building, Miles unlocks arms with me and walks over to Mason, who is still grinning as wide as can be as he stands next to Lily. *Like every groom should be.* The rest of the bridal party veers off to the right toward the reception building. As I look over to where they are walking, I'm surprised to see an outdoor bar and several taller table displays set up near the entrance. I hadn't seen those set up when I had "scouted" the area for Lily. *Cocktail hour for sure.*

"Time to celebrate!" I hear Lily shout from behind me. I turn around to see her and Mason heading straight for the outdoor bar, where the rest of the bridal party is already waiting.

"Hey! Guys!" I hear the photographer say as she tries to catch up with Mason and Lily before they get their drinks. "Let's do one-on-one's real quick!" I scoff. I mean, I understand the need for photos right away, but these expensive professionals are sometimes *too* professional. *Let my girl get a drink first!* If anyone deserves it, it's definitely the bride and groom.

Standing alone at the end of the pathway now, I notice the crowd of guests moving closer and closer to me. A sudden overwhelming feeling hits me as I feel the urge to escape before they surround me. Not that I mind being in a crowd, but I can't imagine my makeup still looks good after what I can only imagine my "ugly crying" looked like. And god forbid, Ryker sees me like this. I don't even know what he'd say.

I swiftly walk up the steps of the main building and rush over to the hallway where the bathrooms are. The hallway, unlike earlier today, is now completely vacant as every hand on deck is now focused on the wedding itself.

I am once again surprised when I take a look at myself in the mirror. Not a single smear, smudge or black streak of mascara. *Damn, these makeup artists really are good.* I quickly fix a few strands of loose hair, shoot a reassuring smile at my reflection and exit the bathroom.

As I walk down the hallway where it merges back into the front lobby of the main building, I get a quick glimpse of the guests through the windows standing in the cocktail area. It's hard to make out their faces through the windows, but I stare for a moment, trying to see if I can recognize anyone. *Ryker has to be in there somewhere.* I straighten myself up, take a breath and take a step.

Just then, my body slowly starts to fall forward as I feel a tug on my arm from behind me. The sudden jolt catches me off guard and I close my eyes tightly, bracing myself for the fall. As if the world starts spinning, I feel myself turn around quickly, my eyes still shut tightly. My body freezes and I'm suddenly hit with a familiar scent that lingers in the air. I feel a relaxing warmth against my bare arm and back and I suddenly realize I haven't hit the ground yet.

"Hey, beautiful."

The familiar voice jolts my eyes wide open and I see Ryker standing over me as he holds my body mid-air. My eyes immediately soften as I stare into his green eyes, just as my heart starts to race. My eyes wander from one eye to the next, then down to his lips and back into eye contact. *He's here.*

"Hi." I softly say, unable to think of any other words as he towers over me, still holding my body up. *When did he get here?*

He slowly pushes his arm against my back, helping me to straighten myself up and land back on my feet, never breaking our eye contact.

"When did you get here?" I ask, slightly surprised to see him here, despite not seeing him during the ceremony.

Ryker lets out a slight chuckle. "I've been here the entire time."

My eyes widen and I tilt my head slightly. "You have?" I can hear my own shock in my voice as I break our eye contact and look up slightly. *Has he really?*

"Yes, of course." He confidently replies.

I take a step back from him, his hand sliding from my back to the side of my body where it stays put, and I look down. My eyes slowly move up his tall figure and I take in the details of his attire. From his black polished shoes up to his freshly pressed black suit, I continue to move my eyes up. Under his suit jacket that unjustly hides his biceps, he's wearing a stark white button down that molds around his pecs. *More how I like it.* At his neck, he's wearing a black bowtie, a choice I definitely expected him to wear when thinking about this day earlier in the week. It gives off a clean, sophisticated look and I had no doubt he would play the part.

Before bringing my eyes up to his face, I notice the bowtie is slightly crooked. I can't help but reach my hands out to adjust it, before I look at him. As I place my hands on his bowtie, adjusting it back and forth, I suddenly feel his eyes on me watching me. It's at that moment that I realize I didn't ask him for permission and that I should look up to acknowledge it, but I keep my eyes down until his bowtie is perfectly centered.

I feel his eyes continue to watch me as I direct my attention past his face and up to the top of his head. I look up at his hair, which looks to have also been freshly cut on the sides and the overgrowth of hair at the top has been pushed back. Not a single hair out of place, unlike myself. My eyes move back down his face, over his dark eyebrows, and quickly past his green eyes. I want to look at them, but I know that I won't be able to think if I focus on them long. I shoot him a quick smile before my gaze moves down to his chiseled jawline, now freshly shaven. A sight that I distinctly remember from our first date together. He watches as I study each part of his appearance and a slight smirk appears on his face, making my eyes immediately land on his lips. I quickly make eye contact with him, realizing I've been studying his features a little too long.

"I saw you got a bit emotional up there." Ryker says with a light chuckle, tilting his head slightly in the same direction. My eyes quickly widen.

"Oh god." I quietly say. *He saw me ugly crying in front of everyone during the ceremony.* I was so focused on Lily and Mason that I had completely forgotten to look around to see if Ryker was sitting with all the guests. It didn't even occur to me that he was watching me cry in front of everyone.

I quickly bring my hands up to my face to try to cover my face. *This is so embarrassing.*

"Hey." Ryker says, grabbing my hands and pulling them down from my face. "Don't worry. I thought it was endearing." Ryker gives me a slight smile.

"That's a lie." I scoff as I roll my eyes at him.

"That's why I followed you over here. I just wanted to make sure you were okay." He says, letting go of my hands, which he had been holding. *Well that's sweet of him.* A smile slowly returns to my face as I feel his arms reach around my back and I can feel his hands interlock to his wrists. "Well, among other things."

With a quick twist of our bodies, I feel him pushing us against a wall and I see his eyes darken. His hand reaches from behind my back, gliding up my waist and up the side of my body. I feel my body shiver. Yearning for more.

As his hand reaches my ribs, I feel him let go and come closer to my face. His eyes focus on my own, then shoot down to my lips. With an instant, he places his index finger below my chin, slightly tilting my face up toward him.

"I haven't been able to stop thinking about you." He says, as his thumb slowly rubs over my bottom lip as his eyes stay focused there. I wait eagerly for his next move.

As his thumb slightly tugs at my lip, pulling it down as he removes his finger, his eyes jolt back to mine and before I can catch my breath, our lips meet. I instantly fold into his hands, which wrap around the back of my neck, holding me in place. I can finally indulge in his sweet aromatic flavor once again as his lips rhythmically dance with my own. Despite it being only a week since I last saw him, I lean in to him, yearning for his lips to dive deeper into mine. This is what I've been craving. What I've been missing since the last time I saw him.

Distant footsteps against the tile break our lips apart as we both shoot our gaze in their direction. We catch a glimpse of the last few steps of a suited man walking into the restroom, completely unaware of this encounter we're having down the hallway. Ryker and I quickly look back at one another and I can't help but let out a small laugh. It instantly makes me think of a high school couple getting caught under the bleachers.

"I've missed this." Ryker says, a soft smirk growing on his face. "I've missed you."

I feel myself instantly blush as my cheeks press against the bottom of my eyes and a large smile plasters my face.

"It hasn't even been a week." I tartly say. I instantly regret the words as I see Ryker's face almost look surprised as well from the words that escaped my lips. *Shit.*

Ryker's facial expression quickly relaxes and he lets out a deep chuckle, which turns back into a smirk. "Should I just leave then?" He playfully says.

"I didn't mean it like that." I quickly say, trying to recover from my own words.

I watch as Ryker's eyes slightly squint and his smirk still lingers on his face. *He's messing with me.* I smile coyly and roll my eyes at him. His hand, which had been resting on my shoulder after we thought we had been "caught," slowly falls back down my back. His arms once again tighten around my body as he locks his hands to his wrists. He inches forward, our eyes staying locked on one another and as I smell his addicting scent, I yearn for him to kiss me once again. As if he can feel the building energy between us, his lips meet mine once again. Hoping it will be like before, I push my body closer to his, but he quickly pulls his lips apart from mine all too soon, only placing a single kiss against my lips.

"I don't want to stay away from you another day, beautiful." He says with a smile as our faces linger just inches apart.

My eyes move down to his lips, then back up his chiseled jawline to his eyes, where I focus on the small golden hue that makes his eyes so unique.

Ryker's hand reaches around from behind my back and his thumb gently slides a loose strand of hair away from my cheek and behind my ear. A strand I must've missed in the bathroom or one that had become loose during our impromptu hallway encounter. I slightly close my eyes for a moment, basking in his touch against my face, but as if I had completely forgotten until a second before, I think back to the last time we saw one another. *He left.*

I open my eyes and cock my head to the side, confusion riddling my face. His hand pulls away and pauses mid-air near my face.

"What's wrong?" Ryker asks, his smirk vanishing as he furrows his eyebrows and pulls back from our close proximity.

"What happened last week?" I say, unaware of the slight raspiness in my voice. "I know you said it was urgent business, but by the look on your face that night, it seemed like something else happened." I raise my eyebrows slightly, waiting for his response. He may have left, but he must have a good reason for it. I mean, he didn't act like he wanted to leave and I certainly didn't want him to, but he turned around and left despite that.

Ryker takes a step back, pulling his arms away from me. Tucking his hands into his pockets, he looks down at the ground for a brief moment before taking a deep breath in. As he lets out his breath, he looks back up at me, our eyes meeting. His brows are still furrowed and I match his expression, anxious to hear the reason. His eyes wander back and forth, as if he is trying to find the answers in my eyes.

"It's -" He says, pausing for a moment as he breaks our eye contact and looks back down to the ground. "Hard to explain." He doesn't look up.

I tilt my head to the side, my eyebrows still furrowed. *What's so hard to explain?* I look at the top of his dark hair, perfectly pulled back at the top. *Maybe something bad happened?* I bring my hand up to rub my fingers through it. As my hand reaches up, he quickly pulls out one of his hands from his pocket and grabs my hand, holding it in the air. He slowly rotates my hand and opens my palm. I can tell his focus has shifted from the floor to my open hand as his head slightly tilts toward it, instead of straight down. He lowers my hand down to my side as his thumb gently rubs the center of my palm. Turning toward my other hand that's resting on my side, he pulls his hand out of his pocket and grabs onto that one as well, rubbing his thumbs over both palms as he slowly brings his head up to look at me. His eyebrows are no longer furrowed as a slight, half-smile grows on his face. An almost reassuring smile. I unfurrow my brows and give a slight smile back, mimicking him.

"I promise I'll explain it to you one day, but just know it will never happen again. Everything's been taken care of." Ryker says, leaning in as he kisses the top of my forehead. "Okay?" He raises his eyebrows with a quick nod as he pulls away from my head.

"Okay." I say with a reassuring smile.

This just got a lot more confusing. *Taken care of?* Maybe he just doesn't want to talk about it right now. I mean, it is Lily's wedding day. If it's sad, it's probably best that I don't hear about it now. I already broke down in tears once today. Best not to have it happen twice. Either way, I don't think it's my business. He apologized before and if he wants to talk about it, he will.

Ryker gives both of my hands a quick squeeze, then releases them as he straightens himself up. Grabbing the bottom of his suit jacket, he gives it a slight tug to straighten it out. As I watch him, I realize that I'm still leaning against the wall from when he kissed me. I quickly push myself away from the wall and straighten myself up in front of him. I look down at my dress, ensuring it's not wrinkled and look at Ryker with a confident smile. Slowly his eyes move down my body and back up again until they meet my own. His eyes slightly squint as his signature smirk grows on his face.

It takes me a moment after straightening myself up, but I realize how much closer our faces are to one another. I let out a slight chuckle under my breath and one of his eyebrows slightly raises.

"What?" He asks, questioning my chuckle.

"Oh, nothing." I coyly say with a smile as I look off to my left then back at him. "It's just -" I pause, then raise both my eyebrows briefly. "You still tower over me even when I'm in heels." I let out a slight chuckle once more.

"Huh." Rykers says, his face almost questioning what I said. His eyes quickly darken and catching me off guard, his arm wraps behind my back pulling me to his chest. He leans closer and his lips brush against my ear as he whispers, "I think I like the boots better." As he pulls away, his smirk quickly reappears as his eyes revert back to mine.

I look up at him, with our faces inches apart, and I purse my lips together trying to hide the huge smile I know is about to pop through.

"Agreed." I let a small smile escape as my lips still press together.

Our eye contact breaks as we simultaneously hear three loud static taps in the distance followed by a muffled man speaking. I squint my eyes and lean my head a few inches closer to the sound and I'm able to make out the words, "bridal party."

Immediately pulling back from Ryker's arm around me, I look up at him wide-eyed.

"Oh shit, I have to go!" I say, grabbing the sides of my dress as I quickly start hustling toward the double doors.

As I'm about to exit, I turn to look back at Ryker who is standing there in his suit with both hands in his pockets smiling in my direction. As if to read my mind, he quickly shouts, "I'm right behind you!" with a wide grin. Shooting a smile back to him, I turn on my heel and head out to the garden where the cocktail hour is being held.

Chapter Fourteen

I arrive just as the last bridesmaid and groomsmen duo that were ahead of Miles and I enter into the reception space. I quickly slip through Lily and Mason, who are standing out in the garden, and slide in next to Miles near the double doors. I lock my arm with his and he instantly looks surprised to see me.

"Oh!" Miles says, pausing. "Hey Paige. Where have you -"

"What should our entrance dance be?" I quickly cut him off, knowing that we both don't have the time for a long discussion when we are up next to enter the room. The music is blasting from inside and I hear the man's voice once again over the speaker.

"Finger guns?" Miles questioningly asks, with a sarcastic tone. I chuckle at the quirky decision, but quickly nod as the speaker says "best man" and "maid of honor."

I raise my eyebrows to Miles, as if to queue us to go, and we rush in through the open double doors. As we get inside, we unlock our arms and start doing cowboy-style finger guns as we separate from one another on opposite sides of a round table that guests are seated at. The room is filled with clapping and I hear cheering grow louder as we dance around the table pretending to blow out the smoke from our fingers.

We meet back together on the other side of the table, where the dance floor sits, and unknowingly, Miles grabs my hand pulling me toward him. A quick spin around and I'm caught off guard as he dips me over the dance floor. While upside down, I catch a glimpse of Ryker walking in through a separate entrance on the opposite side of the room. His eyes quickly widen. It isn't long before Miles pulls me back up onto my feet and he leans down to bow toward the guests. I follow suit, as if we had planned it all along. The guests continue to clap loudly and as I lean to straighten myself up, I catch a glance down at my dress, suddenly seeing it may have been a bit too revealing for that move. I quickly place my free hand over my chest and awkwardly smile at Miles, who is completely unaware of it. He lets go of my hand and turns to walk over to the wedding party's table behind us, where the other bridesmaids and groomsmen have already sat.

After standing on the dance floor alone for a quick second, I hear the man's voice start to announce "bride" and "groom." I look back at the guests and see Ryker smirking from afar. *He definitely saw something.* I purse my lips together, remove my hand from my chest, and grab the sides of my dress as I turn to shuffle over to my table.

As I sit down, Lily and Mason make their entrance, with Mason carrying Lily through the double doors and straight to the dance floor. As they reach the dance floor, Mason spins Lily around in a circle, slowly loosening his grip on her as she glides to her feet onto the floor.

"The bride and groom will now have their first dance." The man over the speaker says.

The song quickly shifts from an upbeat pop song into a slow, heartfelt song. Lily wraps her arms around Mason as they sway back and forth to the music. Despite the occasional dip and them kissing, I quietly chuckle as I watch them dance. In the movies, it's definitely romantic watching the newlyweds have their first dance, but in real life, I didn't expect it to be so awkward. I know Lily loves the attention and is probably enjoying every second of everyone's eyes on the two of them, but I can only imagine if it were me up there, I would feel so out of my element. A one minute dance in front of everyone is long enough, but I can't imagine three minutes. But then again, maybe I would? Especially with the right person. Maybe I'd just forget all the eyes staring at me and focus on the one person right there in front of me. The one person that meant the most to me.

The guests' loud clapping snaps me back into reality and I see Lily and Mason come around to the middle of the table I'm at. I watch as Mason pulls the chair out for Lily, who slides in next to me, her dress covering the entire seat and partially flowing over my own dress. *I don't mind.* Lily and I turn our heads and quickly mirror a small smile toward one another. The sound of opening doors behind me breaks our short interaction as I turn around. Through the doors, waiters dressed in all black enter into the room with platters of salads in tow. As my eyes follow the waiters veering off behind our table, I watch as the other ones divide themselves throughout the room, stopping at several tables.

My eyes scan the room as I look for Ryker again, curious as to where he is sitting. Each table I pass over, I see the guests excitedly looking at the waiters around them, eager for their first courses. Eventually, in the back of the room, I find a table that seems to be rowdier than the other ones. The exclusively men-only table appears to be filled with Mason's friends, some of whom I recall seeing pictures of at Mason's bachelor party when he posted about the weekend online a few months ago. All of them, from what I could remember, came from old money, similar to Mason, and they were all dressed up as if they had been invited to the most formal charity auction of their lives and were there to impress. *My guess? They always dressed like that.*

As I pass through each person at that table, my eyes land on the one person who isn't focused on the food or the rich individuals around him. He isn't looking at the bride or at his friend Mason. He is looking straight at me and I can only imagine he hasn't taken his eyes off me since I left the dance floor. I blush as our eyes meet. His elbow is resting on the table with his index finger and thumb holding the side of his face, with his fingers nearly covering one of his eyes. The positioning is almost as if his head got tired from staring and he needed support in order to not lose his focus. But, what stands out is how he isn't talking to anyone else at the table. He's just looking at me, as if to be in deep thought. Is he remembering the slight embarrassment I just had on the dance floor? Is he thinking about the wedding? Later tonight? *I can only hope.*

As our eyes once again meet, I see the corner of his mouth rise. Can he see me blushing from across the room? *I can't imagine so.* I move my left hand up to my face and lightly press them against my cheeks, as if to try to feel myself blushing. I smile at Ryker, hoping he noticed.

A hand tapping my shoulder distracts me from my focus as I hear, "Pardon my reach, ma'am." I break my eye contact with Ryker as I turn around to see a young, male waiter standing closely behind me holding a salad plate. I blink for a moment at him, quickly lowering my hand from my pink cheek before slightly leaning to the side, allowing him to rest the plate in front of me. As my eyes slowly glance away from the waiter, they meet Lily's as she stares wide-eyed with a big-cheeked, closed mouth smile.

"Excuse me?" Lily asks with a full mouth of salad, her words coming out slightly illegible.

I stare at her, waiting to see what happens. Lily quickly swallows the food in her mouth as her eyes quickly close shut for a moment. As she takes a breath out, her eyes widen again and her grin grows again on her face, no longer puffy from the food in her mouth.

"Paige! Are you blushing?"

My eyes quickly widen as I realize that Lily may have seen the unspoken interaction I had with Ryker from across the room. The hand that had previously been touching my cheek jerkingly rushes back up to its place as I try to hide the color growing on my cheeks. I purse my lips together and turn my face quickly away from Lily's as I grab the fork on the table and stab my salad in front of me. Without a second to rest, I stuff the salad-filled fork into my mouth before looking back at Lily, who now undoubtedly knows I am avoiding the question.

"The food is delicious!" I utter through a smile with a mouth now full of food.

"Hmm." Lily hums, rolling her eyes at me.

Lily slightly looks off into the distance at the other side of the room, then side-eyes me with a smile, finally catching sight of who I was looking at. Instead of saying something else, she slowly readjusts herself in her seat before continuing to eat her salad.

As the other dinner courses were promptly served, the individual speeches that I had been preparing for, were up next. I had consulted Lily about my speech weeks prior and expressed to her how hesitant I was about it. Writing a speech was not my strong suit. Even when my dad had died, I didn't say anything or write a speech. I mean, what does a five-year-old even say in a situation like that? If I had said anything though, it would have undoubtedly made me cry. So when it came to my maid of honor speech for Lily and Mason, I asked Lily what I should say and her advice? *Keep it short, sweet and from the heart.*

Two days ago, I had written out my speech, pulling the words straight from the heart and somehow, I managed to write a lengthy paragraph. I was impressed with myself to say the least. Despite Lily encouraging me to say something simple and short, I wanted to really go all out for her, especially since we had been through so much together. It was the least I could do as her best friend. I wrote it down on a small folded piece of paper and prior to leaving the bridal room with Lily earlier today, I had tucked it in my bra - the only place I had room to hold onto it for the duration of the wedding. However, it wasn't until halfway through dinner that I looked down, only to realize the note was no longer there. The small fear of giving a speech without a "cheat sheet" to look at only made me more anxious as dinner slowly started wrapping up. *How will I get through it? What if I butcher my words as I try to remember it?*

I spent a few seconds looking around my seat and under the table, hoping to find this small piece of paper, just as Miles stood up and started to give his speech. I wasn't worried about the guests watching me or being confused by what I was doing, because their attention was solely focused on him. As I came to the realization that the note was nowhere near me, my eyes moved across the room, retracing my steps from when I came in. I froze as I spotted a small piece of paper folded on the ground off to the side of the dance floor. *Shit.* It must have fallen out when I was bowing after my entrance dance with Miles and had gotten shuffled around by the waiter's feet throughout dinner.

My eyes widen as I look around the room, hoping to find a moment to grab it, but before I'm able to make any kind of decision, the guests suddenly start clapping and clinking their glasses together. Unaware of what's happening, I quickly raise my glass to try to blend in when I notice Miles sitting down after giving his speech. *Shit.* The speaker taps the microphone and the guests turn their attention toward me, as he mentions "maid of honor" over the loudspeaker. *I don't have time. I have to wing it.*

I slowly stand up, my glass still in my hand, as I look around the room. I pick out a few guests who have their dinner napkins up to their eyes and I can only imagine that the speech Miles gave was not only heartfelt, but a tear jerker. If I can say something half as well as he does, I'll be happy. Out of the corner of my eye, Miles reaches behind Mason's back holding the microphone out for me to grab. I quickly grab it from behind Lily and take a quiet inhale and exhale before bringing the microphone up to my mouth.

"Hi." I anxiously say, as I stare out to the guests sitting at their tables.

My eyes quickly fall on Ryker, who has a blank expression on his face. Unsure of what he is thinking, my eyes pace back and forth until I glance down at the dance floor where the note sits. Ryker's eyes follow mine and as soon as he notices the note that my eyes are focused on, he straightens himself up in his seat. I look back at him with worry, hoping he can read my thoughts. *What do I even say?*

As if he can see the desperation in my eyes, the corners of his mouth slightly curve up and he gives me a soft nod - the small encouragement I need. I direct my eyes back on Lily and Mason, who are looking up at me from their seats, and I think back to Lily's encouraging words: Keep it short, sweet and from the heart. *I got this.*

"Hi." I confidently repeat myself as a smile grows on my face. "I'm Paige, Lily's maid of honor." I look back at Lily who appears to be anxious herself seeing what little words have come out of my mouth.

"I know you are all so eager to get out of your seats and dance, so I'll keep this short and sweet." I say with a slight chuckle and I'm quickly relieved to hear several guests let out small laughs as well. *Keep it going. You're doing great.* The small voice in my head pushes me on. I release one of my hands from the microphone and hold it out in front of Lily, who promptly grabs it and holds onto it, knowing I might need a little more encouragement.

"Lily and I have been best friends almost our entire lives and with all the memories we've shared, I consider her to be a sister." I say, confidently smiling down at her. "Today is another great day to add to our memories. Her wedding day." I look at Mason sitting next to her, then give him a quick smile as well before correcting myself. "Their wedding day."

I pause, trying to think of a way to quickly wrap up my speech. I look out at the guests and then my eyes shoot over to Ryker in the back of the room, who has a slight smirk on his face. *From the heart.* I look back at Lily and Mason, who are looking up at me from their seats.

"It's rare to find someone that can complete you, but you two have found it."

I let go of Lily's hand and grab my champagne glass on the table in front of me. Raising it up in the air, I smile down at Lily once again.

"So here's to the bride and groom!"

From my side and out of view, I hear the guests' drinks clink together before clapping starts. I take a sip of the champagne to honor the cheers. Lily quickly stands up and as I pull my glass away from my mouth, she gives me a hug. The clapping slowly fades around us and is quickly replaced by guest chatter. As we embrace, Lily turns her head toward my ear and I hear her whisper, "I think you've found it too." Pulling back, Lily has a devious smile on her face as she looks at me, before turning toward the guests.

"Let's dance!" Lily shouts, raising her arms into the air.

As the music slowly grows louder and louder around us, the DJ glides across the dance floor and grabs the microphone from my hand before heading back to his table near the speakers.

Mason stands up with Lily and they walk out to the dance floor, as a fast-paced pop song plays over the speakers. Several others from the bridal party stand up from the table, joining them on the dance floor. Guests stand up as well, crowding the dance floor within a few moments.

I stand up from my seat and walk along the side of the dance floor as people dance around me, sometimes a bit too close for comfort.

Despite Lily being the more confident one between us two and the one who loves to dance, I was never a fan of dancing. Any time she took me to a party in college, which she had to convince me to go to, she was always the first one in the middle of the room dancing to the music. I had no doubt she had the confidence to go out and dance on her own, but it probably helped that she was more carefree when she was drinking. It always felt awkward to me though. Dancing in front of people as they watched. I always just sat on a couch or hung out in a corner with others that we knew, avoiding dancing at all costs. And I certainly wasn't going to be getting drunk enough to get to my own care-free stage.

So, tonight, I wasn't really looking forward to dancing, but if Ryker wanted to dance with me, I would. I mean, I wouldn't turn down a dance with *him*. I would be an idiot.

As I make my way around the dance floor and weave between several round tables, I finally stop in front of the table where Ryker is at, however, he isn't there. Nobody is. I turn around to look at the dance floor and within a few seconds, I'm able to find several of those old-money men that were sitting here. They all appear to be having the time of their lives dancing to the upbeat music.

I turn back around, glancing quickly at the empty table, before looking in both directions to see if I can find Ryker, but to no avail. Worried he may have left, I glide my hands nervously down the sides of my hips. As I move my hands slowly back up my waist, my fingers are quickly intertwined with ones bigger than my own. Without looking, I know it's him. I feel his savory scent fill my nose once more as his chest rests against my back. His hands, still holding my own, cross over in front of my chest as his arms tightly wrap around my upper body, cradling me against him. My body suddenly no longer feels anxious from the impromptu speech as I feel relaxed within his arms. His head lowers to the side of mine and I'm taken back to the night we first met as I feel his lips brush against my ear. I look down for a brief moment, noticing that his wrapped arms around me have pushed my breasts up. A deep snicker comes out of his mouth and without being able to see it, I can feel a smirk growing on his face. *He noticed too.* I slightly turn my head in towards his lips and I feel his breath against my ear. I suddenly feel warmth radiating through me and my body tingles between his arms.

"We're leaving." Ryker's voice harshly says. Almost demanding. I blink my eyes several times, confused why his demeanor changed so suddenly. *What?*

Ryker uncrosses our arms from in front of my chest just as he pulls his face away from the side of mine. Both hands unwrap from mine, as they rest on the side of my body, before he quickly replaces his hand into mine. Before I can even stop to look at him, he swiftly walks around from behind me and his arm pulls me out through two open double doors that are behind the table he was sitting at. His fast pace gives no rest as I willingly follow him, his strength overpowering my common sense, which would have pulled me back into the room.

As we take a few quick-paced steps out through the doors, the music slowly starts to fade away. We make our way down the opposite end of the hallway from where we met up just over an hour before and even after leaving the room, his pace doesn't lessen. I try to keep up, but suddenly feel my heel catch on the ground and I trip slightly.

"Wait." I say, as my words freeze Ryker in his place. "Where are we even going?" I curiously ask as I adjust myself back to a steady foot.

Ryker turns his head slightly and gives me a brief side-eye, before his eyebrows raise at the realization I had tripped. It's a sudden shift in demeanor from moments before. His brows quickly furrow as he sees my eyes wander around back and forth, confusion still riddling my face. Then, a lift of his lips makes me furrow my brows as I get even more confused. *What is this game he is playing?*

With a swift turn toward me, he steps forward and grabs my body between his hands and gently, but forcefully, pushes me against the wall of the hallway. *Just like earlier.* His forehead pushes against the top of mine as our eyes meet and I suddenly feel the heat coming off of him. This growing urge. This instinct.

"We need to leave. Now." He demands.

With another quick pull away, I'm no longer against the wall but I am held between his arms. My chest pushing up against his muscular figure and thus, pushing my breasts up within my dress. Then it hits me. I look up at him, but this time, I can tell why we need to leave. I know why he is being so demanding. So eager. So filled with want.

"Why?" I playfully ask, batting my eyes.

His breathing is paced as he stares into my eyes and I can tell the harshness on his face is now a growing, lingering hunger. The seductive smirk reappears on his face once again.

"Because." Ryker starts, briefly pausing as he slightly squints his eyes. "If we don't leave now, I don't think I'll be able to keep myself from ripping this dress off of you and taking you right here, right now in the hallway."

The yearning in his voice makes my heart race. My eyebrows raise over my wide eyes and I quickly feel exhilarating chills throughout my body. *Well, let's go.*

As if he can read my mind, Ryker quickly pulls back from our close embrace and turns back around to lead us through the rest of the hallway. I quickly follow, staying closer to him this time to avoid accidentally tripping.

As we reach the end of the hallway, Ryker leads me outside through the entrance of the main building and I quickly look off to the left where the path to my small cottage is located. Ignoring Ryker, I attempt to pull us over in that direction, but I'm tugged back as he doesn't follow.

"Where are you going?" Ryker curiously asks, emphasizing "you."

I turn around to face him, still holding his hand despite being several feet apart from one another.

"I thought we were going back to my room." I ask, furrowing my eyebrows in confusion.

Ryker lets out a deep snicker, then pulls my hand to bring me closer to him. With his other hand, he pulls car keys out of his pocket and turning his head slightly, he drops the keys into the hands of a valet behind him. *Where did the valet come from?*

"Isn't that where we're going?" I ask, tilting my head.

Ryker pulls me against his chest once again and looks down at me, then quickly smirks.

"You're eager, aren't you?" He scoffs. I coyly look up to the sky and then smirk at him.

"You made me wait before, so now I'm going to make you wait a little longer." He quickly winks and I'm suddenly aroused by the sight, thinking back to when I teased him at my apartment while undressing. I turn my head back to look at the cottage and suddenly remember my bag inside.

"What about my stuff?" I say, but before I can fully turn my head back around, Ryker's hand grabs my chin and directs it back toward him.

"Don't worry, Beautiful." Ryker confidently says. "I'll have Turner bring it over for you."

"Who?" I cock my head to the side.

"My driver." Ryker says, slightly chuckling. "I forgot to properly introduce you two the last time. My apologies." Ryker looks up slightly, as if to remember that for the future.

"Oh." I say, nodding my head in agreement. "That works."

I smile at Ryker, who smiles back, just as I hear the purr of an engine and the movement of rocks behind us. *It's more likely going to be a shiny, expensive sports car, I imagine.* Ryker is this big-shot real estate executive, so of course it would only make sense for him to drive something like that. I mean, when Lily and him don't have their driver, that's what Mason drives. Or maybe it's just going to be Ryker's driver, Turner, in his black car.

As the front of the car rolls forward into my peripherals, I quickly notice it isn't the typical vehicle that I see Ryker get picked up in. Instead, I'm caught off guard when I see a car that appears to have jumped out of the 1960's. With a long hood and sports-like back, it's different from the modern vehicles I see around the city. The two-door car is black with low red stripes and there are stark red interior leather seats, a color I never expected leather seats to come in.

"Is this yours?" I ask, tilting my head at Ryker.

I grab my dress on the sides, slightly raising it off the ground and walk forward a few steps to look at the front of the vehicle. That's when I notice the running horse emblem on the grill and finally recognize the brand. I turn back to Ryker, who hasn't answered yet, but has a grin on his face.

"Do you like it?" He asks, raising one eyebrow.

I look back at the car, letting a small chuckle slip.

"What?" Ryker asks, somewhat confused. I look back at him and laugh.

"Well," I say, in a teasing way. "I just expected you to have a sports car like everyone else." I roll my eyes and Ryker lets out a deep chuckle.

"Technically it is a sports car, but I just don't like the brand new, fancy ones." He slightly nods his head toward the car. "I like the classics. The one-of-a-kinds." Ryker looks back at me and smiles. "One of a kind like you."

I feel myself blush as the words come out of his mouth and as I lift my hand up to touch my cheek, I notice a stray hair that has fallen onto my face again. I shyly look down as I pull the stand back behind my ear. As I look up, Ryker continues to smile at me as he holds his hand out in front of me and my nerves quickly start to take over. One second I'm teasing him and the next, I suddenly feel shy and nervous around him. *Who am I?*

As I let go of my dress with my other hand and reach out to grab his, the first thing I think of spills out of my mouth.

"What about your driv- I mean Turner?" I quickly ask.

"He'll be here soon, but I wanted it to be just us tonight." Ryker says, pulling me toward him.

He walks me over to the passenger's side of the car and opens the door for me.

"Watch your head, Beautiful." Ryker says, placing his hand at the top of the roof to sit as a buffer to ensure my head wouldn't accidentally hit the top. He holds his hand out again to help me in as I duck into the car and slide inside. The cold leather brushes against my bare arms as I sit down and I immediately lean forward away from the cold, turning my focus onto the interior.

I could definitely tell it was old, but looking at the condition of the leather on the driver's side as well as the dashboard, I had no doubt it had a lot of restoration to keep up its high quality. The metal wheel and shiny chrome trim around all the hardware definitely felt like I was taken back in time.

I can only imagine that my dad would have loved to have a vehicle like this. He had a small obsession with classic cars, which I imagine most dads do and maybe that's why my dad kept his old Land Rover growing up. You could tell too that it was old, not just by the look of it, but by the interior as well. Not only did some switches not work on the dash, but sometimes the radio would jam up and the only way to get it working again was to give it a small tap with the palm of your hand. I imagine though that if my dad had had a few more years, he could have gotten the Land Rover back up to its quality from when he had first bought it. Or, when we finally had the money to upgrade our car, maybe he would have bought something classic like this, but instead my dad spent money on the one person he carried about the most. *Me*.

"You okay?" Ryker's voice startles me back into the present and I look through the opened window, which I hadn't realized was down. I quickly nod with a forced smile as I sit back into my seat.

Ryker walks around to the front of the car where the valet is standing and after a few brief words between them, that of which I couldn't make out over the running engine, the valet hands the keys back to Ryker. Ryker walks over to the driver's side of the car and I watch him through the window as he unbuttons his suit jacket before opening the door. As he slides into the low car, I pull the seat belt over my body placing my hands in my lap as I wait for him. As he does the same, he grips the wheel with one hand and looks at me, as if he knows what I'm going to ask.

"You know, you still haven't told me where we're going." I say with a snark, raising one eyebrow.

Following a deep scoff, a smirk grows on Ryker's face and I can tell he won't give it away. I quickly roll my eyes at him and I'm caught off guard as his hand, which was resting on the steering wheel, grabs a light hold of my chin. He tilts my chin up until our eyes meet.

"We'll be there shortly." Ryker says, before leaning in to give me a soft kiss on the lips. Pulling back just a few inches and my eyes still closed, he growls, "Then I can get you out of this dress."

I open my eyes and Ryker is smirking as he focuses on my lips, then looks back up to my eyes. He lets go of my chin and leans back into his seat before straightening himself up.

Before I can lean back in my own seat, I'm pulled back as the car pushes forward into drive. I place my hands into my lap and watch as we reach the end of the driveway, only to turn left down the main road, rather than right which leads back to the city. I look around my seat and out the back window in the opposite direction, then look forward at the road. *How long will this drive actually be?*

Chapter Fifteen

Paige

Music plays over the radio, not loud enough to make out any of the words being sung, as we head down the road. It's not more than a couple miles from the venue when we turn off the main road and down a smaller street. The dark, green color of the pines around us slowly fade as colors of orange and yellow peek through the treetops. As we drive down the street further, the fall colors fill the air and cover the road. It's when I catch a glimpse of a house through the trees, that I discover the street we are on is actually a driveway. I tilt my head back and forth, trying to get a glimpse of the house as we inch closer and closer. Crossing over a one lane rock bridge that runs over the top of a small stream, we slightly turn past a large set of trees and emerge in front of the house.

As I look out the passenger's side window, my face nearly touching it, I look up at the house that towers over the car. The two-story house, which appears taller due to the short staircase leading to the front door, is a traditional style home with a bit of a cabin-like feel, especially being in the middle of the forest. The dark, brown stone house has white panel windows, each with an arch at the top. Different areas of the roof peak, notably above a second-story window above the front door.

As we park in front of the driveway that circles the front of the house, I open my door, keeping my eyes glued up at the towering house. A sense of familiarity hits me as my eyes fall down from the top of the house onto the curved archway entrance with two wooden doors. I'm startled when Ryker glides in next to me, as I hadn't paid attention to when he had gotten out of the car.

"Erm-" I say slowly. "Who's house is this?" I turn toward Ryker and cock my head to the side.

"It's mine. I own it." Ryker confidently says, looking at me as if to get my approval.

"You do? How long have you had it?" I ask.

"Probably a couple years now." Ryker looks up at the house smiling. "I don't come often, but it's a nice place to get away once in a while."

Looking back and forth at each side of the house, I realize why the home feels so familiar. Growing up, the home I lived in out in the suburbs was a one-story stone house with arched windows. Not exactly the same at this home that's nearly triple in size, but it has similarities. Especially the wooden doors.

I can picture my parents looking so upset when I was little because I had painted a flower on the corner of the front door. It was before I had had any expensive canvas or supplies and I had thought it would make the home look nice. At least my three-year-old brain thought so. When I had shown them my work of art, I remember them just standing there speechless. I had hoped they liked it, but instead, the look in their eyes told another story. It was probably only a few minutes later that my dad stated that it "gave character to the house" and luckily, their smiles started slipping back to their faces. Nonetheless, it was the start of my artistic journey, from what my mom said.

"The peace and quiet reminds me of-" Ryker pauses.

As I look up, realizing I had been looking down at the ground for a moment, I look up at him just as he shrugs.

"It's funny, if I hadn't bought this house, I'm not sure where the wedding would have been."

"Wait." I tilt my head at Ryker. "Did you help Lily and Mason pick out their venue?"

Ryker chuckles. "I mean, I mentioned the location to Mason, but it was all their decision."

"Huh." I say quietly.

"Come on in." Ryker says, grabbing my hand and pulling me up the short stairway to the front doors. As he unlocks the door, he gestures for me to go inside.

As I step onto the dark-colored wood flooring, bringing that cabin-feel from outside into the home, I suddenly feel small in the large room. Surprisingly different from the outside of the house, the inside feels both homey and luxurious and the room is bigger than I imagined when I saw it from outside.

On one side of the room, a large wooden staircase wraps up to the second floor where a small balcony can be seen. In the middle of the room is a large round table and I catch a glimpse of what appears to be the living room from behind it. Stepping around the table and through a small hallway that goes under the balcony above, I walk toward the living room. Standing behind a large, brown leather couch, I'm in awe as I see large, floor to ceiling windows that overlook a large backyard. But it doesn't even look like a backyard, but rather a continuation of the colorful yellow and orange woods out front.

"Wow, this is beautiful." I say as I look out.

Ryker appears next to me behind the couch and unbuttons his suit jacket. Taking it off and placing it on the back of the couch, he leans over and places both of his hands on the couch edge, while looking out the window with me.

"That's the exact thought I had when I bought it." Ryker says, as I turn my attention toward him and I see a smile appear on his face.

As my eyes wander, I look down at his arms pushing against the back of the couch and notice how tight his shirt appears to be against his large muscles. Higher up on his arms, I'm able to see the darkness of his tattoos on his skin pressed up against the white material. My heartbeat quickly starts racing as I imagine the rest of his clothes off his body. His tattoos that I was able to distinctly see on the night we met, now suddenly visible again. His eyes looking up and down at my naked body just like the last night we were together in my apartment. As butterflies fill my stomach, I suddenly remember the entire reason

Ryker and I had left the wedding in the first place. *It's just the two of us now.*

I step forward to grab onto Ryker's hand resting on the couch, but he suddenly steps back, unaware I was watching him, and walks toward the kitchen. As his muscles press against his shirt with every step, my eyes follow him as he walks away. *Shit, get back here.* I watch as he opens a large wine fridge that's built into the wall, taking a moment to look through the bottles before pulling one out from the middle.

"Wine?" Ryker asks, turning to me, raising both of his eyebrows as he holds up the bottle.

"Actually," I say playfully. "I was kind of curious what the bedroom looked like."

I raise my eyebrows and smile softly at Ryker, who immediately lowers the bottle and smiles back. As I stand there, I use the tip of one of my shoes to slide the strap off the other foot and onto the floor. I keep my eye contact on Ryker, but his focus quickly shifts. Looking down at my shoes, he watches as I step down once my shoe is off and I use my other foot to slide the other shoe off. His eyes slowly move up my dress as I step down once more, my bare feet now on the hardwood floor. I watch as his eyes continue up my body, over my breasts and finally landing back on my eyes.

As we look at one another, I feel my chest rising and falling as my heart rate continues to rise. It was so much easier getting undressed in front of him after we had been together all night and we had just kissed moments before, but this time was different. I feel naked despite still having my dress on and I feel exposed. *Vulnerable.* I took a daring approach before undressing in front of him as he was on the phone, but I don't know if I can do it again. He told me that I had to wait, so maybe I'll make him wait just a little bit longer. No point in showing my body off to him again so quickly. *It's his turn to wait.*

I feel a tingle between my legs as Ryker carefully places the bottle onto the counter and I quickly remember we haven't kissed since we were back at the wedding reception. I had been eager to kiss him again after our impromptu contact in the hallway earlier in the day and it didn't help that I could only look at him from afar during most of the reception. And by now, the anticipation had definitely been building up inside me. I wanted him next to me. I wanted his hands all over me. I may want him to wait, but I don't know how long I can keep my own self from waiting.

He continues to keep our eye contact as he slowly steps toward me and I see a smirk appear on Ryker's face. The last night we were together, it was as if Ryker was unable to take his eyes off me as I undressed. He was like a lion about to pounce on his prey and I had been looking forward to it, until the phone call ruined it, but not this time. That same exact look was on Ryker's face once again and there was nothing here stopping him. Yet, he was still standing on the other side of the room. *Waiting? Watching?* My eyes break our eye contact as I look at the wine bottle resting on the table. He put it down for a reason. I have to do something to make this man crack and have him make the first move.

My eyes shoot back up to his and I lightly squint my eyes at him, as if I'm hatching a plan in my mind. *Will he take the bait?*

Moving my hand up to my cheek, I pull a single stray hair once again out of my face and I slightly open my lips as Ryker's eyes break away from mine and slowly move down to watch. *Gotta hook him in.* I gently pull my teeth over my bottom lip, biting it and releasing it slowly. His eyes darken, just as my lip falls. I form a slight smile on my face and Ryker's eyes shoot back up to mine and they are wide as can be. *I got him.*

As if by a silent command, Ryker places his hand on the counter next to him and leans forward. His eyes stay locked on mine as he slips each shoe off and throws them off to the side before straightening himself back up. Ryker raises his eyebrows and nods in my direction, as his eyes fall on my dress. I look down slightly at my dress, then back up to him, raising my eyebrows back. *Oh no you don't.* I may only have a dress on, but he has several other layers on that I cannot wait to see him remove in front of me. And, I definitely want to watch. *He watched me before so it's only fair.* I slowly nod my head side to side and Ryker's eyes widen, almost surprised by my gesture, as his lips part slightly.

I raise one eyebrow at him, then move my eyes down to his shirt. *Your turn.* Ryker's eyes fall to where my eyes are looking and as if he can read my mind, the corner of his mouth raises as his eyes move back up to my face. He then gives me a short and slow nod, as if to say he will follow my lead.

I move my arms behind my back and grab onto my wrists as I watch him start to slowly unbutton his shirt, starting from the top. As he unbuttons the first button, I notice a small amount of light brown chest chair against his sternum. Surrounding the hair, I am able to see some darkness on his skin, where parts of his tattoos come together. His eyes stay focused on me as he concentrates on giving me the show I've been looking forward to. My eyes watch his hands move down his shirt and with each button, I get a slight glimpse of his body that's been hiding for so long. The curves of his defined pecs are just as noticeable without his shirt as I see more of the tattoos that cover them. My eyes turn toward his arms as his muscles strain against the fabric of his shirt as he moves down the buttons. Looking back at his chest, I notice his tattoos stop at his pecs as my eyes follow down his chest to his well-defined abs.

As he unbuttons the last button, I'm caught off guard when I feel something moving back and forth against my lips. My eyes pull away from Ryker's body as I look down at the moving object only to realize my hand had escaped from behind my back. I pull my finger away from my lips and out in front of me. *Had I been touching my lips this entire time?*

As I look back up at Ryker, I notice his hands still at the bottom of his shirt and my eyes shoot up to his as a flush of embarrassment pools over me. I must have been too caught up in the moment to even realize what my own body was doing. My arm quickly falls down and back behind me. To try to save myself from more embarrassment, I let out a quick puff of air between my lips and form a charismatic smile on my face, hoping he will think it was on purpose, but the look on Ryker's face says otherwise. It's as if the small, unconscious gesture has made him even more aware of how badly I want to kiss him. How badly I want him. And if he didn't know it before, he knows now.

My eyes glance down at my bare feet on the ground, as I try to hide from the embarrassment I've just felt. It was definitely easier to put on a show for him before, but now that I'm watching him, it's only getting harder for me. All I can think about is the next moment. His next move. His eyes locked on mine as he undresses me. I can't be embarrassed now, when this is only the start.

As my eyes stay glued to my feet, I catch movement out of my peripherals and my eyes slowly glance up. Ryker's feet move closer and closer to me from across the room and I can't help but move my eyes further up his body. With each step, I can't turn away as his muscles tighten beneath his unbuttoned shirt. My eyes move up even further as his hands grab the seams, slowly pulling the shirt back, then up to his broad shoulders, now fully on display where I'm able to see the rest of the tattoos that go down to his chest. It's a brief glimpse as Ryker continues to move closer to me, but I'm able to make out a few of the detailed black and white designs. A pair of wings gliding over his collarbone, cursive words surrounded by small trees and half of what appears to be a playing card on the opposite shoulder. My eyes quickly move away from his tattoos when his shirt falls behind his back and his strong, muscular body appears in full display.

Ryker takes one last step toward me and we are only a foot apart, I can't bring myself to look up at him. Not because I don't want to, I definitely do, but because I know what will happen when I do. The moments leading up to this have brought so much expectation and now the moment is finally here. I've been eager for him to touch me. For his hands to caress my body. I want him to kiss my lips. Kiss me all over my body. But my shyness is stopping me.

I've had sex in the past, but the fact that this time it would be with Ryker makes it feel different. *But in a good way.* From the first moment we met, I felt a connection with him that I hadn't felt with anyone else. An invisible string that pulled me toward him. His charming, yet sweet personality made it easy to talk to him and I found myself being open to things I hadn't been before. He even made this time of the year something that I no longer resent. Something I no longer despise, but now can look forward to. And the fact that he genuinely makes my life feel whole again, which I never thought I would feel, makes this moment so much bigger.

I finally bring my eyes back up to his face and I'm surprised when I see a small grin on his face, vanishing my nerves right away. Realizing my arms are still behind my back, I pull them back out in front of me and step forward, smiling at Ryker.

As I stand in front of him and we are just inches apart, I pull my arms up and around the back of his neck against his warm skin. His arms wrap around my back as we stare at one another.

Not wanting to waste another moment, I bite my lip slightly and I'm excited when Ryker's smirk appears back on his face. His charming smirk that called my name earlier. His seductive smirk that just makes me want him all over me. The smirk that tells me he wants it too. *Right now.*

It's almost carnal as Ryker pulls me forward, my breasts pushing up against his bare chest as his lips are suddenly all over mine. *Finally.* As I savor his indulging flavor and kiss him back, I can't help but melt into him as I experience a longing that has been lingering inside me. As our tongues brush up against one another, I stand on my tiptoes to get as close as I can to him, wanting to take in every moment. Between our bodies, I can feel a hardness through his pants, pressing up against me.

Feeling my body pushing up closer to his, I surrender myself to his touch as his hands inch lower down my butt and I feel his arms wrap around my sides. In one swift move, I'm suddenly straddling his strong body as my dress is pulled up to my thighs from the movement. I wrap my arms quickly around the back of his neck, holding onto my elbows. It couldn't have been more than a few brief seconds of us relishing in this moment, but my only thought is going somewhere else. Somewhere private. Somewhere where I can finally give into these temptations.

Without thinking, I lightly suck his bottom lip. Something I've been wanting to do since the last time we kissed. As if triggered, Ryker suddenly pulls back and our lips create a smacking sound from the quick movement. I jolt my eyes open and see Ryker with a startled look on his face. I briefly worry that he didn't like it, but I watch his eyes darken and his devious smirk appears on his face once again. As if by instinct, we both pull forward and back into a kiss, melting into one another's lips as Ryker starts to step forward, still holding me in his arms.

As we continue to kiss between the movements of Ryker's steps, I feel his hands move from my thighs and up onto my bare butt cheeks, exposed around my strappy thong. His warm hands against my bare skin send me whirling and I feel a heat between my legs as he carries me into the front room with ease.

Each second that passes as he walks us forward, I start to wonder how hard the floor would be if he just took me right here, right now. Our bodies intertwined together against the hard floor, with any prying eyes getting quite a show if they passed by the front door. *Who needs a bed anyways?*

Before I can even imagine more, I feel Ryker lifting me up, carefully and cautiously as he takes a step up the staircase that I noticed when we first entered. To help him out, I pull back from our kiss and hold onto him tightly, allowing him to see over my shoulder and watch his step as he climbs the stairs. It's hard to pull away, but I know it'll only mean we'll be in the bedroom sooner.

As we reach the top of the stairs, I feel Ryker take a quick turn and I watch from behind as we enter a room through wooden doors. From my view, the room is darker than the large, window-filled living room downstairs and it has a more rustic look. As we walk a little further into the room, I notice a large white brick fireplace on the wall next to the door and wooden beams on the ceiling, giving that cabin-feel like before. As I look up, I feel Ryker bend over and instantly, I feel the soft bed below me, as his hands slide out from below my butt. Releasing my arms from behind his neck, I place them on the edge of the bed, keeping myself upright.

Leaning down in front of me, he moves his face to the side of mine and wraps his hand around me as he glides the tips of his fingers down the side of my back and up again. The touch forces me to quickly press my legs together as I feel a wetness form between my thighs.

"Are you going to take it off or shall I?" Ryker whispers, as his lips brush against my ear.

His fingertips glide over to the zipper on the back of my dress and he slowly pulls it down, making it easier to get off. As he pulls back and straightens himself back up, he raises an eyebrow, as if to wait for my answer. I stay quiet and give him a silent answer by biting my lip.

The corner of his mouth rises quickly as he bends down and places both of his hands on the top of my knees. He moves his hands slowly up my thighs, keeping our eyes glued on one another as his hands slide under my dress. I feel his hands slowly inch up the sides of my body under my dress and up to my hips as his hands continue up my waist, lightly brushing over the bottom of my bra with his finger tips. As his elbows reach the middle of my thighs, he slowly lifts the dress up and I feel the coldness of the room around me. The change sends shivers through my body, but they are gone almost instantly as I am reminded of Ryker's warm arms resting against me. As he pulls the dress higher, I feel my breasts fall and bounce down and I can only imagine his expression as it happens, but I'm unable to see. As the dress is pulled over my head, Ryker's eyes fall back on mine as he flings the dress to the floor.

Moving his hands back to my waist, he leans in and our lips brush up against one another's ever so slightly. He slowly unhooks my bra and I feel my breasts bounce out as it falls down to my lap. My nipples instantly harden from the lack of material against them. Ryker's hands move from behind my back and below my arms as he slides his hands around and over each of my breasts. I watch as he breaks our eye contact and his eyes fall down to them. His fingers lightly brush over the ends of my nipples and the sensation only makes me wetter, as I indulge his touch around me. My head slightly tilts back in that moment as he rubs over them once more. As I pull my head back down to look at him, I see a small smile on his face, different from his seductive smirk, but he looks as if he is savoring every moment like I am.

His hands glide down from my breasts and onto the sides of my waist as he looks back up at me. He moves one hand to slide the bra off my lap and onto the floor and then both of his hands meet at the top of my thighs. Lightly caressing my leg with his thumbs, he digs his pointer fingers under each side of my thong then wraps his middle finger around the small elastic band. Ryker moves his head to my thigh and places a single kiss on the top of my right leg. The soft touch of his lips against me has my body starting to whirl and I can no longer sit on the side of the bed. I push myself backward to lay on my back and I move my hands from the edge of the bed to above my head. As I look over my practically naked body at him, he looks up at me with a slight smile. His eyes are dark and I can only imagine the look I'm giving him because I am longing for him to kiss me there again. *Please.* He looks back down at my leg and gives me another soft kiss on the thigh, this time a little lower. My head instinctively pulls back as I close my eyes, longing for even more.

As I feel his head get lower down my thigh, I feel a tug on my thong and I desperately raise up my hips, allowing for him to pull my thong slowly with ease down my leg. As he pulls it down, he continues to give me soft, subtle kisses until my underwear finally reaches my knees and he stops. *No, keep going.* I pull my head up and look down at him, eagerly wanting him to continue. He glides my thong down the rest of my legs and off over my feet as we watch it fall to the ground. I bite my lip, hoping for more, but the only thing he does back is smirk. *Playing games once again.*

Ryker leans back, helping himself up from the ground and stands up in front of me. Looking down at my naked body, I watch as his eyes travel from my face down over my breasts and over my bare legs. *It's more of me than he's ever seen before.*

I so desperately want him to continue to touch my body again, but he just stands there, studying my features. I try to keep my eyes glued to his, but I suddenly get nervous that something is wrong as he remains quiet, not saying a word. I quickly lean forward and wrap my arms over my chest, breaking eye contact with him. My jerk reaction must have caused him to notice my concern because I quickly feel his hand land back on the middle of my thigh. I look back up at him, as he leans over me and I see a soft smile appear on his face.

"You're so beautiful." Ryker says, leaning it to give me a light kiss on my lips. I instantly blush as he pulls away. "Every single part of you." Those words quickly put my mind at ease.

My arms relax from around my chest as I slowly move them back behind me, pushing myself up from lying down. I rest my arms against the bed and I give him a tempting smile. This time, I get to watch the show.

Ryker pulls back and as he straightens himself up in front of me, his chest muscles flex as he reaches down to undo his belt from his pants. I hadn't noticed before, but his sex lines above his pant line are more prominent than I imagined and my eyes immediately shoot down to below his belt. The bulge I felt against my body now fully visible as his tight pants rest around it. If this is what it looks like under his pants, I can only imagine what it looks like with them off. As Ryker's hands grab his belt to remove it, I quickly force myself up off the bed and place my hands on top of his, stopping him. *My turn.*

Bending down and onto my knees in front of him, I grab onto his belt and slowly unhook it, as his hands rest on the sides of his body. Dropping the belt onto the floor, my eyes look up at him and I see his lips slightly part as he watches me carefully from above, as I kneel fully naked in front of him. I playfully smile at him, but he doesn't respond, but rather appears to give me permission as his eyes stay focused on mine. *I'll take that as a yes.*

I look back down at his pants and I unbutton the top of them, before slowly pulling the zipper down. Grabbing the sides of his pants, I carefully inch them down his legs. His girth, which is pressed tightly against the fabric of his boxer briefs, is now slightly more visible as I pull his pants past his knees. As his pants fall to the floor, I lean back slightly and look up at Ryker. His eyes meet mine once again as he steps out from his pants and kicks them away with his feet.

As Ryker steps back in front of me, my eyes slowly move down his body. I take in the sight of his tattoos, down to his defined pecs and onto his chiseled abs until my eyes fall back on his pulsing hardness. I move one of my hands over the side of his thigh and rub it lightly over his bulge. As my fingers graze over it, I feel Ryker take a deep breath in, before letting the air slowly fall out of his mouth. I smile, but keep my eyes focused on what's in front of me, aware he can see my expression. Once again, I glide my fingers over his bulge and push my hand against it, rubbing it back and forth over the fabric. The movement triggers Ryker immediately and I watch as he pulls both hands up and over the top of his head, gliding his fingers through his hair. Staring up at his masculine body towering over me, I can only imagine the thoughts racing through his head. What I'll do next. As his hands reach the back of his head, Ryker's eyes fall back down on me and I immediately lock eyes with him. A shadow from his eyebrows falls over his eyes in the room and I'm unable to see them clearly, but I can tell immediately by his look, he is just waiting for my next move. The eager anticipation. The desperation.

I look up at him and direct my attention back down to his exquisite body. I move my hands up to the top of the waistband of his boxers, lightly and slowly pulling them down, over his sex line and past his hips. As his waistband reaches the bulge under his boxers, I quickly pull his boxers down and watch as his full length goes on display. His boxers fall to the floor and I watch as his length pulses in front of me. Just inches away.

Without tilting my head back, I glance up at Ryker and meet his eyes once again. He isn't smirking or smiling, but I can tell he is waiting. Patiently. *He wants it. I do too.* I shyly blink my eyes up at him, trying to act innocent, but the act I plan to do is nothing short of that. *And he knows it too.* I want him to feel the warmth inside my mouth and give in to the anticipation that I'm building. I want to put him into a trance and I know just what will get him there. Keeping my eyes locked on him, I bite my lower lip and feel him take in a quick breath of air. As I slowly release my lower lip, I direct my eyes back to his length, not even waiting to see his reaction.

I grab his long length carefully in my hands and stroke it back and forth for a moment, trying to extend his pleasure for as long as possible, but still trying to tease him just a little bit. It throbs between each stroke. I lick my top lip then move closer to his length, continuing to stroke it slowly. As I reach the tip, I pause, waiting to see if I can feel his eagerness through my hand or hear any breaths of air being pulled into his mouth, but I don't. *He's quiet. He's waiting.* I part my lips slightly and push his tip between my lips, covering the end with the wetness within my mouth. I suck the end of his length just once and hear him take a deep breath. I suck it again, feeling his length quiver between my lips. And again I suck, giving him only a little bit of pleasure, but not enough to relieve himself. His breathing rapidly increases as I feel his abs expanding above me.

Stroking his full length again, I push my lips forward to suck deeper, when suddenly I feel Ryker's hand below my chin, pulling my face up. As I meet his eyes, I see them darken before me and I immediately recognize that look. He no longer wants to be teased. The corners of his lips raise as his other hand rests over mine, still holding onto his length. I slowly release my hands and place them between my warm thighs, as I sit back on my knees before him.

"You've had your fun. Now it's my turn." Ryker says, taking a step back as he releases my chin.

Still looking down at me, he lifts his hand up and taps his pointer finger up to the ceiling, directing me to stand. I willingly obey.

Once I'm on my feet, I lean my butt against the edge of the bed and rest both hands against my side. Ryker's eyes fall up and down my naked body as he holds the smirk on his face. He takes a few steps forward until I once again can feel his hardness against my body. Ryker slides both hands back under my butt, grabbing them with authority, as he pushes me up onto the bed further and my back is once again against the covers. I watch as my breasts bounce down from the rapid push and Ryker's eyes fall quickly onto them, then immediately back to my eyes.

With my legs still dangling slightly over the edge, Ryker glides one of his hands out from behind my butt and slowly moves over my hip and down my thigh, gliding the edges of his fingertips across me. The tingling sensation forces my eyes closed for a second and I want to savor every touch he gives me. But I quickly open my eyes again, wanting to take in the sight before me as well. Ryker's naked body hovering over mine.

I continue to watch his hand move across my body, his eyes following along. As his hand moves down within my thighs, I instinctively spread my legs apart, allowing his hand to move down between my legs. The slow, but gentle caress of his fingertips getting closer and closer will soon fulfill the ache of my yearning.

As the tips of his fingers brush over the tops of my folds, I pull my head back against the bed, closing my eyes, indulging in his touch. At first, he moves his finger gently over them, but as my body squirms beneath his fingers, he can tell how much I want it. How much I crave it. He slides his finger down and between my folds and I immediately feel my wetness being pulled out, as his fingers glide inside me. Carefully, he forces them deeper and deeper and I feel my head whirling as he does it with such ease.

As he continues sliding his fingers in and out of my soaked folds, I feel his other hand slide out from behind my butt. His hand glides up my waist and over my stomach, until one of my breasts is encased within his hand. His fingers brush back and forth over my breast, lightly squeezing it. I want to look down at Ryker, but the sensation of his hands on me and inside of me keep my mind distracted. His thumb brushes over my nipple and he starts to caress it, swirling his finger around until I feel it harden. At the same time, I feel his fingers inside of me curl up and immediately my body pushes me toward the ceiling, deeper into his grasp. The sensation radiating through me jumps into overdrive and I grab onto the covers below my hands, letting my body take over my mind. Shifting my body into a spiral as my heart starts to race, I want to instantly surrender my body to him. To all of him. With his fingers inside me and his hand touching me, I want to give in. I need to give in. Climbing to a peak, I suddenly feel his fingers pull out of me and my mind snaps me back into the room with Ryker.

I open my eyes and lift my head up to look at Ryker, who still towers over my body, and we lock eyes. My eyes are wide and full of anguish as I furrow my brows, hoping he will continue. I need him to continue.

"Don't stop." I longingly say under my breath.

I quickly take several breaths in and out, allowing my heartbeat to catch up from the high I just fell from. I move myself up onto my elbows and watch as Ryker raises one eyebrow and smirks down at me. *Is he playing games?*

I push down on my elbows to lift myself up, but Ryker's hands quickly wrap around the backs of my knees and I'm pulled toward him. His length rests between my open legs and the tip nearly touches the wetness that he created. Ryker pulls his arms out from behind me and places both hands next to my head as he bends over on top of me. I feel a light tickle from his chest hairs as he pushes our bodies together, creating a warmth between our skin. He leans his head closer to mine until I feel his breath against my ears. Just his breath alone causes my body to shake, as I imagine his next move.

"Are we done with the teasing, Beautiful?" Ryker asks as he whispers in my ear.

I nod my head next to his, letting out a quiet "Uh huh."

"Good." Ryker says, brushing his lips against my ear causing my legs to quiver beneath him.

Without wasting another second, I feel his hand glide down between our legs, moving down past my thigh and in between us as he grabs ahold of his length. The throbbing of it against my inner thighs forces my legs to open wider.

"Because the only thing I want is to be inside you. Now." Ryker demands.

At the same moment, he pushes his length between my wet folds and deep into me. I hear Ryker let out a muted grunt beside my ear, which forces me to simultaneously let out a soft moan as I feel him inside me. *Finally*.

Wrapping my legs around Ryker's waist, pulling him in closer, he pushes deeply into me until he is hitting the back of my moist interior and it's almost instantly that I feel the rise in my body again.

The rise that had been cut short from his teasing game, but is now returning.

Tilting his head next to mine, I feel Ryker's lips against my neck, slowly and gently placing delicate kisses as he moves his lips up closer to my face. With each kiss, he thrusts himself inside me. Back and forth. Pushing deeper and deeper with each movement within me.

As Ryker's lips finally reach my own, I release the covers between my fingers and wrap my arms around him, pulling him quickly in so I can taste the sweet scent I crave so much. As his tongue explores the inside of my mouth, his length thrusts further into me and explores my interior. Each push building up the forces within my body as I feel his length throb inside me, as he climbs towards release as well. Inch by inch I feel myself rising. Closer to breaking.

As he takes another deep breath between our lips, I feel the radiant heat of our bodies that we've created as we wrap ourselves around one another. Our scents colliding into one. With one last thrust, I feel my toes curl as my body goes into a frenzy, exploding with pleasure, relieving a satisfaction I've been anticipating all night. At the same moment, I hear the end of a deep moan escape Ryker's lips, as he falls back from his emotional peak. A pinnacle that we reached together.

With our lips still an inch apart, Ryker and I slowly breathe in and out, catching our breath as we come back. Back to reality. Back to just us. Relieved by the moment. Relieved by one another.

Pulling his head back slightly, I open my eyes to see Ryker looking down at me with a smile. A genuinely happy smile and I can only reciprocate it back. We are both in a place that we hadn't been with one another before and the silence says more than words. This is it. This is us. And he's right. I don't want to spend another day without him.

Chapter Sixteen

I open one eye slightly, as a small streak of light escaping from behind the blinds rests over my eye. I don't know what time it is or how much sleep I got, but it still must be early because the light isn't as harsh as I imagine it could be. With my other eye still closed and weighted down against the pillow, I try to adjust my focus in my one open eye, still wanting to stay closed.

As my eye adjusts, I look around to see what's in front of me, keeping my head in place against the pillow. A white brick fireplace. A slightly ajar wooden door. *My house*. My eye moves down to the hardwood floor, where I can recognize some parts of my suit I was planning on wearing to Lily's wedding. Then I see it. *Her dress*. It wasn't a dream.

The covers slide down from over the lower half of my face as I slowly roll over in bed. As I roll, I adjust my other eye to focus on the details of the room. The wood beams above us and the small chandelier. The small light that illuminates the room helps me to focus as my eyes follow my body and finally land on her peacefully sleeping.

The pillow slightly covers a bit of her face as she lays on her stomach, but I keep my eyes focused on her. So beautiful. So perfect. The person I've always wanted and needed in my life.

Her beautiful lips are slightly open as she quietly rests. All I want to do is kiss them again. Her skin, still covered in her makeup from the night before. I can't help but want to rub my thumb against her cheek, wiping the small smudging away. Her dark brown hair slightly covers part of her face, covering one of her eyes. I resist pushing it behind her ear. Careful not to disturb her as she sleeps, I can only watch, taking in the sight of her, and I can't help but smile as I look at her.

Last night was such a dream that it doesn't even feel real. Paige was here with me. I had been looking forward to what we shared last night together. The parts of her that I yearned to see, yearned to touch and yearned to kiss. And it happened. She gave a piece of herself to me and I gave my all to her. I wouldn't have imagined it any other way.

My eyes move down to her bare neck and I suddenly remember that the sheet is covering her naked body. Still hidden, but the thought makes me hard. All I want to do is wake her up and kiss her again. Feel our warm bodies against one another as I taste her between my lips. Feel her hands touching me as I caress her beautiful body. I want every night to be like last night. To have her next to me. To have her in my arms.

A ping from her phone, which is resting on the side table, disturbs her, as I hear a soft moan escape her throat. I imagine her opening her eyes and being pleasantly surprised by me lying next to her. I imagine her leaning in and kissing me as we recreate last night, but the sound does little to shake her from her slumber.

She slowly rolls over to her side facing me, her eyes still closed, and the sheet moves down slightly, exposing one of her nipples. It instantly hardens from the cool morning air surrounding it, which doesn't help the stiffness I'm already holding back beneath the sheets. I take a slight breath in as I watch for a moment, before slowly reaching over to carefully grab the sheet and cover her back up.

As I pull my hand away, her lips form into a slight smile as if she can feel my hand near her, before she rolls back onto her stomach and buries her face deeper into the pillow. I take another breath in just as another smile returns to my face. Slowly removing the sheets from on top of me and sliding myself out from the side of the bed, I keep my eyes focused on her, careful not to disturb her.

When my feet reach the ground, I stand up and I catch a glimpse of my hardness fully exposed. Quickly, I search for my boxers, which are luckily right next to me on the floor and I pull them up my legs, tucking myself beneath them.

Carefully walking over to the other side of the bed, I hear the floorboards creak between my steps, and I shoot my eyes over to Paige, checking to make sure she still hasn't woken. *She hasn't.*

As I reach the side table next to her, I look down at the black screen on her phone. *Who texted her at this hour?* It can't be more than half past six judging by the light coming into the room. Maybe it's her boss asking her about her project? No, it's Sunday. I can't imagine that's the case. I look around the room, spotting Paige's dress on the floor near the fireplace. Maybe it's Lily checking in on her? We left pretty abruptly during the reception last night.

Another ping comes from her phone and I keep my eyes glued to the wall across the room. *I can't look. It's not my place.* My eyes leave the wall and I glance over to where Paige appears to still be soundly sleeping. She didn't move from the noise this time.

I'm not the kind of person to snoop, but curiosity gets the best of me. My eyes slowly move down Paige's body beneath the sheets and fall onto the side table where her phone is now lit up. I turn my head more toward it and focus my eyes on the only text that appears on her screen.

> **Hi hon! I was out for a run this morning and wanted to check in on you again since it's that time of the year. Are you doing okay? I'd love to see you soon. Ma…**

The rest of the text cuts off on her home screen so I'm unable to finish reading it, but my eyes glance up to the name. *Mom.*

I quietly scoff at myself for being nosy and reading her texts, but a sudden feeling of sadness comes over me. I'm happy to see that Paige has a good relationship with her mom, but the fact I'll never get those texts is hard to swallow.

It's been over ten years since I lost my own mother and it's hard not to feel sad sometimes thinking about what it would be like if she was still with me. The last time I saw her, she was so sick. It was almost difficult to see. Your own mother dying in front of you. Her body slowly giving way to the sickness. I can't imagine anyone going through that, but I know I'm not the only one. It's happened to others. It'll happen again. It's an endless cycle that will continue.

At least most others have another parent to fall back on. I sure as hell didn't. I had the kind of father you would dread having. The kind that barely gave a fuck that his wife was dying. The kind that never showed a single emotion. Not a single ounce of remorse. Not a single care in the world. The kind you couldn't imagine your sweet mother being with. But I had that. I wish I didn't, but I did.

Once I found out why he was like that, it all made sense. He never cared about us. He never truly wanted a family. It was all a front. A way to hide what he was really doing. And to make matters worse, he not only took away my mother, but he took me away from the one other thing in this world that mattered to me, which only makes it worse.

Luckily, I was old enough to make a decision. To choose what I wanted to do with my life. And once my mother was gone, I left. I left and I never looked back. All the things that I had in my life were now gone and he was the main factor that stood between me and my future happiness. From that moment, I didn't care what happened to him. It didn't matter to me. He didn't matter.

But I made sure to watch him. To make sure he didn't get anywhere close to the life I was making for myself. I wasn't going to let him destroy anything else I had. Not again. So, I kept him far away. I found ways to keep it like that. He did his thing and I did mine.

It wasn't until last week that he landed back into my life. I had contacts that watched hospital records over the years who were ready to alert me when it happened. It's crazy what you can get once you have money, but I used it to my advantage. Making sure I knew when he was back. Waiting for his moment. His end.

When I got that call from the hospital, it was the night I was with Paige. I never expected that call would ever come and I definitely didn't expect it to actually be him when I got there. But it was. On his deathbed. Going out in the same way he had taken care of so many others over the years. *A truly deserving death.*

I straighten myself up next to the side table and take a deep breath in, before pulling myself back. I slowly make my way over to the door and slide out through the opening as I retreat into the hall. Making my way down the stairs, I am delighted to see Paige's luggage resting against the wall near the front door. Turner must have brought it late last night or earlier this morning.

Rather than going straight to the kitchen like I had planned, I grab her luggage and carry it back up the stairs. *She'll be happy to have it.* As I reach the room, I carefully push the door open with my foot and the door slightly squeaks. I stop in my tracks, hoping the sound doesn't disturb her, but once again I'm relieved when I see her head still pressed down against the pillow.

As my steps carry across the creaking floor, likely caused by the added heaviness of the bags I'm carrying, I try to walk even slower, but it doesn't help. Luckily, it isn't a far walk to the end of the bed, where I place both of her bags gently on top of the bench at the foot. With the heaviness no longer adding to my load, I make my way back over to the door. The squeaking of the floor now is relatively quieter this time around.

Stepping back into the hall, I glance back at Paige once again before I leave. At peace, just as I left her. I slowly close the door in front of me, as a slight smirk forms on the corner of my lips before turning into a smile. *She's mine.*

Chapter Seventeen

Paige

It's dark. I can't see anything, but I'm awake. Or am I? Was last night just a dream? Am I still dreaming? Our warm bodies against each other. Our lips locked as we indulged in one another. And his scent. I can still smell it. Fresh as can be against my face. As if he was right here in front of me.

But I can't breathe. Am I dying? Am I even alive? The air around me feels tight. Constricting.

Suddenly I feel my hand tingling. A weird sensation, but it's recognizable. My hand is asleep. So how am I still asleep? I wiggle my body, trying to escape. Trying to pull back to take a breath.

I wiggle until I can feel my hand again, pressing against my stomach. Then, I feel my other hand next to it and I realize I'm lying on it. Pulling them out from under the weight of my body, I'm finally able to push up on them, releasing my face from the suffocating tightness that surrounded me.

It's bright now. So much brighter than before. I slightly open my eyes and adjust my focus. Where am I?

I blink twice, still squinting my eyes as I look down in front of me. It takes a few more seconds before I am able to see where the darkness came from. To my horror, the white pillow has been stained by makeup, which I must've forgotten to remove last night. *Fuck.*

I quickly push myself up and kneel in front of the pillow. Looking around the room, I recognize it from last night. The once-dark room, now brightened by the sunlight shining through the closed curtain. *What time is it?*

Turning my head to the bedside table next to me, I spot my phone charging. I don't remember plugging it in last night, but maybe Ryker did it for me?

I lean over and quickly tap the screen, checking the time. *8:27.* My eyes move down my screen to the white bubble at the bottom. *Mom.* Pulling my phone off the charger, I bring it closer to my face as I start reading the text message from her.

Since my dad passed away, this time of year has always been hard on the both of us, but especially for me. I thought it affected her more, I really did. She lost not only a partner, but the one person she loved. At least I felt that way when I was younger. I think everyone does. Their parents are the two people they look up to most in the world and it's what every little girl dreams of having when she's older. But, as I got older, that wasn't the case. I mean, they were good parents, but I didn't see the other side of their relationship. Their constant bickering. The late night fights. *The lies.* If I had realized what kind of their relationship they truly had, I could have seen a divorce from a mile away. They never had a chance.

I'm thankful though, as a child, that I didn't see that side of them. I saw them happy. I saw them together. I saw a grieving mother who lost her husband as I had lost my dad. I know she still cared deeply about him when he passed, but there was no longer that "in love" feeling between them. It was over.

I think that was why she was able to uproot our lives so quickly when my dad passed. She had already had it all planned out. Where she would go once they were apart. What she would do. I mean, she had to have a plan in place once their divorce was finalized since she hadn't worked in over six years by that time. She had already been looking for a change in pace. Something she could be good at. And she knew it was time to stop homeschooling me and put me into school. Real school. It was bound to eventually happen.

We sold our house within a month and moved to a small apartment in the city, where she found an assistant desk job right away. It wasn't the greatest pay, but the company loved her organization skills and the job helped pay for the rent. The longer she stayed there, the more she was able to move her way up in the company and over time, she became the director. Not only that, when I moved out, she must have seen that as a sign to change things up for herself again. She was making more. I was no longer living with her. So, she was able to move into a nicer apartment downtown.

We stayed fairly close, but it was definitely different than what I imagined my life to be like.

Seeing all the other kids at school get picked up by both parents. It was hard. It was just my mom and I. But when I met Lily, she did give me a little piece of family I didn't realize I had. A sister I never had. She was that missing piece that filled the empty void I still had in my heart. The void that was created because of my dad. And to that, I am always thankful.

As I read the text through, I watch as the message cuts off. I quickly unlock my phone and open up my text messages to read the rest:

…love to see you soon. Maybe today if you're free? Let me know, okay? Love you!

Today? Despite not seeing my mom as often as I'd like, I do make it a point to see her every time she asks. *But today?* I doubt she remembered Lily's wedding was yesterday considering I'm not in the city at the moment. It'd be at least an hour drive to her if I factor in traffic. *And Ryker.* What would I even tell him? Would he go with me and meet my mom? What would I even call him?

My eyes look past my phone, still resting between my hands, and I catch a glimpse of the unsightly pillow still in front of me. I quickly lock my phone and lean back over to place it on the bedside table. As I sit up on my knees once again, I look down at the pillow. *God, this looks awful.* The unseemly face paint that's been created against the white fabric must be hidden. Without thinking, I flip the pillow over, hiding the stains. I let out a quiet chuckle. *Nobody will ever know.*

My eyes shoot down to the other side of the bed where I see Ryker's suit pants still lying on the ground. No sign of Ryker yet. *Thank goodness.* I can't imagine him seeing this disheveled face of mine. I catch a glimpse of my dress lying next to his pants and I cock my head down quickly, not skipping a beat as I glance down at myself. Still completely naked from last night.

As if my body realizes that it's exposed, I feel my nipples harden as I finally feel the coldness around me. Wanting to cover myself up with something other than the sheet, I twist my body around until I see my luggage resting on the bench at the end of the bed. *When did that arrive?* I shake the thought, then smile, happy that I can go take a shower and have new clothes to wear.

I push myself up from my kneeling position and sit on the side of the bed, my legs dangling. I don't know how much time I have, but I doubt Ryker will be gone long. So I'll try to be quick.

I hop off the bed and quickly walk over to the bathroom, turning the light on as I walk in. As the light flickers on, I pause. I can only imagine how awful my makeup looks this morning and if Ryker isn't here, there's no doubt he's already seen me like this. That wouldn't be good, but this can't get any more embarrassing. I just have to look at myself and see. I tightly close my eyes and turn toward the mirror.

Opening one of my eyes carefully, I prepare to see a monster in the mirror. *It's gotta be bad.* I scrunch my face with anticipation as I open one eye, but quickly both of my eyes shoot open and wide. *Wow.* Expecting to see a disheveled looking mess of a person in front of me, I'm surprised to see how great I actually looked. Barely any smudges. Barely any smearing. I have to say, those makeup artists really are quite impressive if I can say so myself. I'll have to remember to use them for my own wedding in the future, if that ever happens, because they really know what they are doing.

I smile at myself in the mirror, delighted at the sight, then step out of the bathroom and toward my luggage. With enough room on the bench to open my suitcase up and lay it out flat, I unzip it and search through it for my toiletries until I find them. Looking through my clothes, I pull out a nude thong, a bra and a t-shirt, just enough to have something to cover myself up once I get out of the shower.

Walking back into the bathroom, I set my clothes down on the counter and place my toiletry bag next to it, before I remove a single face cleansing wipe from a small baggy. As I start to use the wipe to remove the makeup from my face, I step over to the large, walk-in shower and slightly open the large glass door. Turning the handle all the way to the right, I turn the shower on, before stepping back over to the mirror, giving it a moment to warm up as I finish removing the remaining makeup from my face. As I wipe my mascara off of my eyes, it doesn't take long for the image of myself to slowly disappear from the mirror as the steam from the shower fills the room.

Happy with how quickly the shower warms up, I throw the face wipe into the small trash can beside the toilet and open the glass door, slowly stepping in. At first it's almost too hot, but as I move my arms further into the water, the water seeps over my shoulders and down my back, warming my body quickly. The warmth instinctively pulls my body into it.

Pushing my head into the running water, I cover my face with the water before turning around to let the water fall down my hair. Tilting my head back, I bring my hands up to my face and brush over my chin, my cheeks, my eyes and my forehead as the water comes down. As my hands reach the top of my head, I pull them through my wet hair as I glance up to the ceiling. *A rain shower head.* I can't say I'm surprised to see that Ryker has a house with both the regular shower head and the rain feature. It always felt like a rich person thing, especially when I saw it in the movies.

I turn back around to face the running water, then glance around it, looking for a switch to turn on the rain shower head. *Nothing.* I'm not giving up that easily though. I look for anything else that seems out of place and notice another handle above the faucet handle. *Could this be it?* Pulling it down, the water in front of my face slowly comes to a halt as I feel water start to fall from above me, drenching my back. Definitely better than I could have expected. *I could get used to this.*

As I savor the warmth of the water against my body, I can only think of how it will be now that Ryker and I have had sex. Will it be different between us? Will it feel the same? Will we be closer? I can only think about how I felt last night. How much I want to be around him. How much I yearn to have him close to me. I want him with me every day. For as long as I can have him.

I open my eyes and glance around from beneath the water raining down on me. The hot air within the shower has fogged the glass and I realize I've probably been doing a lot more thinking, than actual showering. I look around and notice a bottle of body wash sitting on a small shelf built into the shower and squirt it into my hands. Despite not wanting to wash Ryker's scent off of my body, I know it'll go away eventually. I can only hope though that he will bring it back to me soon.

With my back turned toward the shower door, I slowly rub the body wash down over my arms, creating suds against my skin. As I rinse it off under the falling water, I step back again and move my hands down onto my ribs and across my stomach before stepping back into the water.

As I step out of the water once more, my back slowly hits something. *Someone.* I freeze my body in place as I feel his hands grab onto my hips, pulling me closer to his wet body. As my back pushes against his chest, I feel his hardness get pressed between my butt and his body. And it's fully erect. *Was he watching me?*

He glides one hand up my side, then slowly back down onto my forearm until he reaches one of my hands resting on my stomach. I relax into his arms as he slides his hand under mine and I follow as that hand glides up and over my breast. His hand opens up slightly, letting my nipple pop up between his fingertips. The water hits it in just the right spot and I feel it harden. As if he notices as well, his pointer finger lifts up and glides back and forth over the tip of my nipple, making my body dance to his motion. I instinctively lean my head back against his shoulder as he plays with it and close my eyes under his movement. Teasing me with every flick of his finger. And all I want is more.

As the water continues falling between our bodies, he takes his other hand and reaches around the side of my face, turning it toward him. I open my eyes and his face is no more than an inch from mine, as I focus my eyes on his lips, which appear eager to touch my own. I try to lean closer, to get our lips to touch, but his hand holds my face still. Waiting for his next move.

Slowly, he pulls his face away, creating distance between us and I feel his hand move down from my face to my neck. My heart starts to race and it feels hotter in here than I remember. I close my eyes again as he inches down my body, his hand gliding between my breasts and over my stomach until he reaches just below my navel.

There's instantly a tingle between my legs and I can't tell the difference between the heat of myself or the water around me. One thing I know for sure though is that I want him to feel me. To be inside of me. My lips part slightly as I try pushing my body up and closer to his hand. But he pauses. *No.*

My eyes shoot open and I look up at him with anxiousness. *Why'd you stop?* I hear the words being screamed in my head. I look down at his lips and the corners rise. *Of course.* When all I want to do is kiss his lips, he's here smirking at me. Playing games again. Teasing me. Does he not realize I just want him? *Right now.*

I close my eyes for a moment and then our eyes meet again, but this time, his eyes are dark. Darker than before. Full of desire.

Before I can comprehend what he's thinking, his fingers quickly slide down between my wet slits and he thrusts his fingers between my folds, immediately causing my eyes to tightly shut as I feel his fingers move into me. With a stark thrust, he pushes his fingers deep into me and I instinctively let out a soft moan as I keep the image of him smirking fresh in my mind. The look he must still have on his face as he sees the pleasure he's giving me.

As I feel his fingers slide in and out of me with ease, my mind shoots up to his other hand that continues to glide over my nipple, flicking it back and forth between his fingers. A thrilling sensation shoots straight down between my legs and steadily increases with every continuous touch. His fingers dance around my nipple, circling it playfully. With every thrust and curl of his fingers inside me, I feel my legs pushing me up higher against his body. Aching for him as he stimulates every part of me. I stand on my toes and his fingers slide deeper into me again, causing me to throw my arms up and behind his neck, pulling my body even closer, as I tilt my head further back against his chest.

As his finger glides back to the top of my hard nipple, I feel his head inching closer to mine. His warm breath against my ear, surrounded by the steam being created in the shower. My heart starts to race as I feel his intoxicating lips draw closer.

"You're mine, Beautiful." He says as I feel his lips brush against my ear. "Every part of you."

I nod my head as he continues each consistent motion, swirling inside me. My moans only growing louder. The falling water above us doing nothing to mask the sound. I would have been embarrassed if it was with any other person, but it's different with Ryker. I want him to hear me. To hear how he makes me feel. How much I crave him. His hands. His body. His touch.

Ryker's lips slowly move down past my ear and onto my neck. He places a warm kiss gently below it as the steam from the shower keeps the warmth in its place.

"I won't go another day without you." Ryker says as I feel his lips inch down my neck. His fingers still deep inside me as his other hand caresses my breast, building up the euphoric pleasure I feel my body reaching.

"You were always meant to be mine." Ryker says. His hands still swirling around both inside and out as his lips reach the top of my collar bone. He pauses.

I look at him out of the corner of my eye, as he hovers over my collar bone, where water is pooling over and down onto my other breast.

"Tell me you're mine." Ryker demands, with a rigid expression on his face.

With my body pulsating between his arms, I watch as he places another gentle kiss on my shoulder and I try to catch my breath as my breathing rapidly increases. My body intensifying with pleasure as his lips rest against my body. His hands still dancing over me under the flowing water above us. I turn my head towards Ryker and I press my forehead against his cheek.

"All yours." I willingly reply, releasing another held in breath.

A moment later, Ryker's hand releases from my breast and grabs onto my jaw, pulling my face up to his. His lips immediately meet mine and I'm once again captured by his aromatic scent that fills my mouth. The taste of him that I've been wanting all morning. *Craving*.

As his tongue swirls between my lips, mimicking his fingers inside me, the sensations pulsating through my body have me in a chokehold. *It's too much*.

As if to tease me once more, I feel Ryker's fingers slowly slipping out from between my folds, pausing as they pull out. *He doesn't want this to end. He wants me to hold out a little longer. To keep my pleasure from rising all the way.* But all I want is for his hands to stay put. To continue touching me. *I'm so close.*

In my head I'm begging. Begging for him to continue. To give me the sensation my body is so eager for, but I can't say anything. His lips are devouring mine. *But I know a way.*

As Ryker's lips slightly part around my mouth, I take the opportunity to bring his bottom lip between my lips and lightly bite it. Without skipping a beat, I feel his hardness throb against my back. Pulsing between us. The singular thought of it pushes me closer as his fingers still linger outside of me. The water tingling the hairs on my body to keep me close. *That'll do.*

His bottom lip falls out from between my lips as I feel his face pull away from mine. As my eyes shoot open to look at him, I'm caught off guard when I see his stunned face. He lets out a deep growl as my eyes travel back and forth between his, eagerly hoping he will see how desperate I am for him to continue. I take a deep breath, as I feel his fingers lightly caress the outside of my folds. *Please keep going.*

Moving his hand from the side of my jaw to the back of my head, I watch as a smirk appears on his face. *He knows.*

Before I can take another breath in, he pulls my face back to his, pressing our lips together while simultaneously thrusting his fingers deep within me.

The tension I held back for only a few moments rises back up to the surface, as my breath starts to intensify once again between his lips. Reaching closer and closer. With one last thrust of his fingers inside me, the exhilaration is finally too much as my body releases itself on top of him and I let out a climactic moan. *Finally.*

Falling back onto the soles of my feet against the tile below, I feel his fingers sliding out from between my legs as his arms glide across my body turning me around to face him. Our lips still locked together in place as my breathing stays heavy.

His hands reach down my back and below my butt, lifting me up against him, as I wrap my arms around the back of his head. Wrapping my legs around his torso, it doesn't take long for the water to start pocketing in the tight space between our bodies. As he takes a step forward, I feel my body inch closer to the shower wall. I arch my back anticipating it to be cold, but as the top of my back reaches the tile, I relax when I find the tile to have been warmed by the steam.

With a quick pull back as I'm suspended against the shower wall, Ryker's lips part from mine momentarily as he grabs his length from below me, pushing it up between my folds and deeply into me. The force causes another strong moan to escape my mouth, as his lips return to mine.

As my body slides up and down against the steamy wall, the pleasure that left me just moments ago, quickly returns with each thrust. With the raining water no longer above us, I feel myself grow wetter than before as I feel his length between my legs. Sliding in and out with ease. Thrust after thrust, our breathing matches one another's as our bodies push closer to the edge.

It doesn't take long for our lips to part as our foreheads rest against one another. Our eyes closed, but our bodies focused on one another. Focused on the growing sensation between both.

I'm unable to keep any more feelings within myself as another moan releases from my mouth. I briefly open my eyes to look at Ryker, whose eyes stay closed, yet he has a slight smirk on his face. The kind that you can tell was caused by the sound that escaped my lips.

Both of our chests continue to rise as I close my eyes again. Our steady pace inching us closer to our breaking points. To our high. Our loud breaths barely silenced by the water falling from the ceiling. But I can hear him and he can hear me. And within a moment, I feel our bodies release themselves as we take a breath in, slowly surrendering to one another.

As our pace gradually begins to calm, I feel Ryker slowly pull his length out of me as he gently pulls me down from him. As my feet hit the floor, I look up at Ryker, who is still catching his breath. A smile forms on his face. Not his seductive smirk, but a genuine, happy smile. I mimic him, smiling back as I keep my hands wrapped around his neck.

As Ryker stands in his closet, only half dressed from the waist down, I watch as his eyes scan my body up and down. No smirk, no smile, but almost as if to focus and remember every detail of me.

Pulling my shirt over my head, I look back up at him and a smile grows on his face as his eyes meet my own. I pull my damp hair out from beneath my shirt and let it drop to my shoulder.

"You're so beautiful." Ryker says, stepping over to me as he pulls his shirt over his head.

Once his shirt is on, I notice his hair has fallen across his forehead. Noticing as well, he runs his hands through his hair, pulling it back on the top. His muscles flexing around his tattoos and through his shirt as he draws closer.

As his hand falls from his hair, he reaches down to grab the side of my waist as he stops in front of me. His body towers over me as I look up at him, surprised at how bright his eyes are from the sun illuminating them in the room.

Pulling my waist to bring me closer, Ryker takes his other hand and cups the side of my face. I watch as his eyes move back and forth at mine, as a light smile crosses his face. His thumb lightly caressing my cheek.

At that moment, I hear a dinging sound off to my right. Our heads both quickly turn and his hand falls from my face as I notice my phone lit up. I quickly turn back to him, hoping the sound didn't ruin the moment, but I can tell it's already been broken.

Another ding from my phone triggers Ryker to look back at me.

"Seems like someone is trying to reach you." He says, raising one eyebrow. "You can check it. I don't mind."

I furrow my brows at Ryker. I had meant to text my mom back earlier this morning, but I had forgotten about it following the steamy moment Ryker and I shared. I know she's probably texting me again to check if I'll be coming over, but I had yet to ask Ryker if he wanted to go with me.

"Okay, just give me a second." I say, slipping out of Ryker's hand still resting on the side of my waist.

I walk over to my phone and pick it up, quickly noticing the texts are from my mom. From my locked screen, I read:

> **Hi hon! What time do you think you'll be by?**

Followed by another text that reads:

> **There's also an envelope here for you. I didn't open it.**

Just like I thought, my mom is already expecting me today. I mean, I was already planning on going to see her, but do I even bring Ryker? I doubt he'll say yes anyways.

I look up from my phone and turn my head around to look at him. From the corner of his eye, he catches me and smiles.

We've been seeing each other for only a couple of weeks, yet we still haven't defined our relationship. I don't want to put this pressure on him, especially regarding meeting my mom for the first time. That would definitely say we are more. But I have to at least invite him, especially if he expected us to be together for the rest of the day. I can't just leave now.

I unplug my phone from the charger and turn around, taking a few steps toward him. I look down at my phone still in my hands, then back up at him, feeling anxious about this conversation.

"So," I slowly start. "My mom wants me to come see her today." I pause, waiting for his reaction, but his face stays stoic, as if he can tell I have more to say. "I was expecting to spend the rest of the day with you, but I can't say no to her. I don't know if you want to come or not." I pause again, holding my hands up in front of me. I quickly continue. "You are welcome to! But I don't want to put any pressure on you about it. My mom can be a lot sometimes and I know meeting family is-."

"I'd love to come." Ryker confidently says as he turns toward me, stopping my sporadic word vomit I was throwing at him.

My lips part slightly and both of my eyebrows raise at the shocking response.

"Really?" I say.

Ryker nods his head and I see a smile form on his face.

"Oh! Okay!" I quickly say. "That's great!" I feel a smile pushing my cheeks up against my eyes. "Well I'll let her know then!"

My eyes shoot back down at my phone in my hands and my smile widens as I see my reflection on the black screen on my phone. I definitely expected him to say no, but this is perfect. Better than I thought it would go!

I unlock my phone and quickly text my mom back, letting her know that I'll be over around noon and I'll be bringing a friend.

A reply quickly pops up below my message:

Sounds good! I'll make you and Lily some lunch!

Yeah, she definitely forgot about Lily's wedding yesterday. I thought about saying I'd be bringing a date over, but then that would have sounded like I had just met him, which I hadn't. I mean, I first met him in Nashville and then we started going on dates a couple weeks ago. So would he be someone I'm dating? Someone I've known for a while?

I lock my phone, deciding to ignore the text. It would be too complicated to try to explain that I'm actually bringing Ryker, considering I haven't even mentioned the name to her whatsoever. I'll just let it be a surprise and on the way there I'll think of how to introduce him. *Yes. That'll work.*

I look up from my phone, expecting to see Ryker still in front of me, but he's gone. I wasn't imagining him here, right? I quickly look around the room until I see him emerging from the closet, now dressed in a pair of blue jeans and suede oxfords. Our eyes meet almost immediately as he turns the light off in the closet.

"I didn't even realize you walked away." I say, scoffing.

"Well," Ryker says, raising an eyebrow as he walks back over to me. He glances down at his blue jeans for a moment and pinches the sides, before looking back up at me. "I don't think your mom would appreciate meeting me in my boxers." I chuckle at the thought as a smirk grows on Ryker's face.

"Want to finish getting ready and I'll meet you downstairs?" Ryker says, stopping in front of me.

I nod my head with a smile as his hand reaches up to my face. Leaning over me, he places a soft kiss on my forehead, before pulling away.

"See you in a bit, Beautiful." He says smiling as he turns and walks out of the bedroom.

Chapter Eighteen

Paige

Glancing over at Ryker, I can't help but smile. I watch as he adjusts his aviator sunglasses on his face and a smile grows on his face as he catches a glimpse of me looking at him from the corner of his eye. I quickly direct my eyes back to the road in front of us and immediately recognize the street my mom lives on.

The rest of the morning seemed to fly by after I walked downstairs. Assuming Ryker would be sitting on the couch waiting for me, I opened my mouth to speak, but as I entered the room, I found him standing in the kitchen. I quieted my steps and closed my mouth, as I realized he hadn't heard me come down. He was staring out the backyard window, with a coffee in his hand. I couldn't see his entire face, but I could see a soft smile on the corner of his lips. He seemed happy. Content.

As I quietly stepped closer to him, I suddenly felt a sharp pain against the side of my hip as the corner of the counter dug into me. *Shit*. As I let out a muted whine, Ryker turned around and the smile quickly disappeared on his face.

"Are you okay?" He asked, setting his coffee down on the kitchen counter, that just punctured my side.

As Ryker helped me up from my leaned over position, I nodded my head as I straightened myself up. The pain ached as I reached down to partially lift up my shirt to see the damage. *Of course, an instant bruise.*

"Do you need any ice?" Ryker asked, turning around toward the fridge before I could answer.

"No, it's okay." I quickly said, holding my hand up to stop him. "Just another typical battle wound that my clumsiness has given me."

Ryker lightly chuckled and I followed suit as I lowered my shirt back over the bruise.

"Are you sure?" Ryker asked again, his eyes filled with concern.

"Definitely." I reassured him with a smile. Changing the subject and somewhat distracting myself, I looked over at his coffee on the counter. "It smells so good in here."

Ryker turned toward the coffee cup, then looked back at me with a smile. "I can make you a cup if you'd like."

"No, it's okay." I said. "Besides, I think we should probably get going if we want to make it to my mom's house on time."

"Right, of course!" Ryker nodded his head as he grabbed his coffee off the counter.

The drive into the city was quicker than I expected as we pull to a stop along the side of my mom's street. I watch as Ryker takes his sunglasses off and places them onto the dashboard. As he sets them down, his phone almost immediately rings.

Pulling his phone out of his pocket, he looks down at it and then up at me.

"Just a moment, Beautiful." Ryker says with a brief smile, quickly answering the phone as I softly nod my head.

I turn my head back toward the closed window of the car and look up at the tan building beside us. I remember how I used to think this building was such a luxurious place to live. I thought it was a hotel when I first saw it. However, that idea of luxury quickly went through the roof once Lily showed me where she planned to live with Mason. Now *that* was luxury. Does Ryker live in an apartment like that? One that just exudes that the people living in it have money?

I look back at Ryker just as his call wraps up.

"Thanks Turner. Talk later." Ryker says, before hanging up the phone.

"How's Turner doing?" I ask, tilting my head with a smile.

"He's good. He's bringing your suitcase over to my place." Ryker says.

"Your place?" I say, furrowing my brows.

"Yes, here in the city." Ryker says, nodding his head with a slight smile. "Is that okay, Beautiful?" Ryker raises an eyebrow.

"Definitely!" I say, almost a little too excited. "I'd love to see where *the* Ryker Blackwell lives." I chuckle as I finish my sentence.

Ryker scoffs at me and his smile grows into a smirk.

"You're kind of a big deal here in the city from what I'm told." I say, raising both of my eyebrows quickly with my own smirk growing on my face.

"Not at all." Ryker lets out a deep chuckle. "Come on, let's go."

"Whatever you say, Mr. Blackwell." I say sarcastically as I see Ryker roll his eyes at me with a smile as he opens the driver's side door.

As Ryker gets out, he quickly walks around the front of the car and over to the passenger's side door. Opening it, he holds his hand out for me to grab and I willingly grab it as I step out.

Walking through the lobby of the apartment complex with my hand still in his, we make our way up the elevators to my mom's floor. As we walk down the short hallway, thoughts quickly flood my head. I've never brought over any guy to meet my mom, let alone a man like Ryker. Will she even like him? I know how strong my feelings are toward him, but what if my mom doesn't think he's right for me?

Ever since my dad passed, my mom has written off being in relationships. Maybe just because she doesn't want it to end the same way? Or the way it would have ended in a divorce if he hadn't died. So for as long as I can remember, she's never truly given me a lot of advice on what I should look for in a relationship. Except one time. I do remember her telling me one piece of advice when I was in college: If they aren't all in, then you shouldn't be either. I never really understood what she meant by that, until I met Ryker. If I could guess, Ryker was all in from day one. There's no doubt about that. Even Lily could see it. So, if my mom can see it too, then I can't imagine her not being happy for me.

I take a breath in as I lift my hand up and knock on the door to her apartment. Almost immediately, the door opens.

"Paige! You're early!" My mom says as she looks down at the ground adjusting her earring. She doesn't even notice Ryker towering behind me as she steps aside to let me walk into the apartment. "Here, come on in!"

As I step through the doorway, she turns away and quickly shuffles back into her bedroom.

"Nice to see you too Mom!" I shout, as she exits the room. I turn around and shrug my shoulders at Ryker as he steps into the apartment, closing the door behind him.

"I don't even have lunch ready!" My mom shouts from her bedroom, as I hear a cabinet door slam from her room.

"It's okay Mom. We're a little early anyways." I say, as I walk into the living room with Ryker following closely behind me.

When I reach one of the two armchairs that face the window, I rest my hand against the top of the chair as I turn toward my mom's bedroom door that's slightly cracked. I turn my head to look at Ryker and raise my eyebrows.

"That certainly wasn't the introduction I had imagined." I say with an uneasy laugh. Ryker slides in next to me and interlocks our fingers on my other hand. "Maybe she just didn't notice?" Ryker purses his lips together, staying silent.

"How have you been Lily?" My mom shouts from the other room, as I hear the sound of unknown items dropping in her bedroom.

"She definitely didn't notice." I quietly say, letting out a loud chuckle as Ryker smiles down at me.

I turn my head back toward the bedroom.

"Mom!" I yell, with a slight chuckle in my voice. "Lily isn't here!"

I hear the bedroom suddenly go quiet. The only thing I hear are my mom's footsteps as she paces around her room. Within a moment, the bedroom door slowly widens as I see her poke her head out of the door. Her eyes immediately widen.

"Oh!" My mom says without haste. She steps out from behind the door with a smile and straightens herself up as she walks over to us. Cocking her head as she turns toward me, she raises an eyebrow, then looks up at Ryker.

"Paige!" She says with an amused look on her face. "You didn't tell me you were bringing a man over."

"Surprise." I say, with slight sarcasm in my voice as I find my assumptions were correct.

She hadn't even registered that Lily wasn't with me because she had become so accustomed to Lily joining me over the years. More so, Lily was basically family so Lily wouldn't have cared if my mom hadn't finished getting ready. She would have just made herself at home while we waited. So this time, when she assumed Lily was with me, she went about her normal routine, completely unaware of the new person that had entered her apartment.

"And who might you be?" My mom asks Ryker as she raises her eyebrows.

"This is-." I say, just before Ryker cuts me off.

"Ryker. Ryker Blackwell." He says, holding his hand out to my mom. "I'm Paige's boyfriend." My head immediately turns as I look up at Ryker, my eyes as wide as can be. *Boyfriend? Did I hear that right?*

My mom shakes Ryker's hand and I feel her eyes glance back at me, as if she is also surprised by the words.

"It's nice to meet you Ms. Palmer." Ryker confidently says, ignoring the questionable look that I'm giving him.

"Please, call me Allison." My mom says, as she lets go of his hand. Her hand immediately goes up to her chin as she tilts her head. "You look very familiar. Have we met before?"

"Not that I'm aware of." Ryker says, raising his eyebrows.

"Really? I swear I've seen your face before!" My mom purses her lips as if to think.

"You know Mom, maybe you've read about him?" I quickly chime in, as my mom continues to study his face. "He's apparently a pretty big deal when it comes to the city's real estate department" I turn to Ryker and wink.

"Erm, maybe." My mom pauses. "That has to be it!" My mom straightens herself up again and a genuine smile appears on her face. "Well it's so lovely to meet you Ryker."

"You as well." Ryker says, nodding his head with a smile.

"Well, you two came for lunch so let me go get lunch ready!" My mom says, as she claps her hands together.

She walks around us and heads toward the kitchen. We follow her into the kitchen and sit down at the large dining table, where four other chairs remain empty. Despite my mom living alone, she always appeared to have everything fit and ready for when guests came over. The house was always clean, there was always food readily available and she was always perfectly put together for when guests arrived. Well, except for today when we arrived early.

"Do you need any help in there?" I ask, peering into the kitchen as I see her quickly pulling pots out from the lower cabinets.

"No, I've got it!" My mom says, as she paces over to the kitchen. "Just make yourselves at home!"

"Okay, if you say so!" I say with a small chuckle as I shrug my shoulders at Ryker.

"So, before I start, is Lily still coming for lunch though?" My mom asks as she stops in the middle of the kitchen, holding a block of cheese in one hand and a cheese grater in the other.

"Mom!" I say through a laugh. "Lily got married yesterday!"

"Wait, was that this weekend?" She says, as she looks up to the ceiling, as if to think.

Pulling her hand, which holds the cheese grater, up to her head, she uses the back of her hand to rub her forehead before looking back at me.

"I could have sworn it was next weekend!" She says, letting out a slow sigh.

Her arm slowly lowers back to her side, before she turns around and starts quickly getting back to making lunch.

"Would you be able to give Lily her wedding gift for me? I'm not sure when I'll see her next!"

"Of course, Mom!" I say, letting out a small laugh. *I knew she forgot about Lily's wedding.*

"Ryker, have you met Lily yet?" My mom asks as she fills a pot with water from the sink.

"Yes I know her." Ryker says, turning his body in the chair to face toward her in the kitchen.

"She's such a lovely girl!" My mom says, turning to look at us with a smile. "Did you know she's been Paige's best friend for as long as I can remember? Practically her only friend."

"Mom!" I say, putting my hand up to my forehead with my elbow resting against the table.

"Well, except for that one boy when you are little." My mom turns back toward the pot filling up and carries it over to the stove top. "What was his name?" She looks up toward the ceiling again. "Oh it's on the tip of my tongue!" She turns back toward the stove and turns on the burner.

"You remember her childhood friend?" Ryker asks, raising an eyebrow.

"I remember a lot from her childhood." My mom says. "My memory has served me well, except for recently that is. I really should have written down Lily's wedding date on my calendar. Not sure how I missed that." She says with a sign. "But yeah, everything from her childhood is fresh in my mind. It's just his darn name I'm forgetting!" My mom chuckles.

I shift my focus away from my mom and look at Ryker, whose eyes turn toward me. Only light banging from the kitchen can be heard as my mom continues to cook. Ryker places his hand onto the dining table, with his palm open. Moving my hand off of my forehead, I reach out and grab it. He gives my hand a light squeeze and we both smile at one another, as a silence fills the room.

"Ace!" She shouts, practically making me jump. "That was his name!"

The startling noise causes my hand to pull away from Ryker's, but he tightens his grip, keeping my hand in place. His head instantly shoots over to look at my mom.

"You and Ace were such cute kids." My mom says, as I hear her stir the pan next to the pot. "You practically spent every day together."

"Do you remember him?" Ryker asks, tilting his head as he looks back at me.

My mom turns around just long enough to catch Ryker staring in my direction and I realize she heard what he said before I can reply.

"Of course you do, Paige!" She chuckles. "I remember they even formed a little club. It was so sweet! Paige, do you remember you even drew a logo for your club?"

I raise my eyebrows and look up at the ceiling, trying to think of the memory, but I can't. My memories from when I was younger continue to be so foggy in my mind. The loss of my dad really made me forget a lot of it. Only small memories here and there tend to come back into my mind, but nothing regarding a kid named Ace. I shrug as I shake my head to Ryker.

My mom puts the spatula down on the countertop and turns around to face me.

"You know, I think I have a photo of it somewhere!" My mom says, walking out of the kitchen and into the living room. "Let me see if I can find it!"

Walking over to a small side table, she opens the top drawer and pulls out a box that is overflowing with photos, as they pool over the top. Resting it on the table, she starts to quickly flip through the photos with her finger, pausing several times to pull a photo out to check it. As she goes through the photos, I hear the pot on the stove start to boil, quickly bubbling around the top.

"Mom, the water is boiling!" I say, looking around Ryker to see if she is finished.

Before I can call her name out again, she rushes back into the kitchen and turns the knob down on the stove.

"Are you sure you don't need help in there?" I ask, slightly standing up from my chair to peek into the kitchen.

"No hon. It's okay!" My mom says, without turning to look at me. I slowly start to sit back down in my seat. "I'll look through the photos later and send it to you! You'll have to show Ryker! It's so cute."

My mom turns back to look at me and notices Ryker's hand holding mine. A wide grin grows on her face as she looks at me, then directs her attention to him.

"So, Ryker, where did you grow up?" She asks before turning back toward the stove.

I also wanted to know. From all the times Ryker and I talked, I never really got a chance to ask him about his childhood and where he grew up. It was still a mystery to me. I didn't mind telling him about my life when he asked, but now I would get to hear more about him. *Thank you, mom.*

"Erm," Ryker says, tilting his head to the side. "Up north."

"Oh! Where up north?" My mom asks. I turn to look at Ryker and rest my cheek into my hand as my elbow sits on the table.

"Here and there." Ryker says, scratching his head. He turns his body in the chair and faces forward, staring straight at the wall. *Well, that doesn't tell me much.*

"Do your parents still live up there?" My mom asks, turning her head to look at him for a moment.

"No." Ryker says quickly. Without taking another breath, he adds, "They are no longer alive." *Woah. That's news to me.*

This entire time, I never really thought to ask him about his parents. I just assumed they were both alive. I had lost one of my parents when I was a child, but I couldn't imagine losing both of them. Yet, Ryker had.

"Oh, I'm sorry to hear that." My mom says, turning the rest of her body to face him. Ryker nods slowly, almost ignoring the words that my mom said. "Was it recent?"

Ryker's head stops nodding, and for a moment he blinks a few times as he stares toward the wall. Then, he quickly shakes his head. "My mother passed away when I was 18."

"And your father?" My mom asks, placing one of her hands behind her neck. She appears to be rubbing her neck and I can tell she also feels like these questions have gotten a little too deep. I know I do.

Ryker stays silent for a moment. As I look at him, his face quickly grows cold. A shadow I've never seen in him before crosses his eyes. He doesn't blink his eyes and he remains stoic as he stares into the distance. Like the words my mom said were a trigger that pushed him into this state. While he seemed to be already uncomfortable with the conversation that was progressing, I can tell we may have hit a nerve. Which nerve, I'm not sure.

I squeeze his hand to help reassure him I'm here if he needs me and it's as if my squeeze snaps him out of the trance he's in. He blinks for a moment then turns his head to look at my mom, before speaking again.

"Last week." Ryker says bluntly. "He died last week." *What?* Ryker turns his head back toward the wall.

Why didn't he say anything to me? If I had known he had lost his father, then I could have helped him through a hard time. I know when my dad died, it was one of the most difficult things I had ever been through. It made me feel like a hole was punched through my heart. *Why would he keep this a secret from me?*

Then, I remembered. There was only one moment I could think of: The night Ryker left. He had received a phone call from someone and he had the same cold appearance on his face. He didn't look like he was expecting that call that night, but could that have been from a family member? Was that when he found out his dad had died?

As I sit quietly next to him, I slowly start to see it in his face. He didn't have to tell me anything, but I could finally see it. The hatred. I expected to see Ryker saddened by the words that he so easily said, but the words carried no empathy. No sadness. It was as if the words he had said tasted like a bad meal coming back up. He wasn't close to his father. He couldn't have been okay so quickly after his father died. That's got to be the reason.

"Was that what the phone call was about? The night you left?" I ask slowly, being careful with my words.

"Yes." Ryker says softly, turning to me. His face slowly starts to warm up as he looks at me. His brows furrowed together. "I was going to tell you, but-"

"You weren't close to him." I say quietly. Ryker's eyes widen as he hears my words, almost like he's relieved that he didn't have to explain it to me.

"Not at all." He says in a cold tone.

Ryker takes a breath in then squeezes my hand, reassuring me with his answer. "I hated the man." He says in a low voice, emphasizing the word "hated." He didn't need to say it because I could already tell, but hearing it out loud from him was still surprising. This time, I could clearly tell he didn't like the words even coming out of his mouth. It finally made sense why he didn't bring up his parents before.

"I'm sorry for your loss, Ryker." My mom says, taking a deep breath in and out. She definitely didn't hear the conversation between just Ryker and I. "If you need anything, please let me know!"

"Thank you." Ryker says, not breaking our eye contact. Taking another breath in, he musters a smile and I softly smile back. Then, he turns back around to my mom and stands up from his chair.

"Here! Let me help you with lunch!"

Ryker walks over and stands next to my mom, who gladly gives him the spatula to help stir the pot, while she jumps into making the rest of the food.

"How thoughtful Ryker!" My mom says, turning to give me a wide grin. I roll my eyes, then sit back in my chair as they prepare lunch in the kitchen together.

***

Luckily, the rest of the afternoon's conversations were light. I could tell my mom didn't want to accidentally get into a touchy subject with Ryker again, so she stayed quiet as I led some of the conversations. I told my mom about how Ryker and I had met, how my project was going at work and all about Lily's wedding. She seemed happy to hear about what was new in my life, since it had been a while since we last spent so much time together.

Once we finished lunch, Ryker took over the conversation topics and started asking my mom questions about her life. My mom happily obliged and couldn't wait to share all the details of how I grew up. It was slightly embarrassing when she brought out the photo albums, but I could tell she enjoyed talking about our life together.

"Wait!" I hear my mom shout from her bedroom, as we walk over to the door. "I almost forgot to give you this!"

We stop next to the door as she walks out of her bedroom carrying a large present in her arms. The present, which is wrapped in white wrapping paper, has shiny, purple ribbon around the sides and at the top is a large purple bow. I had no doubt it was for Lily, considering her favorite color was purple.

"This is for Lily!" My mom says, holding out the large present for me to grab. "Please tell her I'm so sorry I missed her big day."

"I will." I say, holding my arms out to grab the present.

As my mom hands the present over, I hear a swoosh as I feel something hit the top of my foot and slide onto the floor below me. I turn my body to the side and notice a large brown envelope lying on the ground between us.

"Oh! This is for you." My mom says, picking up the envelope from the floor. She slides the envelope between the present and my hand, securing it in place.

"What's in it?" I ask, tilting my head to the side as I attempt to read the writing hidden between my fingers. My eyes glance up at the upper righthand corner of the envelope where I see several colorful stamps. None that I've seen before.

"I'm not sure. It came in the mail for you." My mom says, stepping around the present to give me a side hug. "I love you hon. It was nice having lunch with you." My mom steps back. "And Ryker."

"Thank you so much for lunch, Ms. Palmer." Ryker says, as my mom leans in for a hug.

"Please! Call me Allison." My mom says as she hugs him. Pulling back, she leans over and grabs the knob to the front door. "You are welcome any time!" She says, looking toward Ryker with a wide grin.

As the door opens, Ryker walks through and I follow him through the door, careful not to fall as I look over the large present in my arms. As I turn slightly, I see my mom standing in the doorway.

"Love you!" I say, smiling at my mom. She quickly smiles back at me and closes the door behind us as we head back toward the elevator.

Chapter Nineteen

Paige

It's felt like a daydream the past couple weeks. Like I'm on cloud nine. Ever since the day after Lily's wedding when Ryker not only met my mom, but called me his girlfriend, I've never felt happier.

Typically, this time of the year was my least favorite. A time I dreaded. The changing trees reminded me of my past and the season only brought sorrow. But that's no longer the case.

Since meeting Ryker, I feel like a part of me that felt empty has finally been pieced back together. It had a slow start, but it quickly was filled and became whole again. A feeling I haven't felt for as long as I could remember. A feeling I never thought would come back. Has it all been because of him? I'm no longer dwelling on the past. No longer dwelling on what my life could have been like. Can I now truly feel happy? Feel like I can move forward in life?

Just yesterday, I was able to complete my project at work. I had emailed the photocopied pages I had illustrated to my team lead, Anna, and started working on smaller projects that my coworkers were behind on. It was a proud moment to say the least.

I didn't expect to finish as fast as I did, but the past couple weeks, it's felt as if the book basically illustrated itself. While it had been a slow start to begin with, I had gotten to a point where illustrating the children's book, which took place during the fall, became easier. My imagination flowed as the pages were filled with colors as bright as the trees that scattered the streets below my office. As the story continued, I found creative ways to incorporate various elements of the manuscript into the pages of the book, which impressed even myself as I drew them.

I look out the window from my office desk and take a quick sip of breath in. Out the window, I watch as white specks slowly fall from above. Lightly dancing down. These specks of white used to be a sign that fall was ending as winter approached around the corner. But, now I see them as a sign of the future. Of what could be.

After that Sunday afternoon at my mom's apartment, I had Ryker make a quick stop at my apartment, despite my suitcase being sent over to his place. I knew if he was already planning on having me stay over with him, I might as well grab some additional things that I may need. Well, a little bit more than a little.

As Ryker waited in his car on the street below, I unlocked the door to my apartment, as I balanced Lily's present and the envelope from my mom in my other hand. I had only been gone for the weekend, but it felt like forever since I had last been there. The last time I was at my apartment, I was so rushed when I left to get to Lily's wedding that I barely had time to clean. Luckily, I did remember to close the curtains before I left, but the darkness made it difficult to see as I took another step inside, hoping I could reach the light just a few more steps away. Unfortunately, as I took another step forward, I tripped over a shoe lying near the door, sending my body down to the floor and Lily's present across the room. *Shit.*

Still lying with my stomach against the floor, I looked back at the shoe on the floor. *A black stiletto.* Before I had left, I was debating between two different sets of heels and had forgotten I had switched my shoes out right before I left the apartment that day. *Of course I tripped over it.*

I turned my head to face forward and noticed Lily's present. *Shit, shit.* Not only was the present across the room, but it didn't look good. I quickly stood up and ran over to the present on the floor, which now looked like it had been hit by a car. The purple ribbons that wrapped around it were hanging off and the bow appeared to be misshaped. The box itself was no longer perfectly squared and had several dents in the corners.

Taking a breath in, I picked up the misshaped present off the floor and walked it over to the counter, carefully setting it down to ensure it wouldn't be damaged more. I never asked my mom what she got Lily, but I truly hoped it wasn't fragile.

Walking over to the window, I opened the curtains to let in some light from outside and it immediately brightened the room. As I looked at the present on the counter from across the room, I realized the envelope had also disappeared. I spent a few minutes trying to find the envelope, but despite my best efforts, it was nowhere in sight.

I walked back over to the window and looked down at Ryker's car parked on the road. Ryker was outside of his car now and he was leaning against the passenger door. I noticed him looking up at the building, but I doubt he was able to see me through the window. However, I quickly walked into my bedroom to collect my things, as I could only assume he was waiting for me to come down. *I'll have to find the envelope another day.*

As I walked into my room, I definitely didn't realize how messy I had left it. The bed was unmade, there was a pile of clothes sitting on a chair in the corner and you could tell I left the bathroom in a hurry, as several items were scattered across the counter. There was definitely some cleaning that needed to be done, but I knew I didn't have enough time at that moment to do so.

I gathered some additional toiletries from my bathroom and placed them into a small duffle bag that I had grabbed from beneath my bed. Searching my closet, I grabbed several pieces of clothing that could be mixed and matched for both dates and work and stuffed those into the bag, completely neglecting to even attempt to fold them. As I zipped up the duffle bag and threw it over my shoulder, I shuffled some clothes and shoes around on the floor, as I cleared a path back to the doorway.

When I got downstairs, Ryker was in the same place as I had seen him, waiting against the passenger door. A wide grin grew on his face as soon as he saw me walk out of my apartment complex. I couldn't help but smile as he opened the door for me.

I imagined Ryker's apartment to be similar to Lily and Mason's place. Penthouse apartment. Clean and modern. Large floor to ceiling windows with an incredible view. The typical penthouse apartment that any rich person would love to live in. However, Ryker's place was almost surprising.

As we came to a stop, Ryker got out and handed his keys to the valet, before coming to open my door. As he opened my door, the first thing I noticed was that we were across one of the biggest parks in the city. The leaves on the trees had started to scatter the ground as the weather slowly grew colder and if Ryker lived in one of these tall skyscrapers, the view would be phenomenal.

Ryker grabbed my duffle bag from my arms and with his other hand, he grabbed mine, leading me down the sidewalk. As I turned to walk into a large, brand new apartment building next to his car, Ryker's arm quickly pulled me away.

"Isn't this your building?" I asked, looking up as it towered above us. Ryker let out a deep chuckle.

"Actually, it's the one next door." He said with a smile, pulling me toward a red brick building.

As we walked inside, you could tell the apartment building was older. It had an older smell to it and was definitely a different style compared to the clean and contemporary look in the one that Lily and Mason lived in. It was still large inside, but it was just different than what I expected it to be.

As the elevator opened to his floor, which was still at the very top of the building, I was surprised to see how different it was to what I had imagined. It still had a modern look to it, but it was industrial with its brick walls and tall black arched windows. The ceiling was lined with wood beams running across the top and several lights hung between the beams, brightening up the room. A staircase near the entrance of the apartment led to a second floor and I could see several decorated spaces up there from where I was standing.

Many of the furniture pieces that sat in the front room had wood incorporated in them as well and on a wall in the distance was a beautiful, large fireplace that rose to the ceiling.

The beams continued across the tall ceiling as we walked into the kitchen, where the modern industrial look continued. The counters were a dark, black granite resting above dark wood cabinets and the most eye-popping thing in the room were the stainless steel appliances.

As I walked over to the windows, I was delighted to see the view that I expected. None of the tall buildings around us obstructed my sight of the park, which made me smile. As I stepped closer to the window, I noticed something different about Ryker's place. Not only did it have a beautiful view, but he had a large balcony that wrapped around the outside of it.

I quickly walked out through the back door onto a concrete patio that had string lights hanging from above. The patio was surrounded by trees and plants, which lined the edge of the short brick wall at the edge of the balcony and there was a small area with patio furniture over a large rug. If I hadn't known it was a balcony, I would have thought it was a regular backyard despite its concrete floor.

As I looked out at the park, I noticed the sun setting in the distance and the lights above me quickly flickered as they came on. Growing up, we had string lights hanging across our backyard and I remember it always made the backyard brighten up as the sky grew dark. I had always wanted to add string lights to a small apartment balcony, but I never found an affordable place that came with one, so that was put on hold. However, Ryker did have the space. It was as if there was a little reminder of home here at Ryker's apartment, not that he would even realize it.

As I stood outside looking out into the distance, Ryker came up from behind and wrapped his arms around me. I leaned my neck into his chest as he kissed the side of my forehead.

"I could get used to this." Ryker said, taking a breath in.

"You see this view all the time." I scoffed. "It's probably nothing to you anymore."

Ryker chuckled, then turned his head to the side to look me in the eyes.

"I meant having you here." Ryker said. "I wouldn't care where we were, as long as you were here in my arms."

A smile formed on my face at the words and Ryker leaned in to give me a soft kiss on the lips.

As the weeks passed, Ryker's place felt more and more like home. His large bedroom upstairs reminded me a lot of the house he owned outside of the city and it made it that much easier to get used to.

While I wasn't actually living with him, it truly felt like it as I kept a lot of my clothes at his apartment. I would stop by my own place every now and then to grab what I needed and switch out some of my outfits, but I always went back to his place each night. I had forgotten how lonely it had become in my own apartment since Lily had moved out, so having the option to stay with Ryker was a comfort for me.

Also, it was a bonus that I got to wake up every morning to see Ryker lying next to me. While most days, I'd inch closer to him to rest my head against his chest as I fell back asleep, on occasion, I would take an extra moment to take in his physical features. Remembering all the parts of him.

I'd watch as his chest rose and fell below my head as he soundly slept. His breath lightly blowing against the hair on my head. I'd look at his arms wrapped around me, holding me closely, as I studied the tattoos that covered his arms from the wrist up. Wondering what each one was for and what it meant.

I'd turn my head up and look at him. His dark hair, slightly hanging over his forehead. His memorable green eyes hidden beneath his eyelids. His thin lips, slightly parted open.

I focused on all these details because I never knew when it would be the last. When he would disappear in my life. That was a thought that always crept up from inside of me. Found its way into my mind in those early mornings. I had lost someone before and it destroyed me. Someone I loved. I didn't want to lose someone again. But, was this love?

I had no doubt I was falling for him. It was easy for me to see that. But it was different from the way I remember falling in love in the past.

In my previous relationships, I said I was in love, but that wasn't love. It was lust. It was the idea that someone else was caring for me in my still-broken state and I grew attached to the idea. To the concept that I had found love again.

This time was different though. I was no longer that broken girl with a piece missing from her heart. I felt like myself, which made all the difference. Falling for Ryker was different. It felt easy. It felt natural. And it was almost as if it happened the moment I saw him. As if an invisible string pulled us together. And as we grew closer, that string between us shortened, twisting us into a knot, tightly bound together. With him, I feel back at home. Back to a place where I felt safe. Where I felt loved. Where I am loved. So falling for him wasn't hard. It was inevitable.

A smile spreads across my face, as I start to close my eyes, drifting back into a deep sleep within Ryker's arms. *I could get used to this.*

A ping from my phone sparks me out of my memories as I'm reminded that I'm sitting at my desk at work. Staring at the window, I blink a few times before shifting my body up into my chair.

I'm not sure how long I had escaped into my thoughts, but my laptop screensaver had just switched to a black screen as my eyes focused back in front of me.

Once again, I hear the ping from my phone as I see the screen of it light up. I grab it, hoping it'll be from Ryker, but instead I see my mom's name above the text with just the words "I found it!" followed by an attachment.

Opening my phone, I go into my mom's texts and see a photo she sent me. Although blurry, presumably from my mom trying to take a clear picture of the printed photo, I'm still able to get an idea of what her text is about. The printed photo, which has an illegible date in the bottom right corner, shows me hugging a light brown-haired kid, who is a little taller than me, as we stand in front of a large sheet. I can only assume it's that "Ace" kid that my mom mentioned when we came over.

I squint my eyes, trying to focus on the sheet behind us in the photo. The sheet has what appears to be a black marker drawing of an ace of hearts playing card with a palm tree in the center of it. Above the drawing are the words "Ace of Palms."

I stare at the drawing in the photo, faintly recognizing it. I don't remember taking this photo whatsoever, however, the drawing is somewhat memorable. Maybe my mom has shown me this photo before? Maybe I'm remembering this subtle memory from my childhood? It's hard to tell, but I feel like I've seen it before today.

"Hey Paige!" I hear off to my left, startling me as I push back into my chair. I turn to look up at the voice and immediately smile, seeing my team lead, Anna, standing next to me.

"Yes?" I quickly reply, placing my phone down on my desk.

"Do you have a moment to speak with me in my office?" Anna asks, smiling back.

"Definitely!" I say, standing up from my desk as Anna turns around and walks back to her office. I willingly follow as I can only presume she wants to go over my drawings for the frog book I finished yesterday.

As we step into Anna's office, she gestures for me to sit in the chair in front of her desk.

"Please take a seat."

The words spark déjà vu in my mind as I'm reminded of the last time Anna called me into her office to talk. My anxiety was through the roof thinking she was going to fire me, but I was delighted when she had given me the opportunity to do solo work on the illustrations for a book. This time though, it couldn't possibly be bad. I just gave her some of the best illustrations I had ever come up with.

Sitting down across from Anna, my hands immediately grip the seat as I clench my jaw. *Please only good news.* As if Anna can sense my tension, she quickly speaks again.

"Don't worry! It's good news again!" Anna says, chuckling.

I immediately relax my body in the chair as I let out a breath, not realizing I was holding it in. Anna slides her laptop, which was sitting directly in front of her on the desk, off to the side.

"I looked over the remaining pages you sent me and-." Anna says, pausing. She clicks a button on her computer, then looks back at me, placing both of her hands on the desk in front of her. "I just have to say, wow!" She holds her hands up in front of her, with her fingers spread apart.

"So you like them?" I ask, leaning forward in my chair as I raise an eyebrow.

"Like them? I love them!" Anna says, smiling at me.

She turns back to her laptop and appears to be scrolling through a series of photos, which I assume are the pages I sent her.

"You have really shown your true colors with this work!"

"Thank you!" I say, smiling as I lean back into the chair, interlocking my hands tightly in front of me on my lap.

"I have to say, I really liked how you interpreted the frog's story." Anna raises her eyebrows. "Most people would have just drawn what the notes called for, but you really brought the story to life through the pages! It was exactly what we were hoping for."

"I'm glad you think so!" I say, pressing my lips together.

"Well, let me just get right to the point." Anna says, chuckling. "I think it's time you take the lead. Your own story. Your own illustrations."

"Wait, what exactly do you mean?" I slightly lower my head.

"You know how we were planning to add a full-time artist to our team? Well, we think you'd be the perfect fit for the position."

"Really?" I say wide-eyed with a smile.

"Definitely! You've proven to us that you are more than capable." Anna says, turning her head to click a few more keys on her keyboard. "So, is that a yes?"

"Of course it's a yes!" I say, taking a breath in.

"I thought you'd say that." Anna chuckles. "I went ahead and sent you an email with everything you need to know, including information about your nine percent pay raise, but overall, you have free reign. I know you will excel on your own projects."

I lean forward again in my chair.

"Thank you so much! I won't let you down!" I say, fidgeting as I try to contain my hands in one place, with my excitement making me want to jump up and down in my seat.

"I know you won't." Anna says, standing up from her chair.

I stand up from my chair as she walks over to the door. As she opens the door, I walk over and stop in front of her.

"We'll have touch points each week to go over the work you do, but let me know if you need anything. I'm always here to help." Anna smiles.

"Of course! Sounds good." I say, smiling back as I walk out of her office door.

As I reach my desk and sit down in my chair, I immediately see the wide smile across my face as I stare into my reflection on the black screen of my laptop. *Did that just happen?* My smile grows bigger until I feel a pain in my cheeks. I take a deep breath in and out, before moving my lips back and forth to try to bring some feeling back to my face from smiling so hard.

After all the hard work I've put in, I'm finally getting the chance to do my own projects. My own stories. They offered me the full-time artist position, no questions asked. Not only has this been something I've been looking forward to since I started working here, but it just makes me think of how proud my dad would be. Knowing that I finally made it. I finally got to have my dream job. *This has to be a dream.* I pinch my arm quickly and scrunch my nose as I feel the pain. *Nope, not a dream.*

As I click my laptop to turn it back on, my hand pauses above the keys as the screen opens up. I know I should start jotting down story ideas, but how can I when I'm so excited? I need to at least tell someone. *I have to share the big news with him.*

I grab my phone, which is facing down on my desk, and I smile immediately as I see the text from Ryker:

> **Hello Beautiful! It'll be a late night for me as I have a few contracts I have to write up, but I'll see you back at my place.**

Followed by another text that reads:

> **But, to make up for it, I'll take you out for lunch tomorrow! Deal?**

I quickly open my phone and start typing, but pause.

While I could easily tell him the news over text, I don't want to distract him while he's busy at work. That wouldn't be fair to him. Also, it may be better to wait until I see him to give him the new life update, that way, we can celebrate together in person.

I hold down the delete button, then simply reply "Deal," followed by a smiley face emoji.

Chapter Twenty

Paige

Just like all the nights before, I wake up to Ryker by my side. I hadn't even heard him come in last night, but it must've been late, judging by his atypical sleep attire: suit pants and a plain white tee.

I roll over and look up at the large windows that fill the walls. While darkness still surrounds us, I can see a small glimpse of light peeking through the sides of the window shades.

Every moment I've spent at Ryker's apartment, I've become more and more used to it. The old sounds that the building makes. The oak smell that lingers from the wood beams on the ceiling. The bright mornings that shine through the smallest cracks of the window shades as the sunrise flows over the horizon.

As my eyes adjust to the light entering the room, I glance over to my side at the clock resting on the table. *My alarm isn't set to go off for another hour.* A smile grows across my face at the thought.

I roll back over to Ryker, who is lying on his back, and I close the distance between us as I pull myself next to him, resting my head against shoulder. I close my eyes for a moment, then carefully lift my hand up as I place my pointer finger on the center of his chest.

Tracing my finger over his defined pecs, my finger glides over his white shirt and down his chest as the material ripples beneath my finger. I brush over his sculpted pecs and I feel Ryker take a soft breath in and out as I move my finger from left to right. As my eyes follow my hand's movements, I briefly glance down past his waist, where I see a bulge growing under his pants. I continue to trace my hand up and down his chest, slightly moving closer to his pant line with each go. Ryker takes a deeper breath and this time, I know he's awake.

As my finger moves back down his chest and toward his pant line once again, I catch my breath as his hand suddenly grabs ahold of my finger. I watch, waiting for him to move my hand or say something, but he remains quiet. Pausing us in that moment. *Does he want me to stop?* I wait for him to say something before tilting my head to look up at him. Our eyes meet and instantly I feel a force against my hand as I'm quickly pushed onto my back.

"Good morning, Beautiful." He says softly, as he hovers above me. His eyes locked onto mine.

I glance down at his smirking smile and focus on his lips. I can't help but lightly bite my lips as I think of his pressed against mine. His lips devouring me in every way. Every part of me, up and down my body. I lean forward to kiss them, but I'm helpless as I feel Ryker's hands pressing against my wrists, holding me down. All I can do is wait for his move.

Ryker leans down and I take a breath, anticipating that his lips will meet mine soon, but his attention turns as I feel his lips press against the base of my neck. Slowly, he places a kiss on each side of my neck, followed by one at the top of each of my collarbones.

As his head moves down my chest, his hands release my wrists as I feel his lips place a kiss at the tops of my breasts, partially exposed from the deep neckline of my sleep shirt. I immediately place my hands into his dark hair as one of his hands moves to cup my breast and the other holds his body up.

His lips move from left to right, as he places a gentle bite at the top of my breast tissue and I cross my legs tightly as his mouth moves down my chest. Holding my breast in his hand, his mouth passes over my nipple and he pushes it into his mouth. Although it's separated by the light fabric of my shirt, I feel my nipple harden as his mouth pulls away.

Moving down my shirt, Ryker's lips trace my body in the same way my finger traced his. As he gets lower, my hands fall to my side as I feel where his head is moving. As his lips inch down to my waist, I feel his hand squeeze my breast slightly, then slide down past my ribs and my hips, before resting along the fabric of my shorts. The tips of his fingers move slowly up and under the base of my shirt, revealing to him the lower half of my stomach. I feel his lips place a single kiss on my navel and immediately I feel a wetness between my inner thighs.

But then, Ryker pauses. Long enough that I take notice, because the growing sensation in my body starts to dissipate as I wait for him to continue.

Lifting my head up, I glance down at Ryker. Our eyes meet as he hovers above my navel.

I watch as he takes a breath in and a soft smile grows on his face, as if to say "hello" in a way that has us not speaking a word to one another.

My eyes move back up to his eyes as I focus on the small hint of gold in them and I feel myself smiling too. His eyes soften.

I didn't expect it, but since Lily's wedding, Ryker and I have spent every single day together. Every moment we could with one another. And with that, you can't help but develop strong feelings for someone. *Has he fallen for me too? Was it as easy for him as it was for me?*

Before another thought crosses my mind, I feel his hands move down the sides of my hips and under my shorts, cupping my butt within his hands. Before I know it, I'm pulled toward the end of the bed as I watch his eyes darken. With my legs dangling off the side, his hands slide back up my hips, gripping the cotton shorts around my waist. He pulls my shorts down past my thighs, over my knees and I feel them drop to my ankles, all while his eyes still hold their gaze on mine as his face lingers above my navel.

His eyes turn away from me for a moment and anticipating his next move, I slowly inch my feet down the side of the bed as I feel his lips move down past my hips and onto my thighs. The slow and carefully placed kisses surge the wetness beneath my thong, as he moves his way down. As my feet land on the floor, he slowly opens my legs and I feel my breathing intensify as he places another kiss on my inner thigh, moving his way back up. The sensation builds within my body as each moment passes.

Pushing myself upward into a sitting position on the side of the bed, I quickly place my hand on his head, stopping him in his place. *It's my turn.* I push his head backward, as he kneels on the floor in front of me, and I smirk at him as our eyes meet. He immediately returns the expression, knowing the game I'm playing.

Placing my hands out in front of me, he grabs a hold of them and pulls himself up from his kneeling position. As he stands up, I pull myself up from the bed and place my pointer finger onto his chest. With our eyes locked on one another, I slowly use my finger to push him back, step by step, until our bodies have rotated 180° and his back is now facing the bed.

I might still be wearing my thin sleep shirt and only a pair of thongs, but I want him to be naked in front of me as he waits for me to make the move.

Kneeling in front of him, I slowly unhook the button on his pants, keeping my eyes glued up at him as he watches me. I move my hand down to his zipper and pull it down. Moving my hands back up to his waist, I grab ahold of the sides and slowly pull his pants down. As they fall to the floor, his length presses against his boxers and I press my lips together at the thought.

Standing back up from my knees, I glide my finger up the side of his body, while my eyes reconnect with his. Ryker takes a deep breath in and out as I trace my finger across his abs and back up to his chest, where I pause between his pecs. With one more push of my finger, his body is pushed into a sitting position on the side of the bed, in the same position I was in before.

Moving my finger back down, I take my other hand and grab ahold of the bottom of his shirt. Slowly pulling it up his body, I'm delighted as his muscular body is put on show and his chest becomes exposed. As I pull the shirt up past his pecs, his eyes leave mine as he assists me with removing the rest of his shirt, pulling it over his shoulders and head.

Once his shirt is off, he throws it onto the floor as he grabs ahold of my hips. Pulling me closer to him, I watch his head close the gap between our bodies as he leans over to kiss between my breasts.

As his head tilts slightly toward one breast, lightly kissing around my nipple still covered by the thin fabric of my sleep shirt. My eyes move past his dark hair and onto his right collarbone, where a tattoo of a pair of wings is etched in his skin. Ryker's head tilts once again as he moves over to kiss my other breast and my eyes move to his left shoulder.

As I look down at the tattoo on his shoulder, my lips part and my eyes widen. My entire body becomes frozen in place as I stare down at Ryker's shoulder, completely numb to his lips still against my body. *Where did he get that tattoo?*

While my heart was racing with anticipated satisfaction just seconds ago, it is now fuming with anxiety. I close my eyes and take a breath in. *Am I imagining it? Is this a dream again?*

Opening my eyes, I know I'm not dreaming. I know this is real. I know this is what I see. It's the same exact drawing. The same one I drew as a child. The one in the photo that my mom sent me earlier today. *It can't be.* I blink a couple times, staring down at the ink marking Ryker's skin. *It definitely is.*

While the tattoo is a bit more intricately designed, there's no doubt it's the same. There's an ace of hearts playing card with a palm tree in the center. *That's my drawing.*

Panicking, I quickly take a step back from Ryker and his arms fall from my hips as I keep my eyes glued on the tattoo on his shoulder.

"What is that?" I frantically say. "Where did you get that tattoo?" I point to his shoulder, but I can't help but look at it with fear. Fear as to how he got it. Fear as to who he really was.

Ryker immediately stands up from the bed, recognizing the look on my face.

"I can explain." Ryker says, taking a step forward. I immediately put my hand up in front of me, creating a space between us. Ryker stops.

"Explain what!" I yell, my eyes still wide. "You have a tattoo of a drawing I drew from my childhood!"

Ryker is silent as he rubs his hand across his face. As I watch him, I only feel rage fueling inside of me. Building more the longer he stays quiet.

"Who are you?" I yell.

Ryker steps back to sit on the edge of the bed. He places his elbows on his knees and rubs his hands over and through his hair. I turn around, as his attention is no longer on me, and immediately grab the blanket from the basket behind me, wrapping it around my half-naked body. I feel my chest rising and falling as the silence grows, killing me inside. *Who even is this man? This person I thought I knew?*

He takes a breath in and as he lets it out, he softly says, "I didn't mean for you to find out this way."

"What?" I shout, trying to get him to speak up.

"Our meeting wasn't a coincidence." He says, slightly louder as he picks his head up from between his arms, while still staring down at the floor. "None of it."

"What does that mean?" I say, as I take deep breaths in and out to calm myself down, while trying to ensure I don't have a panic attack.

He lifts his head up and I feel his eyes on me, but I can't bring myself to look at him as he continues speaking.

"My father called me 'Ace' when I was younger." Ryker says slowly and calmly. "I always hated the nickname." Ryker scoffs slightly.

I immediately recognize the name as he says it. *Ace.* The kid from the photo. If I was as close to him as my mom said I was, then why would Ryker keep it such a big secret? He could have told me that from the start. I may be a little creeped out by it at first, but maybe he has a reason that he's back in my life? Maybe he came across my social media account and wanted to reach out? *Right?*

"So, what? You found me online and wanted to reconnect?" I say with a light scoff, hoping the words that came out of my mouth were correct. *This has to be the explanation. It has to be.*

"Well yes, but also-." Ryker pauses. "I had to tell you the truth once I found out."

"What truth?" I say. "That you did some casual internet stalking and then wanted to meet again?" I awkwardly chuckle.

I finally look him in the eyes, however, he doesn't seem to find my joke funny. Instead, his eyes are filled with sorrow and regret. The same way he looked when he spoke about his mother no longer being alive.

"No, the truth about your father." Ryker quietly says, as tears well in his eyes. I immediately step back further from Ryker.

"My father?" I snap at him. "What does this have to do with him?"

"I'm so sorry, Paige." Ryker says, shaking his head as he looks down at the ground. *Paige? He never calls me that.* He slowly lifts his head back up and furrows his brows as he takes a breath in. "Your dad's death wasn't an accident."

"What do you mean? Of course it was. You know that." I say, trying to dismiss the words he just said.

"But it wasn't." He says, taking another breath in and out. *Is he trying to be funny? This has to be some fucked up joke.*

"What are you trying to say?" I ask, as I feel a tear well in the corner of my eye.

"My father." Ryker says. He pauses and I watch as a single tear falls from his eye. "He was hired to kill your father and he staged it to all look like it was just an accident."

"No, no, that's not what happened." I say, trying to keep myself from falling apart. "Why would you say that?" I start to feel tears fall down my face, soaking my cheeks.

"I'm so sorry, Beautiful." Ryker says, shaking his head.

"No!" I yell at Ryker. "You can't just say that to me!"

My dad died in a car accident. That's what I remember. How could Ryker make up something like this? Something that would bring up the past and hurt me again? *This can't be real. Please let this be a dream.*

My legs immediately give way as I feel my body fall forward and my knees hit the hard floor below me. Still covered by the blanket, I bend over, wrapping my arms tightly around myself.

"Once I found out the truth, I wanted to tell you. I truly did. I tried. On our first date, but I just couldn't find the words." He pauses. "Once I found you, I made sure to take care of you. To help you in every way that I could."

"Stop." I say quietly, but Ryker can't hear me. *I feel sick to my stomach.*

"But then I couldn't keep myself away from you. It was as if I was being pulled toward you. I couldn't stay away."

"Please." I say again, still too quiet for him to hear me. *I can't take this any more.*

"When I finally had the guts to tell you the truth, it was too late." Ryker says. "I had already fallen for you. You were back in my life again and I didn't want to lose you. Not again. Not like before."

Slowly, but heavily against the floor, I hear Ryker's footsteps as he inches closer to me. His hand reaches down and touches my shoulder through the blanket and I immediately feel a chill run down my spine. A feeling I've never experienced from Ryker's touch. A feeling I never thought would be caused by him.

I quickly look up at Ryker standing above me, through my tear-filled eyes, but I no longer recognize the person in front of me. It's as if someone I barely knew just touched me. Or someone I thought I knew. But, I guess I truly don't know him. I don't know what other secrets he's hiding.

As Ryker sees the tears stream down my face, his hand reaches down to wipe them from my cheeks, but I pull myself back before his hand reaches me.

"I'm sorry. I'm so sorry." Ryker says, standing above me.

I push my hands against the floor, forcing myself back from him even further. As I start to lift myself up to stand, Ryker immediately steps forward and lightly grabs my arm.

"Don't touch me." I shout, pulling my arm quickly out of his grasp.

As I stand myself up, I see him take a few steps back, giving me more space. Space to breathe. Space to think. Space away from him.

He slowly falls to his knees as his eyes quickly meet mine. He can see the pain that's coming back. The pain of the past pushing its way back in. The confusion. The trust. The lies. The fear in my body that's making me sick. The feeling that the room is closing in on me. I can't be here. I'm trapped and I need to get out. I need to escape.

I race over to the end table and grab my phone, still holding the blanket tightly around my body. I turn back and walk past Ryker, whose head hangs down as he stares at the floor, and I quickly grab my work clothes from the chair near the door, which I had set out the night before.

Without another thought, I swiftly exit the room and make my way toward the elevator door, which opens right into the apartment. I click the button and the doors open immediately. I step inside and click the button for the ground floor.

As I stand there, I know this is the end. This will be the last time I see Ryker. The last time I will be here at his apartment. But, I can't stand this place anymore. I can't be around him. He lied to me. He kept this dark secret inside of him. This secret that completely breaks the only memories I had of my dad.

The only ones that I thought were happy memories. But, were they really?

I still have so many questions. Why did his father kill my dad? What did my dad do to deserve it? Why didn't he tell me from the start? *I need to know what actually happened.*

With my back turned away from the elevator door, I slowly start to turn my head to see if Ryker is there. To see if he has come over to explain it to me. To see if he can answer these questions that race in my mind. But, as I turn my head, I watch as the elevator doors close. Separating me from the one person that knows what truly happened.

Chapter Twenty One

Ryker

I've lost her again. And this time, I don't know if I can get her back. I can't run after her and tell her how sorry I am for hiding this from her. Tell her how sorry I am from keeping this dreaded secret from her that's been tearing me up inside. I can't tell her how much I wish I could have told her earlier. I can't.

I could only watch as she walked out of my bedroom. Out of my apartment. Out of my life. And I don't blame her. How can someone stay when they learn a secret like this? This thing that makes you rethink everything you thought you knew. What you thought had happened, but actually didn't.

I remember that night like it was yesterday. While my mother was cooking dinner at home, my father asked me to go on a drive with him. I didn't know why, but I felt compelled to go.

After a short ten-minute drive, he pulled over on the side of a narrow road with several miles of farmland surrounding us. I recall asking him why we had stopped, but the only response he said was to "sit down and shut up."

As we sat there on the side of the road for what felt like half an hour, I passed the time by counting the cars that drove past us as we waited. Three, I counted in that time. It was a quiet road, so when another car started toward us, I got excited to add another one to my count. I remember my father leaning forward in his seat, both hands tightly gripping the wheel, as the car approached. But, as the car drew closer, I started getting an uneasy feeling. Like we weren't supposed to be there.

Just then, the car, still about a quarter of a mile away from us, started to swerve back and forth across the road. I'm not sure how the driver lost control on such a straight road, but all of a sudden, the car flipped over and skidded forward. As it eventually stopped in the center of the road, my eyes widened. *Was this even happening? Was I dreaming?*

I turned to my father, whose eyes were glued to the car on the road, confirming it wasn't a dream. But, why wasn't he as shocked as I was? This car had just gotten in an accident in front of us and someone could be hurt. I quickly tried to open the car door, but my father grabbed my arm forcefully.

"Don't." He said in a stern voice.

"We need to do something!" I cried.

"Don't you dare." He said, glaring at me with his dark eyes.

I wanted to say something. I wanted to tell him we needed to call someone. We needed to help, but I knew what could happen if I disobeyed him. I knew what he was capable of, so I kept my mouth shut. I stayed silent as I leaned back and into my chair, his hand still tightly holding my arm.

"Good boy, Ace." He said, turning back to watch the car.

As the car stopped less than 1000 feet in front of us, I watched as it slowly started to catch on fire, with smoke pouring out of the passenger side windows. I couldn't see the driver's side, but I knew it wasn't going to end well. I just watched in disbelief as the fire quickly built up around the car, engulfing it in flames.

As my father released my arm, I had hoped that we were going to help. That we were going to do something. But, I shouldn't have thought that. My father didn't care. He never seemed to care about anyone but himself. He quickly started our car back up, made a U-turn and started driving back down the road from where we came. Completely ignoring what we just witnessed. I turned and watched as we drove away. Nobody around to help as the fiery vehicle lit up the road against the setting sun.

When we got home, my father got out of the car and walked into the house. Not another word to me about what we just saw. As I followed him inside, he sat down at the table and acted as if our drive was similar to a quick grocery store trip. Like we didn't just see a car get into an accident and catch on fire. It was like he had completely forgotten the entire thing.

When I tried to bring it up in front of my mother, he immediately quieted me down and told me to forget about it all. I didn't know why, but it just didn't sit well in my stomach. *How could he just tell me to forget it happened?*

Later that night, I saw the police cars outside of Paige's house. *Did something happen?* I thought back to the accident from earlier, trying to piece together the details in my mind, and it was in that moment that I made the connection. The same color. The same model. *It couldn't be. It can't.* Did my father know it was his car? Did he intentionally not help? And if so, why? What was his reasoning?

Then, I got the news we were leaving. I was told I needed to pack everything up and that we would be gone the following day. *Why now? Why do we have to leave now?*

One thing I knew for sure was that all I wanted to do was run next door and comfort Paige. I couldn't leave her. She just lost her father and she needed me. She needed someone to be there for her. But, how could I go over there knowing the truth? How would I tell her I saw the accident happen and didn't do anything about it? She would be even more devastated. Even more heartbroken.

So, when the next day came, I didn't say goodbye. We just left. I just knew it was for the best. I couldn't break her heart more than it already had been broken.

Then, I found out the truth. It was after my mother passed away that I finally learned about my father. What he did. Why he did it. Nothing about that day was an accident. And when I found out, I knew it was time to tell her. I couldn't just keep that inside of me. I had to tell her the real truth.

When I started looking, it wasn't hard to find her. It was actually pretty easy. She had just started college and I was happy to see that she was doing well. She looked happy. I didn't want to drop into her life at that time and bring everything up again. I couldn't. So, I kept my distance. At least for a few years.

When I found out that she was looking for an apartment after graduating, I wanted to help her in any way that I could. I had started getting into real estate at that time and making a name for myself when I discovered Florian Apartments. It needed some work, but the location was perfect and it was a good deal at the time. So, once the purchase went through, I had to find a way to push it towards Paige. Subtly, of course.

I hadn't known Lily at the time, but I knew how close she and Paige were, so I went with my gut that they would be looking for an apartment together. That afternoon, I had my assistant send her an email with a promotion for Florian Apartments. It was too good to pass up, so I hoped Lily would take the bait. Luckily, she did. I had my property manager set everything up for them and they moved in within a week.

If I could, I would have offered her to live in the apartment for free, but I know that would have looked suspicious. You can't just get an apartment that size, with the view and location, for free. But, I did make it cheap. Cheap enough for her to want to stay there in the long run. That way, I could always know she was safe. Comfortable. Happy.

As the years passed, I continued to keep my distance. Keeping the truth from her. Hoping there would be a moment one day for me to tell her. But, something always stopped me.

Then one day, I met Mason. I don't recall how we actually met, but he was around a lot of the same high class people I knew. I would see him at social events and functions, but never really knew him. When he took over his father's business, it was almost immediately that he reached out to me, asking me for help to find several new office buildings for the company.

Since he came from old money, we didn't have much in common. I didn't have many friends, so I tried to get to know him a bit more, but he was always a closed off person, so I didn't push too hard. Until one day when he mentioned he met someone. I didn't even ask him and didn't think he saw me as a friend, but he must have thought differently because he told me all about her. And, as soon as he said Lily's name, I knew. I knew an opportunity had been dropped in front of me.

As Lily and Mason grew closer, he and I grew closer as well, as his father's business expanded under his control, and thus, only helped my business even more. Then, he was engaged and he asked me to help him and Lily find a place to live. That was my ticket to getting closer to her, which would get me closer to Paige.

I honestly didn't know Paige was in Nashville at the time I was there. I had gone to close on some contracts and decided to grab a drink afterward. I figured I would check out what all the hype was around Nashville. But, I figured I'd have some fun with it so I dressed up and played the part.

Then, I saw her. Not only in a different city, but in the same exact place I was drinking at. She looked so beautiful that night. So mature. So confident. I couldn't help but watch her from under my hat as she stood at the bar. And maybe it was the alcohol or the fact that it was the first time since we were younger that I was in the same room as her, but I had to go over to her. To say something to her.

As soon as she turned around and I felt her hands against me, I was done for. This girl that I knew from my past was finally back in my life. Finally there in front of me, so I barely noticed the drink pooling on my shirt. It didn't matter. I just wanted to touch her. To make sure this wasn't another dream I had created in my head.

As I reached out in front of me, I grabbed the bottom of her chin and lifted her face up. As our eyes met, my thoughts were confirmed. She was actually there. All I wanted was to be near her for the rest of the night. To have her back in my arms. To hold onto her and never let go. But, it was cut short. Shorter than I would have liked.

Seeing her again and feeling her in my arms, I knew that couldn't be the last time. I knew there would be a moment again. And once we finally had our first date, I didn't want to be away from her. Not for a single second more. This girl of my dreams was finally back in my life. And now so beautiful. But I still hadn't told her the truth. I hadn't told her what really happened.

Soon, it was too late. Each second that passed with her, I couldn't help but fall for her. The past that strung us together only brought us closer. It felt like that missing piece of me had finally returned, so I fell quickly. I fell for her quicker than I could have imagined. I fell in love with every piece of her. Every moment I looked into her blue eyes. Every moment our lips touched. Every moment she was in my arms. I couldn't stay away from her. She was my addiction and I craved each moment I had.

And with each moment, the strings pulling inside me only got worse. There was this guilt that started growing. This guilt that she had started falling for me, but didn't know the secret I was hiding. She didn't know the truth that continued to drag me down.

As soon as her mom mentioned my nickname at that dinner, I knew that our time together was limited. That these last few days or weeks would be our last. That if I couldn't get the guts to tell her myself, she would find out on her own.

I didn't expect it to be this morning, but it finally came out. She knows everything. She knows it all. It's over.

And if I could say anything to her, I'd say thank you. Thank you for being you. Thank you for giving me all of yourself. Thank you for letting me back into your life and for being the best thing that's ever happened to me. For bringing me happiness. For getting rid of my pain. Every second with you was something I cherished because you quickly became my world. Loving you was so easy and an experience I will never forget, even till my last day.

Chapter Twenty Two

Paige

I lied and I never lie. Well, it was only a white lie. I was actually feeling sick on Friday morning, just not with the flu. But it sure felt like my guts were being ripped out when I went home and threw up. But how do you tell your boss the truth? That the man you've been seeing has been lying to you. Keeping a secret about who he really was. That you just found out that your father's death wasn't an accident. That he was actually killed. Even thinking of the words sends chills down my spine. *Murdered*. And not by just anyone, but by your boyfriend's father. You can't tell your boss that. *Nope*.

So I called in sick. I called in sick on the very first day after my promotion. I couldn't go in. I just couldn't. So, for the weekend, all I did was think. I let my mind wander. But really it was racing. Racing around trying to piece together some sort of explanation. Some sort of reason why my dad would be murdered. Some sort of reason why someone would do that to him. I let my thoughts go back to the darkest times in my life to see if I could remember something. Remember anything to help me get those questions answered. But, I couldn't. Especially after more than twenty years.

So when Sunday came, I called Lily and I'm so thankful she answered. She had been on her honeymoon for the past couple weeks, lounging it up in Greece, while I had been back here, pretending to live with a man that I thought I knew. And the timing couldn't have been better when she got back home on Sunday afternoon. I must have sounded so frantic on the phone spitting out everything that happened. All I wanted to do was tell her every little thing I knew. Every little thing that I found out. Luckily, she was able to calm me down yesterday, at least long enough for her to recover from jet lag and meet up with me before work.

Despite the quiet atmosphere on this Monday morning at Hanley's, I stare at the door, waiting for Lily to walk in. I know it'll be easy to spot her when she arrives, but I don't want to look around. I don't want to accidentally catch a glimpse through the windows and there be a possibility of spotting him walking by. It was bad enough getting here this morning. I was practically staring at my feet as I walked here.

My eyes glance down from the door for a moment as I look down at my coffee, which is still filled to the brim. I always got a coffee when I met up with Lily, but this time, I couldn't even bear the taste. Let alone anything really this past weekend.

A bell chimes from above me and my eyes shift back over to the door, as I see Lily walking in. She gives a thoughtful smile as she walks over and I try to muster one back, but I find it a little more difficult. As Lily gets to the table, I open my mouth to say something to her, but I'm stopped as she leans down and hugs me. The small gesture makes the corners of my mouth curve slightly, knowing that I can finally talk to someone about everything I've been feeling.

Once Lily pulls back and sits down across from me, she rests her elbow on the table and rests the side of her face against her closed knuckles.

"How have you been feeling?" Lily asks, furrowing her eyebrows. I take a breath in.

"Like shit." I say, letting out my breath. Lily immediately chuckles and my eyes widen.

"I'm sorry." Lily says through her chuckle before coughing to stop herself. "No, I am." She straightens herself up in the chair. "It's just that you didn't act like this with all the other jerks you were with."

"Ryker isn't a jerk." I murmur, looking down at my coffee, which I assume has now turned cold.

"Well, in my mind, anyone that hurts you is a jerk." Lily says, raising one eyebrow as she crosses her arms. I scoff slightly. "Did he ever mention anything about you two knowing one another?"

"I mean, no, not really." I say furrowing my brows, but Lily can't see as I continue to stare down at my coffee. "He told me a little about his past, but never went into detail."

"Hey!" Lily says, putting her hands up in front of her. "If I had known that this random dude that sold us our apartment knew you from the past, I wouldn't have set you two up on a date."

I look up at Lily, take a breath in and out, then lean back in my chair.

"But I'm glad you did." I say, tilting my head back as I look up at the ceiling. "I mean, he was exactly the kind of person I wanted to be with. He finally got me out of my funk and I genuinely felt like myself again. Like I hadn't lost anyone. Like I was happy. And I think." I pause. "I think I loved him."

"You loved him?" Lily leans over the table and I see a smile forming on her face.

"I did." I say nodding slightly. I take another breath in and out, then feel myself sliding down the chair, trying to hide. "Well, I still do."

I feel my body reverting back to how I felt throughout the weekend. When I felt alone. Like I had been shattered into a million pieces and nobody was there to pick me up. Like how I had felt back when I was a child. When I lost someone so close to me. Someone who I loved.

As if my body has used all of them up, not a single tear falls from my eyes at the thought. But I want to cry so badly. It's the only thing that helps. It's the only thing I can think of to help me recover. To somehow find a way out of this pain.

"Well, he doesn't deserve your love!" Lily says angrily. "I mean, how could he keep something like that from you? That's not a small secret!" Her eyebrows raise as she straightens up in her seat.

"I have no idea." I say, shaking my head as I pull myself out of my slumped over position in the chair. I pull my hand up to my forehead and rub my temple with my thumb. "I don't know what to think any more."

"Well, how about I come over later this week and we can have a girl's night? Okay?" Lily says, smiling as she places her hands flat on the table. "Just you and me!"

"That sounds nice." I say, slightly smiling as I look down at the table.

"Yay!" Lily says, pulling my hand off of my forehead. I'm caught off guard slightly as she pulls my hand to the table. "And if you need anything before then-."

My eyes glance up at the clock on the wall and I quickly stand up. *Shit.*

"I'm sorry, I'm late for work!" I say frantically, as I grab my bag off the floor.

I may have been able to call in sick on Friday, but I know I couldn't avoid work anymore. *How would that look?* I take a step forward toward the door, but forget Lily is still holding onto my hand on the table.

"Seriously." Lily says, sternly looking me in the eyes. "I'm here for you if you need me!" She smiles.

I turn away and start walking toward the door. As I reach for the handle, I turn to look back at Lily who is taking a sip from my cold coffee and the thought of her claiming my coffee as her own makes me smile. A genuine smile. *It'll be okay. I'll be okay. I have to be.*

Chapter Twenty Three

Paige

When I was assigned the project about the frog book, it took time for me to bring the author's story to life. While I would have normally found it easy to illustrate another story, maybe it was the nerves or the fall setting that was throwing me off, but it took me some time to find my rhythm. I hated all the pages I drew and didn't feel like it fit the theme. What was I supposed to do? I had been given this opportunity, but never felt like the drawings matched the words on the pages. That is, until I met Ryker.

When he showed me the view from the rooftop of my apartment complex, it was as if he showed me the start of my inspiration. The start of where my ideas could flow freely. I mean, he said it was where he came to think. To get away from everything. Maybe it could help me finally get the right ideas into my head? So, I started going up there when I could.

I brought a small folding chair up from my apartment and set it next to the ledge that overlooked the park below. I'd bring my sketchbook up with me and use the ledge as a table, with my favorite view in front of me. It was frightening at first, being up so high above everything around me, but the height started bothering me less and less.

When I wasn't with Ryker, I was up there. I mean, how could I not be? It was as if the words from the book filled my mind, dancing in and out of me, until they reached my hands and drew themselves. It quickly became my favorite place to get away. To escape. To find inspiration.

But, I haven't been there in over a month. Once I started staying over at Ryker's, I didn't get the chance to go up there. And I didn't need to. I found inspiration elsewhere. *In him.*

Yet nearly two weeks since we broke up, I still haven't been able to think of a single thing to write about for my own book. And I desperately need inspiration. But, I know I can't go up there. I know if I took one step onto the roof, all the feelings for him that I've tried to drown away would rush back in. All the moments we shared. I did enough crying the weekend following our break up and I know it will cause me to fall back into those emotions. I can't do that to myself. I just can't.

As my mind wanders elsewhere, hopelessly trying to find an idea somewhere in the back of my brain, all I can do is hope I'll find inspiration again. In anything. But, I won't be finding inspiration here. Not at my apartment. So I try to stay at work as long as I can. Spending longer hours at the end of the day, hoping even a sliver of inspiration will come and I'll finally be able to start this damn book. *Nothing so far.*

On the weekends though, I find ways to distract myself. To pass the time even just for a little while. I had left my apartment in such a mess prior to Lily's wedding and with the free time I finally had, I just started to clean. And when I say clean, I mean *everything*.

I started with the basics, just tidying up and putting things away, but I quickly dived deeper as I found areas of my apartment that called for deep cleaning. It was like therapy to me. Something that helped relieve my stress, but was also productive. I had only wished I could have discovered this simple coping method when I was a child.

Lily was there to help too. She got the rest of my belongings from Ryker and brought them back to my apartment the week following our break up. As our girl's nights increased, it felt like it did before. When she was living with me. I can't imagine how Mason has been feeling, knowing his new wife has been spending so much time back at her old apartment, but I hope he knows it's been helping. Making things a little easier.

As I'm vacuuming the rug in my living room, I look around at the furniture sitting on top of it. My couch, my two chairs and my coffee table. I pull the vacuum back from the rug and click the button to turn it off.

"I need to move all of this." I say to myself out loud. I can't think of any time I've ever moved my furniture off the rug to clean it deeper, but now is always a good time to start.

I grab the back of one of the chairs and slide it off the rug, grinding it against the floor in the process. Then, do the same with the other chair. I walk over to the couch and my first instinct is to grab the sides and pull it, as I did with the chairs, but as I lean back, the couch stays in its place. Not moving a muscle. I lean back even further, angling the couch toward the floor and I feel it slightly raise up on the opposite end, but it still won't pull toward me. Rather than pulling, I turn around with my back against the couch and opt to push it off. Bending my knees, I arch my back against the side and push with my legs against the floor and the couch starts to move. One inch. Two inches. Three inches. Until finally the couch is nearly off the rug.

With another push, I think I can get it where I want it, but as I look down, a brown piece of paper catches my eye. I tilt my head and look at the small corner that pokes out from beneath the rug. *What is that?*

I push myself up against the couch, sliding my feet back and pulling my body into an upright position, not taking my eyes off the paper on the floor. As I bend down to grab it, I'm surprised to see that the small piece of paper isn't as small as I thought, but it's rather large. And not just a piece of paper, but an envelope. *The one from my mom.*

"So that's where it's been hiding." I sigh with a slight chuckle. That must've been where it went when I tripped over my shoe.

I flip the envelope over and immediately recognize the colorful stamps that I had noticed when my mom first gave it to me. One with several birds. Another with the ocean on it. And a few that are standard stamps I see. *This came a long way.*

My eyes glance over to read the return address, but the words are illegible. As if water damage occurred in the corner, the ink is severely smeared and the only thing I can make out on the second line where the address should be is: FM6.

The mailing address is addressed to me though, but I'm surprised to see the address below my name. Not my mom's current address, but my previous address. Not the one from when I met Lily or for my current apartment, but an address I haven't been to in over twenty years. The address for the house I lived in when my dad passed away. I glance down at another sticker on the envelope and it shows the post office forwarded it to my mom's apartment. *But, who is this from?*

I walk over to my couch and sit down, quickly tearing open the envelope. As I tear it open, several things fall out and onto my lap, but I choose to ignore them, looking for some sort of information as to why this has been sent to me.

As I stick my hand into the envelope, I feel a thicker, folded piece of paper at the bottom. I'm able to grab it between my middle and index fingers and pull it out, placing it on my lap. I look back into the envelope and find that it's now empty, so I place the envelope onto the cushion next to me. Grabbing the folded paper, I open it and I'm surprised to see a date in the top left corner that reads October 18, 2022. *Two years ago.* I quickly start reading it.

Hey kiddo, it's dad. I've been sitting here for weeks trying to find the right words to say. I mean, there's so much to say. To you, it probably felt like such a long time ago, but to me it hasn't felt like long. It feels like just yesterday that I left you. I wish I hadn't, but it was what had to happen.

I don't even know where to start, but I'll try to tell you from the beginning. To tell you everything.

I'm so sorry you have to read this and this may be hard to hear, but I survived the accident. I was driving home from work when one of my tires blew and the car started to swerve. I tried to get it under control, but I couldn't and the car flipped on the road. I must've hit my head as it flipped because at that moment, I thought I was dead. I must have passed out for only a moment, but when I woke up, I was hanging upside down in my seat and I saw smoke start to fill the inside of the car. I had broken my arm pretty badly, but I managed to take my seatbelt off and pull myself out of the broken driver's side window onto the street. I knew the car was only moments away from catching fire, so I tried my best to get as far away from the car as possible, hiding in a ditch next to the road. As I crouched down in the ditch, I noticed a black car just down the road and recognized it immediately. It was at that moment that I knew that my accident wasn't an accident at all and that it had all been planned out.

Just before the accident, we weren't doing too well. We were struggling financially and I was afraid of what might happen to us. I tried to be a step ahead and find a better paying job, but it was just never the right time. Then, something happened. I stumbled upon a file that wasn't encrypted and learned about the shady dealings going on with the business I worked for and its CEO. I was desperate so I used the information against him. I didn't want to, but I had to. We needed the money and he needed the information I knew to stay private, so it worked out well. And we were finally doing better financially. Better than we ever had been, but as soon as those neighbors moved in next door, I had a bad feeling. I knew I was being watched and as the weeks went by, I could tell that someone was following me. I wanted to stay out of it, but my CEO started pulling me deeper into his business dealings, using me as a cover for anything new that they were planning. When it became too much, I knew that one wrong move could end badly for me and I had to get out. So, when I saw our neighbor's car after the accident, I knew that it was set up. I was meant to die in the accident. And honestly, I wish I had died in that accident because then I wouldn't have had to do what I did, but I knew it was the only thing I could do. I had to pretend I died. And not just to them, but to everyone. Even both of you. I knew that if there was any trace that I was still alive, they would have looked for me. So I fled. I got away as fast as I could and left everything behind.

Years later, that business closed and everyone involved, including the CEO, were finally imprisoned for everything that was going on when I worked there. But, I knew that there was still one person out there that knew what happened and couldn't know I was alive, so I stayed low. I stayed quiet to protect you. And in that time, I quietly followed your life and achievements on social media. I held onto the things that I had left of you and cherished them. I wish I could have been there to watch you grow up, but I needed to stay away. I needed to know you were safe. But, I'm so proud of you. So proud of the woman you've become. You've done so well for yourself. I just wish I could have been a part of it.

I'm so sorry again. I wish I could have told you this in person. I know it's been a long time, but I can't imagine what you went through. What you and your mom went through. It was probably a lot, but it needed to be done. It had to be done in order to keep you both safe. I couldn't put you in more danger than you already were. If I could, I would have stayed. I wanted to stay. I truly did. I wish I could have had the chance to be in your life once again, but I won't ever get that chance.

By the time you receive this letter, it'll probably be too late. I'm dying. For real this time. I am nearing the end of a year-long battle with stage four pancreatic cancer and probably won't last much longer. But it's okay kiddo. If you are receiving this, it means you are finally safe. The only person left that can harm you is no longer a threat. No longer someone that can hurt you.

I love you kiddo. Always remember that.

I drop the letter to the floor and wipe the tears pouring down my face, blurring my vision in the process. My heartbeat is racing and I can't tell if I'm angry or heartbroken over this. Everything I knew was a lie. Everything I thought I knew was a lie. *My dad didn't die in the accident?*

The forgotten memories of my dad rush to the front of my mind for the first time since I was a child. Everything that I closed out. Everything that I tried to hide. Everything that I thought I forgot about because it only hurt me more.

I look down at the items still sitting in my lap. A colorful bracelet I made with my mom that I remember gifting to my dad. A small picture I painted of the trees in our yard. All from my childhood. All things that he kept to remember me.

I feel my brows furrow and I wipe another tear from my cheek.

I went through so much pain as a child thinking I lost my dad. I thought I lost him in a tragic accident. I went to his funeral. I buried him in the ground. And to think, he kept this a secret from me. This dangerous thing that nobody would expect their own father to hide from them. And to make me think for the last twenty years that he was alive. Watching over me. Knowing I was still suffering from his death. *How could he?*

I take several deep breaths in and out, trying to control myself from hyperventilating. There had to be another way. We could have all moved with him. Started a new life. Stayed together. But now, he's gone. He's actually gone. I'll never get that chance.

It had to be done in order to keep you both safe. The words echo through my head.

As I try to stop myself from crying again, I think about how my father mentioned our neighbor. Ryker's father. How he was the one hired to follow my dad. How he was the one that set up everything for the accident. And Ryker knew all of this and didn't tell me. He kept this a secret too. He's just as bad as my dad. They both lied to me. They both kept it a secret until now. But, my dad didn't die. He hid the real truth. *But, did Ryker know that too?*

As my mind circles trying to connect all the missing pieces, I feel my body crashing. I feel it giving out. With another deep breath, I lean back onto the couch, giving into the exhaustion. *It's all too much. Everything.*

Chapter Twenty Four
Paige

I thought the past was the past. At least that's where I thought it should stay. Back in a time when I was a child. When I didn't know how big the world could get. When I thought I knew everything, but knew so little. I didn't expect anything from my past to come back. I didn't expect anyone to come back. Let alone, *him*. But then I received the letter.

From the moment I opened the letter, my past changed. My past used to be filled with sorrow. It used to be filled with hate. I used to shutter those memories into the back of my mind, making myself believe that I forgot them, but they were always there. *He was always there.*

I could be angry and upset and mad about everything he did, but I'm not. If I had known the circumstances, would I have been okay with it back then? Probably not. But, I don't want to hate him because of what he did. I know he did what he thought was best. At least I try to see it that way.

Before, it felt like I lost something. Like a piece of me was missing. But, knowing that I never really lost him changes things. He was still with me always. Still watching over me. Still making sure I was safe. That's the only way I can think about it now.

There's one thing left though that I need to fix and only I can be the one to fix it. I didn't know that my dad survived. I didn't know what kinds of things he got himself involved in. I thought he had died in a tragic car accident. I didn't know the entire truth. And neither did Ryker. He deserves to know the truth as well.

Ryker always had the best intentions in mind. All he wanted to do was keep me safe. Watch over me like my dad had all those years. And yet, if he had told me his truth earlier, he may have unknowingly put me more at danger. To think he beat himself up over this for his entire life. Feeling like he was hiding a dangerous secret that would crush me. Feeling like he couldn't get close to me again because of what he knew. I can't imagine that kind of weight on someone's shoulders.

But, Ryker was never in the wrong. He always hated his father and had wanted to tell me the truth. He tried. And when he finally told me, I shut him out. I left him and told myself I would never interact with him again. But that's no longer the case. I can't stay away from him. I can't be apart from the one person that I still have from my past. The one person that's here. The one person that isn't gone.

I roll over in bed and grab my phone sitting on the table next to me.

When I thought my dad had died, Lily was my support system. She was there with me during my time of grieving. She would understand. *She has to.*

I go into my contacts and click on her name, dialing her number. She immediately picks up and before she can get a word in, I start word-vomiting the entire story to her, not leaving out a single detail of what happened only a week prior.

I was almost surprised I hadn't brought it up to Lily earlier in the week, but it took me a while to come to terms with everything myself.

After a silence on the other end that feels like it will never end, I sit up as I finally hear her speak.

"Woah, that's one crazy story." She says on the other line.

"Yup." I say, slightly chuckling as I rub my temple.

"Well, you need to talk to Ryker!" Lily says. "Let him know the truth!"

"I know, I know." I say, taking a breath in. "I just don't know how."

"We need to come up with a plan!" Lily insists.

"What? Why do we need a plan?" I say, chuckling.

"Well every good story ending shows a plan for the couple to get back together with one another." Lily says. I can tell she is smiling through the phone.

"This isn't another one of those romance movies. This is real." I say, laughing.

"Maybe." She laughs. "But, I have the perfect plan."

I roll my eyes. "Fine. Let's hear it."

"So even though you guys broke up, I couldn't stop Mason from still doing business with him. I mean, he is the best in the industry as you now know."

I slightly nod my head, but Lily can't see me agree through the phone.

"Mason has been in the market for a new office building for contract workers so Ryker has been helping him look for one."

"I don't see how this relates to anything." I say, furrowing my brows.

"Hold on! Hold on!" Lily says excitedly. I scoff.

"What if Mason sends Ryker a listing he likes and asks him to meet there. You know, to go over the details in person? But then, Mason tells Ryker that he can't make it and that I'm going to meet him instead."

"Okay?" I slowly question.

"So then I can text Ryker and let him know I'm running late and instead of me showing up at the listing, you can!"

"What-" I am quickly interrupted.

"And then you can tell him everything and you can make up and have a happily ever after."

"That sounds complicated." I chuckle.

"Hmm. You're right. Scratch that. How about-" She says.

"You know what? I'm just going to text him." I say, cutting Lily off.

"Oh! I had such a good idea though!" Lily sighs, almost upset that she didn't get to tell me. Before I can say another word, Lily speaks again, "But don't text him! That's too easy."

"Too easy?" I say, laughing. "How about I just go over to his place then? Does that plan work for you?" I raise my eyebrows.

"I guess that works." Lily says, disheartened.

"Did you just roll your eyes?" I laugh.

"No." She says, but I can tell she's lying by the sound of her voice.

We say our goodbyes over the phone and as soon as she hangs up, I quickly roll out of bed to get dressed.

As I walk into Ryker's building, I immediately feel my heart start to race. I can't help but think about the last time I was here, yet I know this time will be different. I just know it.

Despite everything that happened, Ryker had never asked me to give back his spare key card. I could have easily thrown it away, but I didn't. I'm not sure why, but I'm secretly thankful I kept it in my wallet. I scan the key card as I step into the elevator and as I watch the numbers flash across the small screen, I start to think of what I will say to him. How he didn't know the entire truth of it all. How I didn't either. I imagine he'll be surprised at first, but he'll be happy I'm back. *Right?*

As the elevator opens to his apartment, I'm surprised at how different it looks. It's quiet and the curtains in front of the arched windows are closed, letting in barely any light from outside. I cautiously take a step inside.

"Ryker?" I quietly say, as my voice echoes through the hallway into the living room. There's no answer.

I walk over to a light switch at the end of the hallway and turn it on, brightening up the living room.

"Are you home?" I ask, hearing my voice echo back to me. Once again no answer.

I look around the room and I'm surprised by what I see. What used to be a well-kept, tidy living space is now cluttered. I know he has a cleaning service that comes and goes, but it appears as though they haven't come in weeks. There are left over glasses on the coffee table and several of his button down shirts laying on the back of the couch. On the couch itself is a pillow from his bedroom and a throw blanket, halfway falling onto the floor.

While I found a way to cope by cleaning, it didn't appear that he had the same mindset. And I wouldn't blame him. I didn't see it until now, but he had lost everything. Everything he had known. Everyone. And then, he lost me. The last person he still had in his life. I can't imagine how he's been feeling since we broke up. And by the looks of it, not very good.

I take a breath in and out, as I walk around the rest of the apartment, calling out again to see if he's home, but still no reply back. I decide to leave, rather than awkwardly waiting around for him to return, and decide to head back to my own apartment.

On the cab ride home, I remember what Lily said about Mason needing a new office building and how he's had Ryker help him out. Maybe Ryker has been focusing all his attention on work? Maybe that's been his coping method?

I pick up my phone and do a quick web search for his office phone number. Clicking on the number, I hear a dial tone before a woman answers the phone.

"Hello, Blackwell Realty and Property Management. This is Debra, how can I assist you?" I hear her say. I never met his assistant, but her voice sounds older. Similar to what I imagine my grandma to sound like if she was still alive.

"Hi, is Ryker- I mean, Mr.Blackwell available?" I ask timidly.

"Hi dear, Mr.Blackwell took the day off today for personal reasons. However, if you leave your name and number, I can have him return your call when he is back."

"No, I'm okay. Thank you." I say, quickly hanging up the phone.

Considering he wasn't at his apartment, I was sure he would be working today. I think back to what Lily said about texting him. *No, I can't just do that.* I need to talk to him in person. This all has to be said in person.

As the cab stops in front of my apartment complex, I step out and look over at the small park down the road. The trees are lit up from the setting sun, but most of them are nearly bare with the trunks of the trees submerged in about a foot of snow. A sign that winter is here.

In the past, it would have been a welcoming sight to see. To know that the hardest time of the year for me had passed. The time of year that I had grown used to hating. The time of year that I always dreaded. But that had changed all too quickly when I met Ryker. And now, looking at the trees, I couldn't help but miss the signs of fall. It had given me the feeling of hopefulness for the future rather than being stuck in the past.

Walking inside my complex and into the small elevator, I feel disappointed that I didn't find him. That I can't talk to him today. All I wanted to do was to tell him what I knew.

As I'm about to click the button to my floor, I pause as my finger hovers in front of it. I tried the two places I thought for sure Ryker would be, but he wasn't there. I had created this idea of how we would reunite in my head, all thanks to Lily's fairytale imagination, and I was only let down.

My eyes glance up at the buttons in front of me and I fall onto the letter "R" on the keypad. *Roof.* And for the first time in over a month, I click it.

As soon as I step through the double doors of the white rooftop room, I see him. Standing on the other end of the rooftop with his back turned toward me. I can't see his face, but I know it's him. Everything in my body is telling me it's him.

I wrap myself tightly in my wool coat as I feel the wind hit my skin and slowly start walking toward him. An invisible string pulling me closer and closer to him once again.

With each step toward him, I feel my heart pounding out of my chest and I feel more nervous than the night we first met. Never could I have imagined we'd be apart. And after the weeks that have passed, it feels like it's been a lifetime away from him.

Once I'm within six feet of him, I stop. Waiting for him to turn around. Hoping he'll see me. My mind begs for him to turn and look at me, but I watch as he continues to face out toward the setting sun, unaware that I'm there. I watch as Ryker's body stiffens in front of me. Does he not realize I'm here? His body relaxes for a moment, but I can't stay quiet any longer.

"Ryker?" I quietly say and it's as if my voice snaps him out of his imagination.

Ryker slowly turns his head and his eyes widen immediately as our eyes meet. At that moment, every feeling and thought that I've had about him that I've been pushing down since we broke up, comes back up again. And all I want to do is run into his arms and apologize to him. Apologize for everything that's happened and to tell him the truth. The real truth. But, as I take a step forward, I pause.

He quickly blinks and takes a step closer to me, his eyes moving back and forth, as if to make sure it's actually me standing in front of him.

"You came back?" He says, with slight sorrow in his voice, almost surprised by me being there. I take another step closer until I'm within arms reach of him.

"I had to. I needed to show you this." I say, taking a breath in as I slightly raise my eyebrows. He quickly furrows his brows.

"What do you mean, Beautiful?" He asks, taking a deep breath in. *Beautiful.* I shyly smile as I hear the nickname once again.

I reach into my pocket and pull out part of the letter from my dad, handing it over to Ryker. As he reads it, I watch as his facial expression quickly changes from concern, to shock, to sympathy.

"How did you-" He asks, looking up from the letter with his eyebrows raised.

"We both didn't know the truth." I say, smiling at him. "You kept this secret for so long, but you never knew the real truth. Neither of us did."

I hold out my hands in front me and Ryker slowly grabs a hold of them, squeezing them slightly as I look down at them and back up to him.

"And I can't imagine how much this killed you inside. For so many years. All you wanted to do was protect me. To keep me safe and I shut you out. I shut you out because of what I thought I knew. But I didn't know the half of it. Will you forgive me?"

Ryker's eyebrows slowly raise and I hear him quietly exhale.

"There's nothing to forgive. From the moment I met you, I wanted you in my life. Someone as beautiful as you only comes once in a lifetime and nothing could keep us apart, no matter how much time had passed. So when you left, it destroyed me. I felt like my heart had shattered. I lost the one person I loved most in my life and having you back was the only thing that ever mattered to me. All I wanted was your forgiveness, yet here you are asking for mine." Ryker chuckles, lowering his head slightly.

"I just don't want to lose you again." I say, lifting my brows as I look up at him.

Suddenly, a smirk appears on his face and I feel my body being pulled into him by my arms. I squeeze my arms around him tightly and I press my head against his chest. Taking a breath in, I recognize his sweet scent against my face just as I feel him press his lips against the top of my head.

"You are my past, my future and my now and I promise I'm not going anywhere. I was here before and I'll be here till my dying breath. I can promise you that, Beautiful."

I hadn't cried since I read my dad's letter, but being back in Ryker's arms quickly pulls a tear from my eye as I feel it roll down my cheek.

From the moment I met Ryker Blackwell, I didn't know that our paths had crossed before. I thought he was just someone random that I met in a bar. I had felt like a piece of me had been missing for most of my life. Not just a piece, but a person. And not just anyone. *Him.* I thought that person was my dad. Someone I thought was taken from me all too soon. My dad was always there. Always watching over me. Even till the end. But I was wrong. The person who was missing from my life was Ryker. *Ryker Blackwell.*